Praise for
Jack Stinger and
The Haunting of Whitlock Manor

"Unexpected twists—like taking a ride on a roller coaster!"

—LitPick Book Reviews

"Phillip Wolf creates an ambiance that draws you in and does not let you go until you discover the secrets held within the depths of Whitlock Manor."

—Readers' Favorite

"It's fast-paced and then really keeps your attention."

—Owl Book World

"Loaded with compelling characters and 'I didn't see THAT coming!' plot twists."

—Laura Hofford

"The slowly unfurling mystery keeps the reader so encapsulated in the story from the beginning until the twist ending!"

—Matthew Gill

"The deeper you get into the book, the more intense it gets. I loved the ending."

—Jade

THE REAL WOLF MAN

ALSO BY PHILLIP WOLF

Jack Stinger and the Haunting of Whitlock Manor

Jeremiah the CHD Aware Bear and Friends

The Man I Never Met

God Gave Us a Promise: The Story of a Little Fighter

DOCUMENTARY FEATURES

My Barbara

Silent Cries: Breaking Through CHD Awareness

THE REAL WOLFMAN

PHILLIP WOLF

WEP PUBLICATIONS
WolfEntertainment.NET

An Imprint of Wolf Entertainment Productions, Inc.

First WEP paperback edition June 2025

Manufactured in the United States of America

1 2 3 4 5 6 7 8 9

Library of Congress Control Number: 2025904939

ISBN: 979-8-218-63545-9

For Mom,
staying current with constantly changing technology.
You're doing great!

"I didn't have time to write a short letter,
so I wrote a long one instead."

—Mark Twain

CONTENTS

INTRODUCTION

When I attended junior high school in Allen, Texas, everyone on the athletics team liked my last name. Some called me Wolf, but most nicknamed me Wolf Man. To this day, Wolf Man has stuck with me.

Despite being one of the shorter kids in school, I excelled at high jump. I sprinted in the 220-yard dash and 100 hurdles (short and high). I was the quickest at sit-ups in grade school, completing more than sixty per minute. After everyone's fitness test one day, the coach asked me to do them again in front of the entire class. I was shocked when I completed about sixty-five or seventy sit-ups after doing them only minutes prior.

I also had a knack for climbing up and down a fifteen-foot knotted rope hanging from the beams in the gymnasium faster than anyone else.

Those were the days when times were simpler.

Even today, I remember when I was born. No one believes me whenever I bring this up in random conversations. There was nothing, and then there was something. It was the weirdest feeling. That's all I can describe.

I recall most of my childhood. But, since age twenty-five, I can't remember shit from a week ago.

The one thing I kept up throughout my life was reading and writing—mostly writing. Writing takes me back to simpler times. I enjoy including my childhood experiences in the stories I write. I'm only a kid once, so why not be a kid forever? Writing keeps me in that bubble where I can relive the 1980s as much as I like. If I could revisit the '80s for real, I'd return in a heartbeat.

I read an introduction to a book by Stephen King where he mentions that "an author has endless opportunities to revise and improve his work. His stories are never perfect until his final breath or when he can no longer tell stories. Only then can his stories be considered complete and final." This rings true as I reflect on most of the stories I've written for this collection. I can continue tweaking them, adding new characters, improving descriptions, rewriting endings, etc. But I will most likely not revisit these stories when this publication is out. I will continue to revisit them in my head, however.

The stories included in this collection have never been previously published. They consist mostly of horror and are not intended for young readers. So, before little Johnny comes running up to you in a bookstore with this book or asks you to order it online, don't let the innocent cover fool you. Each element on the front and back cover represents a macabre tale.

"Prey for Escape" was the closest I got to being accepted for publication in an issue of *Worlds of Fantasy and Horror* (formerly *Weird Tales*). I received a personal response from the editor, which was rare and exciting compared to the usual form letters that came with my rejection notices. In those days, I kept a log of all my submissions to various magazine editors and rarely received personalized rejection responses. Editors didn't have time to respond to every submission, especially before email was widely available. I would write new stories while waiting for responses (ten to twelve weeks or longer). Of all the rejection notices I received for my story submissions, only two editors provided me with personal and encouraging feedback on how I could improve my writing: Darrell Schweitzer from *Weird Tales* (in the 1990s) and Marion Zimmer Bradley, founder and editor of *Marion Zimmer Bradley's Fantasy Magazine*. These responses were like small victories in my eyes and motivated me to keep writing.

My strategy for becoming a full-time writer was to publish some short stories in magazines before writing my first book and mailing the manuscript with a query letter to literary agencies.

Growing up, I spent years buying new editions of *Writer's Digest* books and magazines, attending author seminars, reading, researching, and submitting stories to editors. Alas, I found myself going in circles.

In 1992, I enrolled in a creative writing class as an elective during my junior year of high school. I wrote some short stories for the class and continued submitting manuscripts to editors. In 1994, I took another creative writing course during my first year of college. I remember vividly halfway through the class when the professor announced his first science fiction novel was being published. He had been trying to publish it for ten years. He was so excited that day when he shared his good news.

I was jealous.

I never kept a folder or binder containing the stories I wrote during college the way I did in high school. But over the years, I dusted off my old high school creative writing binder and skimmed through it to reminisce about those pivotal years when I wanted to be a writer.

I'm fifty as I write this, and I've cracked open that one-inch binder again to decide which stories and assignments I wanted to revise for this book. As I sifted through the pages like an editor and their discard pile, I came across an assignment I wrote about myself. It is both nostalgic and bittersweet to revisit my younger self and see how much has changed.

I was filled with conflicting emotions when I began this collection of twisted tales. On one hand, I'm excited to rewrite my stories and see them in a new light. But I'm afraid of what these tales may reveal about my weird, creative mind. Will I be able to honor my past while accepting where I am now? It's a daunting task, but one that I must face head-on.

Many of these stories are the ideas that drove my previous book, *Jack Stinger and the Haunting of Whitlock Manor*, into existence. If you've read it, these tales should be familiar to you. Consider them as Easter eggs.

For example, Jack Stinger was the pen name I would use if I ever became a full-time writer. Since I chose another creative career path (video production), I introduced Jack Stinger as a character instead. Thus, he makes his debut in *The Haunting of Whitlock Manor*.

Jack Stinger and the Haunting of Whitlock Manor was initially titled *Whispers Through the Broken Window*. I wrote a treatment and three sample chapters from the book to send to my literary agent in 2007. Unfortunately, the agency went out of business before the proposal reached them. So I stashed the book away and never picked it up again until the world shut down during the COVID-19 pandemic in 2020.

Before we begin this journey, I leave you with some advice. Never give up on what you love doing in your spare time because it can transition into a full-time career later. To this day, I still receive rejections for my writings and films submitted to contests and festivals. As a professional, I learn from my mistakes and move forward.

I write for myself but allow others to enjoy it. If someone doesn't agree with my writing style or subject matter, I don't let it get to me. It's been this way for thirty-eight years. I'm thick-skinned, so I can take a criticizing punch. I'm always satisfied with the results once I finish a story and it's out of my hands.

Growing up, I was fascinated with horror and fantasy genres—mostly horror because that was me. Today I still enjoy reading a good horror story or book or watching a scary movie because this is me.

I am the real wolf man.

During a creative writing class in high school (1991–1992), one of my assignments was to write a story about myself in the present tense. This class was my favorite since I loved to write.

It was the only writing program I could choose as an elective (aside from the required English literature courses). I wrote my stories for this class using a word processor on an IBM desktop computer my parents bought me through the Home Shopping Network (HSN) advertised on late-night TV. The monitor on that thing was huge (bulky and shaped like an alien head). When turning in my assignments, I printed them on an oversized dot matrix printer. I miss those days.

The following is how I became a writer from an assignment I wrote at eighteen in 1992.

MYSELF

I

It's 1987, and a banana-yellow 1974 Camaro pulls into a parking space in front of Waldenbooks in Carrollton, Texas. Vince gives the throaty engine a couple of revs, lets it idle for a few seconds, then turns the key in the ignition and cuts off the motor.

In the passenger seat sits Vince's little brother, Phil. He's a skinny, blond-haired, blue-eyed twelve-year-old wearing glasses. He's a bookworm. A nerd.

Excited, Phil quickly unbuckles his seatbelt, pops the door lock, pulls the handle, and pushes the heavy car door open.

"What's the hurry?" Vince asks. "The store isn't going any-where."

"I know," Phil says, stepping out of the vehicle. He peers back inside at his brother. "I'm itching for a new book. So hurry and get out. Let's go!" He slams the door shut.

Vince cringes before stepping out of the car. He peers over the hood, scolding Phil for slamming the door. "I'll give you something you can itch."

Something about the cold weather made Phil want to look at books that day while he and his brother were out and about.

The brothers walk into the bookstore and part ways. Vince heads to the magazine racks and checks out the automotive publications, while Phil scouts the books in the fiction area.

With both hands sunk into the pockets of his jeans, Phil walks up and down the narrow aisles, transfixed, looking for any book cover that would leap out and catch his eye. He migrates to the science fiction section, and toward the end of the aisle, a book finally leaps out to him: *Robocop*.

Phil's eyes light up as he reaches for the paperback and flips through it. "Damn!" he mumbles to himself. "Mom wouldn't let me see this movie. I can read the book instead!" He holds on to the movie novelization, rounds the endcap, and browses the next aisle.

Approaching the horror section, Phil scans the rows for a book cover he hopes will catch his attention again. He takes it slow because the horror selections are limited.

Finally, he stops before a thick book with the image of a green-clawed hand protruding from a sewer grate. A paper boat floats in the street alongside the curb toward the hand. *IT* is the title, and Phil reaches for the book.

"Stephen King," Phil says. "Hmm." The book is heavy as he flips through the thin pages.

"Hey, dumbass." Vince's voice carries from the opposite end of the aisle, interrupting Phil's moment. "I've been looking all over for you!"

Phil closes the book and walks toward his brother. "I've been over here the whole time. I'm ready to go."

"It's about time, shithead," Vince gripes. "This place is for nerds."

II

Over the next several months, Phil reads *IT*. His mind floods with imaginative ideas that could inspire his own stories. Reading the book also sparks an obsession with collecting Stephen King's works, stories, and articles published in various magazines, like *Cemetery Dance*, *Weird Tales*, and *Writer's Digest*.

Phil's future career path becomes clear. He wants to be a professional full-time writer.

III

Phil sits at the dining room table at his family's new home in Allen, Texas. His mother's electronic typewriter is perched on the table before him. He's determined to begin writing his first book.

Phil carefully loads a crisp sheet of typing paper into the typewriter, its keys stained from countless letters his mother has written over the years. With a deep breath, he gazes intently at the blank page, his mind whirling with possibilities. After contemplating for several minutes, he strokes the first key and begins typing the title of his first short story:

CURSE OF THE RED PAW
The Best Mystery Story
Written by Phillip Wolf

Little did he know, Phil's first short story plagiarized a Saturday morning episode of the *Scooby Doo* cartoon.

He's gotta start somewhere.

January 24, 1992 / Revised August 27, 2024

I was thrilled when one of my earlier creative writing assignments in school was to write a short story of at least ten pages. To me, the assignment was gravy. And so, on February 19, 1992, I began crafting *The Rat Hole*.

Looking back on the story, I realized it might not be well-written enough to publish verbatim. Some plot holes needed filling. Therefore, I changed the title and gave the story a facelift to fit the times. But it will always be *The Rat Hole*—a testament to my early days as a writer and a reminder of how far I've come.

CHEESY DEMISE

Within the cramped confines of Danny Benton's one-bedroom apartment, a piece of cheddar cheese rested on the trigger of a mousetrap. Its pungent aroma drifted through the hole at the base of the wall to lure in the curious critter with its irresistible scent.

Danny's ears had been relentlessly bombarded for a week by the sharp skittering of tiny claws across his bedroom floor each night. The sounds kept him awake and on edge. The urge to rid himself of this torment grew stronger with each passing night until it was all he could think about. Despite the fact that he was a habitual video game player, the repetitive noises had begun to grate on his nerves like never before. He couldn't understand why they bothered him. In some ways he felt like an old man, prematurely plagued by grumpiness and irritation.

In hopes of regaining peace of mind at night, he decided placing a mousetrap inside the hole in the wall might solve the problem. He was determined to silence the constant commotion once and for all. After setting the device inside the mouse hole, what followed were nights filled with anxious anticipation as he waited for the trap to do its job, longing for the blissful silence that would follow.

The hole in the wall was small and unassuming, resembling the arch of Jerry's beloved mouse hole from the classic *Tom and Jerry* cartoons Danny watched on Saturday mornings as a child. It held a nostalgia for him now. And the anticipation of dread, for he knew what fate awaited the rodent that dared succumb to the temptation of the delightful snack within the wall.

Danny lay in bed, the soft blue glow from the television screen filling the bedroom and casting shadows on his face. He scrolled through the endless options on Netflix, searching for something new and exciting to watch as he waited for the inevitable sound of the sharp crack of the hammer slamming against the mousetrap's wooden platform. It would startle him, piercing his ears like a whip. But in the end, satisfaction would prevail, and he could finally get some much-needed rest. He'd dread the sight that would follow and the mess he'd have to clean up—a lifeless mouse trapped and mangled beneath the metal jaws of the trap. It was a gruesome and unsettling image Danny did not look forward to seeing. But it must be done.

The same sounds simultaneously had woken him for seven consecutive nights. Despite keeping a clean and tidy apartment, there seemed to be no explanation for why this visitor had chosen his place as its nightly destination. Did the creature have a hidden nest somewhere in the walls? Maybe a neighbor's pet had escaped and found its way into his place.

With each passing minute, Danny's frustration grew, not because of the mouse this time, but due to the choices of movie titles. He had seen many of the movies already. If only he could afford other subscriptions like Max or Paramount+, maybe he wouldn't be stuck cycling through the same old flicks every night. But with a dead-end job and constantly rising inflation, it seemed impossible to get ahead. Financial pressure hung heavy on him, and he could barely afford his monthly rent for the past three years.

Another day of monotonous work awaited him tomorrow. Still, Danny knew he couldn't quit yet, not when he had bills to pay and a dream of one day making it out of this crappy apartment and into something better.

With a defeated sigh, he shut off the TV, settled under the covers, and closed his eyes. In just a few short hours, he'd start another day stocking dairy products at the supermarket with a fake smile while taking heat from disgruntled customers questioning him about out-of-stock products.

2

Waking to the soft, rhythmic pitter-patter of tiny feet scurrying across the floor, Danny sat up in bed. It was happening again—short bursts of sleep like he was power napping. He *must* get rid of that pesky rodent!

Danny glanced at the digital clock on the nightstand beside him with blurred vision.

3:05 a.m.

He rubbed his eyes and yawned, mentally preparing himself for another night of dealing with his uninvited guest. His yawn was cut short when he witnessed the small creature dashing out from underneath his bed toward the hole in the wall.

Danny flung the covers off and hung his legs over the side of the bed. *Oh, I'm gonna get you tonight!* he muttered under his breath, focusing on the hole in the wall. His ears strained for the deathly *snap*.

But all was quiet.

Danny heard the faint hum of the internal fan in the laptop, which he had forgotten to shut down before turning in for the night.

He inched out of bed, careful not to make sudden movements that might startle the mouse. Danny moved slowly over to his desk in the corner of the room and opened the drawer, sifting through clutter until he found a small flashlight. With a click, a light beam illuminated the room, and Danny stepped closer to the mouse hole. He shined the light along the floor and crouched, aiming the light directly into the small hole in the wall.

"Ugh, not what I was hoping for," Danny said. He could see deep inside the hole.

It was empty. Not a creature was stirring.

Then it dawned on him the mousetrap was missing!

With a double take, Danny blurted, "Where'd the trap go?" He panned the flashlight left and right inside the wall, careful not to get his hand bitten should the mouse be hunched against the inner wall out of sight. Contracting rabies was not something he wanted to add to his already miserable lifestyle. "No way that thing could've moved the trap without getting whacked!"

Something again caught Danny's eye just before he decided to click off the flashlight and return to bed. A slight, furtive movement within the mouse hole at the edge of his vision drew his attention to a thin, twitching tail that flopped down inside the hole. Danny thought maybe the rodent had stumbled back and crashed, taking its last breath.

Without hesitation, Danny repositioned himself flat on the floor in a splatting position, his body tense with anticipation. He held his breath as he watched for the tail to move again.

A few seconds passed.

No movement.

Was it dead? Had Danny finally rid his place of the annoying creature?

Danny went hands-free with the flashlight and placed the end of it in his mouth. "Gotta be sure," he mumbled with the flashlight between his teeth as he reached inside the small hole. His hand was too big to fit inside and clogged the hole at his wrist. He didn't even think about protecting his hand with a glove or anything.

Although his hand could not fit inside the mouse hole, Danny could've easily made the hole bigger by grabbing the inside edges and ripping apart the sheetrock. But why cause more damage over a stupid pest? He didn't own the place, so he'd probably be billed for the repair. No sense in adding yet another bill to the mound.

A mix of determination and curiosity quickly transposed to frustration as Danny stretched his fingers inside the wall as far as he could, hoping to at least touch the tip of the mouse's tail. He could pinch it between his fingers and remove it if he could feel it.

After an eternity of fumbling around inside the partition, Danny felt the rodent's tail against his fingertips. He pressed down, the creature's tiny muscles squishing beneath his touch. Then, excitedly, Danny withdrew his hand from the mouse hole while sliding his fingers firmly against the floor. If the mouse wasn't dead and he raised his fingers even slightly off the floor, he'd risk the rodent escaping, and he would be back at square one.

The flashlight hanging from Danny's mouth illuminated the tiny archway when he removed his hand from the mouse hole. His face lit with triumph. The tail curled outside the hole and rested against the baseboard. Proof of a successful catch.

Grinning from ear to ear, Danny pushed himself up from the floor and leaned against the wall with a sense of accomplishment. He set the flashlight on the floor next to him. Finally, a good night's rest for once. And maybe with some much-needed sleep, he would have a decent day at work, too.

Without further ado, Danny pinched the tip of the mouse's tail and pulled . . . and pulled . . . and pulled, like it was a thin, three-hundred-foot cable on a spool. It never ended!

This was not the little rodent's tail Danny thought he had caught. "What the hell is this?" he grumbled. It looked like a speaker wire he was pulling from the wall.

With a heavy sigh, Danny released the wire. He gave up. The

flashlight lay abandoned on the floor next to him, its beam piercing through the darkness. He swiped the flashlight off the floor and clicked it off before placing it on the nightstand.

Danny crawled into bed, rested his head on the pillow, lifted one side to cover his mouth, and let out a scream muffled by the fabric. All the pent-up frustrations from the night's events were captured in his soft pillow, and the silence within the room was broken only by his ragged breathing.

3

The blaring alarm jolted Danny awake as if signaling a DEFCON 5 emergency. He slammed his hand down on the off button before the sun's rays even had a chance to peek through his bedroom window.

Turning to look at the small hole in the wall was a daily part of his morning routine. Weekday mornings were methodical, almost like Danny had been diagnosed with obsessive-compulsive disorder. He would jump out of bed and yank the corner of his bed sheet back toward the pillows, making the bed quickly. Then he would shuffle across the floor barefoot to the bathroom, using his big toe to push open the door and let it hit against the door stopper with a satisfying thud. After taking care of business and washing his hands, he would spend a few minutes styling his hair before drying his hands with a towel. Next was breakfast—French toast sticks in the toaster oven and a tall glass of milk while scrolling through social media on his phone. After breakfast, Danny would shower and partially dress for work. He'd sit on the edge of his bed (always in a specific spot) and slip on his underwear, followed by socks. Then came brushing his teeth with exactly four passes for two minutes while still clad in socks and underwear—a perfect balance. The final step was slipping on his work uniform: black slacks, a long-sleeved white button-up shirt, and a tie—although not necessarily in that order.

But today, something backfired in Danny's routine, triggering an intense wave of anger within him. As he reached for the wire he had pulled from the hole in the wall, he realized it was gone. Just like the mousetrap, mysteriously missing.

"You sneaky little bastard," Danny growled, glaring at the tiny rodent's front door. He knew the culprit had snatched the wire back into its hiding place. Who else could it possibly be?

Frustration mounting, he grabbed his trusty flashlight from the nightstand and knelt at the mouse hole. He turned on the beam with a forceful click, shining it deep inside the wall. He scanned every inch of the dank, dark space with intense focus, squinting and moving back and forth, hoping to catch even a glimpse of the elusive critter.

Danny shook his head in disbelief and clicked off the flashlight in frustration. "Ugh! You're gonna make me late for work!" He rose from the floor and returned the flashlight to the nightstand. "I guess I'll call the property manager to get pest control over here." The thought of involving the apartment manager only added to his annoyance. Still, he knew he couldn't continue living with this pesky intruder disrupting his rest at night.

4

Danny trudged inside the apartment later that afternoon, weary from another stressful day at work. He flung his keys onto the cluttered kitchen counter and slumped into the worn, discolored recliner with a heavy sigh. The weight of tomorrow's impending repetition of the same mundane tasks added to his already mounting anxiety.

A glance at his watch revealed the pest control company was due to arrive any moment. He had barely made it home to let them in, and he couldn't wait to finally witness the exterminator pulling that pesky mouse from its hiding spot in the wall. The thought of ridding his space of the rodent brought him a slight sense of relief.

With a determined spring in his step, Danny grabbed a broom from the kitchen pantry and tidied up the place. He didn't like his apartment disorganized for guests, especially pest control. He worried they would blame him for the cause of bugs and mice from a filthy space.

Danny swept and dusted every nook and cranny of his apartment for ten minutes, determined to rid the place of dirt and cobwebs.

Just as he finished picking up the bedroom, a gentle knock sounded at the door. Danny rested the broom against the nightstand and traversed the living room. His eyes widened in surprise when he opened the apartment door.

A young woman stood before him with a smile lighting her face. Her long chestnut hair was pulled back into a ponytail, revealing rosy cheeks and bright hazel eyes. She wore a beige jumpsuit, reminiscent of a Ghostbusters uniform, with a bulging backpack slung over one shoulder. "Hi there, I'm Janet with Runaway Rodent," she sang cheerfully.

Danny couldn't help but feel energized by her infectious enthusiasm. His jaw slacked. The pest control lady was cute!

Janet maintained her irresistible smile. "You called for the removal of a mouse?"

"Oh, yes," Danny said, finally managing to focus. He swung the door fully open and gestured for her to enter. "Please, come in."

Janet was cautious when stepping into the apartment, as she always practiced. She glanced around, taking in the somewhat neat and organized space. This apartment starkly contrasted some places she'd been called to.

Danny watched her with a mixture of curiosity and admiration. She seemed so at ease, as if entering strangers' homes to catch rodents was the most natural thing in the world.

"So, where did you spot the critter?" Janet asked, still glancing around the living room.

"In the bedroom," Danny said. "This way." Leading her into the bedroom, he pointed down toward the mouse hole.

"I see," Janet said and removed her backpack. She set it on the floor near the bedroom doorway and crouched, rummaging through it. She pulled out a small flashlight, a small foldable cage, and a pair of latex gloves.

"You do this often?" Danny asked to break the silence in the room. He couldn't help but notice how graceful Janet looked, her movements fluid. "You know, catch mice."

Janet stood and spun to face him as she slipped on her gloves. "Every day is a new adventure in the world of pest control," she replied with a wink. "You never know what you might find." She unfolded the small cage and placed it on the floor beside the mouse hole.

Danny found himself smiling despite his earlier frustration.

With the flashlight in hand, Janet knelt and peered inside the hole in the wall, her brow furrowing in concentration as she scanned the dark crevice. Then, moments later, she murmured, "There you are, little guy." Her voice was soft yet determined.

Danny winced and blinked his eyes in awe. *No way she caught that thing already*, he thought. But his mind was not playing tricks on him.

Janet carefully reached into the mouse hole, her gloved hand disappearing into the darkness. Then, after a few tense moments, her face broke into a triumphant smile as she extracted her hand from the wall, holding a squirming mouse firmly in her grasp. "Here you go!" she said, rising to her feet. Janet raised the mouse to eye level.

"He'll never bother you again."

Excited yet dumbfounded at how quickly Janet caught the mouse keeping him awake the past several nights, Danny watched as she placed the rodent in the trap. She secured the small door to the portable cage, removed her gloves, stashed them in a pocket of her bag, and zipped it closed.

"How'd you do that so easily?" Danny asked, still in disbelief. He couldn't help but admire Janet's calm demeanor and skillful approach.

Janet let out a soft chuckle. "Years of practice. But it also helps to have a knack for it. Also, the mouse hole should be clear so you can seal it up. I didn't notice a nest or anything as far as I could see."

"Great!" Danny said. "Well, I can't thank you enough for taking care of that little troublemaker."

"It's all part of the job," Janet said warmly. She slung her backpack over her shoulder and carried the cage under her arm, the mouse darting back and forth with what little room it had to move. She stopped at the front door that Danny held open for her and turned back to him. "If you have any more pest problems, please let your landlord know, and they'll contact us."

Janet turned and stepped through the doorway. But Danny couldn't let her leave just yet. He had to ask. "Wait!" he spoke up, his voice slightly breathless with nerves. "Can I… take you out for coffee or something? As a thank you, I mean." He felt a rush of warmth to his cheeks at his boldness, but he couldn't help but feel drawn to the beautiful woman before him.

Surprised, Janet turned back to face him, her eyes flickering with curiosity before a soft smile spread. "That sounds like a date," she assumed, used to receiving such invitations from single clients. She held up her left hand and turned it to present the ring on her finger. "Sorry, my fiancé probably wouldn't approve."

Danny's heart sank, but he tried hiding his disappointment. "No problem." He forced a smile. "Sorry to have asked. Not sure what my gut was telling me."

Janet returned his smile with a pleasant one of her own. "It's okay," she reassured him. "Have a nice day!" And with that, she turned and glided out of Danny's life.

5

Danny lacked the proper materials to seal the mouse hole. He'd have to make a trip to the home improvement store tomorrow after work to get what he needed. In the meantime, he improvised by placing a stack of books on the floor to block the opening. It was a makeshift fix, but at least it would do the job for tonight.

With a satisfied sigh, he prepared for a restful night's sleep and popped an antacid pill into his mouth, chasing it down with a glass of water. He knew all too well the consequences of indulging in a late-night frozen pizza—the fiery burn of heartburn and the uncomfortable churn during an acid reflux attack. But tonight, he was determined to avoid such discomfort and enjoy a peaceful slumber.

As Danny got comfortable, he rested his head on the plush pillow and let his eyes adjust to the dimly lit room. He strained to listen for scurrying or munching noises, but there was only silence.

He closed his eyes and drifted off to sleep.

6

SNAP!

Danny jolted awake in the middle of the night. The sound reverberated through his room. He strained to listen for other noises, instinctively knowing they would come from the same place. *The mousetrap*, he thought grimly. *There must be another mouse!*

Janet had insisted there were no other pests behind the wall, but Danny couldn't shake off the feeling of unease. He reached for the flashlight on the nightstand and swung his legs over the side of the bed. Shining the light toward the makeshift barricade of books placed over the mouse hole, Danny cursed under his breath, seeing them scattered across the floor. His heart pounded as he directed the light toward the hole in the wall. To his horror, the wall had burst apart, the sheetrock in a pile on the floor. And then Danny saw them—a pair of glowing yellow eyes staring back at him from the darkness within the large hole in the wall.

Before Danny could register what was happening, a massive rat's sharp claws curled the inner partition as leverage to pull and wriggle itself free, dragging behind the broken mousetrap clamped at the tip of its tail. The mousetrap looked like a clothespin compared to the size of the severely oversized rodent.

This was no ordinary rat; the creature was enormous, its matted fur caked with dirt and grime, its teeth sharp and menacing. Danny felt a chill run down his spine as realization dawned on him—he had not been dealing with a small pest all this time. It was something more sinister and terrifying, a demon living behind the wall like a secret hidden from sight. It seemed the huge rat used mice as scouts like bucks do with does, sending them out in the open first to be sure the coast was clear.

Danny's pulse quickened as the giant rat's eyes fixed on him. He sprang into action without a moment to lose, adrenaline coursing through his veins. He grabbed the broomstick he left leaning against the nightstand when he cleaned the apartment before Janet showed up. With white knuckles from his tight grip, Danny faced the monstrous rodent.

The giant rat let out a guttural growl, its claws flexing as it prepared to lunge at Danny. With a swift movement, the creature charged toward him, its foul breath filling the room. Danny dodged just in time, narrowly avoiding the sharp claws that grazed past him.

Heart pounding, Danny knew he had to act quickly before the rat could strike again. Summoning all his courage, he lunged forward with the broomstick, aiming for the beast's head. With a sickening squelch, the broomstick connected with one of the rat's glowing yellow eyes and pushed it deep into its skull.

Danny clenched his teeth and gave the broomstick a swift twist. The oversized rodent collapsed with its legs splayed on the floor, a final exhale of breath seeping from its gaping bloody mouth.

Danny slowly released his grip on the broomstick, his hands and legs shaking. He stared down in horror at the giant rat. Its matted fur was soaked in the puddle of blood gushing from its skull. And the stench. The awful, sour stench made him want to puke.

But Danny's feeling of retching where he stood was suddenly interrupted by a voice from behind.

7

A feminine voice echoed in the room. "Hey! Are you okay?"

Danny's vision blurred as he stared down at his wet hands, the icy liquid seeping into his skin and numbing his fingers. His body trembled from the cold. His toes felt like blocks of ice. Slowly, he turned to the source of the voice and squinted to try and make out who it was. "Janet?" he croaked.

"Um, yeah? What's wrong with you, Danny? You've been cleaning up this mess for over fifteen minutes now. We have customers to take care of."

Danny slapped his numb hands over his face, trying to shake off the exhaustion plaguing him for days. The mysterious noises in the walls of his apartment had robbed him of precious sleep, leaving him constantly on edge and struggling to keep his grip on reality.

As he blinked away the blurriness in his vision, Janet's figure slowly came into focus. But something was different about her. Instead of her Runaway Rodent Pest Control jumpsuit, she wore a crisp white button-up shirt and loose-fitting black slacks. A name badge pinned to her chest proclaimed her as "JILL S. STORE DIREC-TOR."

Impatiently tapping one foot, she snapped at Danny, "What's taking so long? I need those milk and eggs stocked pronto. Chop chop!" Her sharp gaze scanned down to Danny's feet.

Following her line of sight, Danny's heart sank as he saw the mop handle lying on the ground, surrounded by a pool of spilled milk. There was no large rat with a gouged eye. Nearby, a gallon jug lay toppled over where it had fallen from the shelf. He sighed heavily as he turned back to face Janet with a defeated expression. "I'm on it," he muttered in a monotone voice.

Jill's scowl deepened before she spun on her heel, her shoes squeaking loudly against the sticky floor as she stormed around the corner.

The nauseating stench of spoiled milk and harsh cleaning solution assaulted Danny's nostrils. He picked up the mop handle and resumed mopping inside the dairy cooler. Each stroke felt like an eternity during his never-ending shift at the grocery store.

February 19, 1992 / Revised August 12, 2024

During my senior year of high school, I took a co-op class. This meant attending school for only half a day so I could work and gain valuable experience. I made $5.00 per hour.

I still recall my first day. I was trained to be a cashier, and since there were no conveyor belts yet, my trainer had to keep pulling the basket of groceries closer to the counter for me to scan them properly. My instinct was to leave a gap between the register and the basket, but my trainer kept reminding me to stay close and keep the process efficient. "Work smarter, not harder," he'd say.

I would take a step toward the basket, lean in to grab an item, take a step back to the register to scan it, push it down the counter for bagging by the clerk, and then repeat with the rest of the items in the basket.

I also met some interesting people when I worked retail. I remember vividly a lady who caught my eye with her well-endowed figure. I couldn't help but take my time ringing up this customer's order. When she handed me her check at the end of the transaction, I had to hold back my laughter when I read her last name: "Titless."

Playing it safe, I politely asked how to pronounce her name because we were required to thank every customer by name if it appeared printed on their receipt or they wrote a check.

"How do you think it's pronounced?" the lady replied with a knowing smile.

Feeling flustered, I blurted out, "Tit-less?" Her large tatas were right there before me, her cleavage exposed beneath an open-chest tank top. I didn't mean to offend her.

To my relief, she corrected me and said her name was pronounced "Titles." I completed the transaction and wished her a nice day (by name, correctly) before moving on to the next customer.

No matter how much I learned about the grocery industry, I never thought I'd spend sixteen years working for one company. I worked my way up to a service manager position and on to the person in charge when the store director was away. I took on every task imaginable: ringing up purchases at the register, bagging groceries, re-stocking dairy, frozen foods, and produce, working overnight shifts to replenish shelves, wrapping meat and slicing cold cuts, unloading trucks, crushing boxes and creating bales, managing office tasks, overseeing a team of over eighty employees, hiring new staff members and providing thorough training, even becoming the district photographer and earning numerous awards for my dedication.

I was capped at $14.85 per hour during the last two years, and those days were especially tough as I grew to hate my job because of the absurd micromanagement.

When I was an overnight stocker, I wrote a story about my experiences working in retail. The story that follows is me venting about the industry. But it will always hold a special place in my heart for incorporating bits and pieces from my experiences with my first job.

Would I ever work in a grocery store again? Absolutely not.

MONSTERS IN THE BOX

12:00 PM

As I made my way through the automatic sliding doors of the store, I was greeted with the familiar sight of six cash registers and two express lanes. It had become routine for me over the past sixteen years to enter through the northeast doors and walk down the main aisle. This demonstrated my punctuality and set a good example for other employees. However, in the last two months, I had switched things up by entering through the northwest entrance and heading for the time clock to punch in for my shift. Chattering and beeping machines filled the air as employees scanned grocery items.

Despite my usual routine, I couldn't shake the feeling of discouragement caused by the constant micromanagement procedures recently implemented at this job. Every day felt like a struggle to stay motivated and not get lost in the mundane environment. The company had been bought out twice since I started working here, and each new owner seemed to make things even more difficult with their strict policies and procedures.

I entered my employee number on the keypad in the break room and then logged into the computer at my desk to check emails. Corporate had sent a mass message to all the managers about changes to bagging procedures. Changes were happening quickly as the company implemented new rules to cut costs. The email announced that we would no longer use paper bags and required plastic bags to be filled with at least eight items without double bagging. In other words, we had to stuff the customers' bags, or we would be written up. Last week, we changed bagging supply manufacturers to a company that made thinner bags than we've always used. I knew the rollout of the new bagging procedure would be a shit show. I could picture myself only leading a horse to water with the many high schoolers working this job. Most of them weren't eager to work here in the first place. It was often their parents who pushed them to get a job. The only ones who stayed for an extended period were the students taking co-op courses as part of their education.

I had no choice but to follow the new procedures and policies handed down to me. It was my job to lead by example. But it was always a hassle. On the management side, these policies challenged our time management skills. For instance, instead of simply walking around the store to place orders for the next day's delivery, we had to count all the out-of-stock items on the shelves first. Some managers tried to save time by moving items to cover up empty spaces. Still, they always got caught later when the district manager paid a surprise visit to the store and audited us as we counted. We were written up if there were more than ten out-of-stocks in each department. The purpose of the count was to place a practical order. If the product's manufacturer was also out of stock, we were still held accountable at the store level.

After shutting down the computer and pinning my name badge to my shirt, I walked past the store manager's office. The store director, Jill Sheffield, looked up from her desk and alerted me.

"Tony, can you come in here for a moment?" Jill asked.

I entered her office and took a seat across from her desk. "What's up?"

"Can you cover Danny Benton's shift tomorrow in the dairy department?"

"What time?" I inquired. This request was unusual, as it wasn't typical for the store manager to have the front end manager work in another department. The store was known for its high turnover rate and desperate need for help, but pulling from the busiest area with such short notice made me question things.

"The morning shift, six to two," Jill replied. "Danny has been acting strange lately, like he hasn't been getting enough sleep, and it's affecting his ability to keep the department stocked and conditioned. It'll just be for tomorrow, and Ronald Daniels can watch the front end for you while he stocks the short aisles near the registers until your other service manager comes in. I'll have someone from another store cover the rest of the week until Danny can get a head on his shoulders again."

I had experience stocking dairy before; it was simple but tedious.

I wouldn't get a bump in pay for it, but at least it was less stressful than running the front end. "Sure, I can work in dairy tomorrow," I confirmed.

"Great! There won't be any orders to place, either. I'll take care of it if you have everything stocked by noon."

"No problem," I said. "Anything else?"

Jill's smile lit up as she glanced at her computer screen and then back at me. "Actually, yes," she said. "The company is introducing a new job title that we need to fill internally. I have to submit a candidate's name to corporate by the end of this week."

"What's the title?" I asked, intrigued, sensing Jill was hinting at something.

"Person In Charge," Jill replied. "We'll call it PIC for short. You already do most of the work, so there wouldn't be much learning curve. You'll still oversee the front end but will be the point of contact when the assistant store director or I am unavailable. You'll receive cross-training in other departments, too. And you'll be pulling applications for interviews, conducting new hire orientation, and cashier training."

"How ironic," I chuckled, thinking about my recent agreement to work in the dairy department in the morning. "Does this come with a pay increase?"

Jill raised her finger and arched an eyebrow in amusement. "As a matter of fact, it does." She clicked a few times on her mouse and pulled up a file on her computer screen. "It's a one-dollar raise per hour, plus you're guaranteed five hours of overtime each week. The catch is that you'll have to work forty-five hours per week minimum. So, should I put your name forward for consideration?"

The thought of guaranteed overtime hours was enticing. I could use it, and I was pleasantly surprised to learn that the company was implementing this program.

Without hesitation, I reached across Jill's desk and shook her hand. "Let's do it," I said with a wide grin.

12:20 PM

I made my way down the hallway to the staircase and exited onto the sales floor by the cash office, each step becoming more dreadful the closer I got to the front end. The store was always busy. I counted the customers in each line as I headed to the service desk facing the cash registers. If there were more than three customers in a line, we were required to open another register, regardless of who would be operating it. With all registers already open, my next step was to redirect customers to other departments for checkout, such as the floral department, customer service booth, video department, or even the food service department.

As I began my shift and spotted a department manager working at one of the registers, I knew I needed to consult the schedule quickly to prepare for the day. It was clear the store had been busy before I arrived; some cashiers hadn't taken their breaks, and the front end was a disaster.

The floors were dirty, items like candy, gum, and magazines were scattered about, and shopping carts were abandoned in various aisles. I was never informed about any callouts, so I discovered them by noticing a missing staff member or having another manager tell me at the last minute. Poor communication has always been my biggest frustration, and this was one of the most irritating situations.

Ron Daniels, the department head of general merchandise, seemed distressed as he worked at register eight. I could see him muttering to himself while quickly scanning a full bascart of groceries.

From his body language, Ron had been interrupted from placing an order for his department to come up front and help with the busy checkout lines. But he was a cool guy with a good sense of humor. I always appreciated management personnel who could take a joke because that's my style. I liked to keep things light and crack jokes sometimes at work, but never in front of customers unless they initiated it first.

Ron was tall and lanky with a goofy appearance and a thin mustache. He was an older gentleman, and I knew he had been in retail for most of his career because of his thoroughness and knowledge of the industry.

When I approached him to take over his register, his face lit into a colossal smile. "Thank God you're here!" he said as he flipped through the produce book, looking up the code for kumquats. We sold these by the pound but always wondered why they were never packaged and assigned a barcode. "It's been absolute madness today. And your pal Larry down there on register four has been driving me insane, paging me every fifteen minutes."

Ah, Larry. He was a one-of-a-kind cashier. He was a friendly kid at heart, but he tended to grate on the nerves of whoever was in charge during morning shifts. But what can you do? Larry was only available for early mornings. Finding someone with an open schedule for this type of job was rare. It was a scarce resource that only came around occasionally. If all employees had the same level of availability, we would have fewer issues and be able to complete our work more efficiently. But I was sure the company would still find a way to make our lives miserable.

Larry was an employee who always followed the rules by the book and had no regrets about calling out others if they weren't doing the same. Many of the employees knew him as a tattletale. I knew him as a person with a developmental disorder that people just needed to accept and be respectful of. Yes, Larry got on my nerves daily, but I could control how I responded to his needs.

"Well, tell the company to get rid of the maximum of three customers per lane," I suggested to Ron as he totaled the customer's bill. "I can't get anything done, either."

With a polite smile, Ron handed the receipt to his customer and thanked her by name. As he signed out of the register, I took my place behind it and quickly logged in with my numbers.

Ron slapped my back and said, "Welcome to hell," before deftly swiping his ordering gun off the counter and striding back to his department.

2:00 PM

Before I knew it, two hours had passed, and my feet were already starting to ache. I ran the front end, scanned groceries for customers, and handled any disputes or issues arising at other registers. I also covered breaks and lunches for cashiers and answered phone calls while managing my register. It was a skill I acquired over the years of doing the same repetitive tasks daily.

The afternoon rush was finally starting to taper off. I shut down my register and cleaned up the front end. Breaks and lunches were caught up. The morning shifts were ending, and I was about to lose two cashiers, only to be replaced by three more in thirty minutes.

As I updated the sheet for assigning breaks, there was the familiar sound of bascarts clattering near the entrance. We called them bascarts instead of baskets because they were carts with wheels. Baskets were used for carrying groceries. I looked up and saw Brian shuffling toward me from the northeast entrance.

Brian was an older employee who enjoyed collecting bascarts from the parking lot. This task and cleaning were his strongest skills, so he remained a bagging clerk throughout his time with the company. As he approached the service desk, Brian's face glistened with sweat. "It's time for my break," he said in a monotone voice.

I glanced down at the break sheet and ran my finger over his name to check his scheduled break time. Sure enough, I had missed sending him on break by two minutes. "Oh. Sorry, Brian. Yeah, go take your break."

"Who will collect the carts from the lot?" Brian asked.

I scanned the front end. There was only one other bagger on duty. "Andrea and I will take care of it, my friend. You go ahead and take your break."

"Are you sure?" Brian's eyes widened as if concerned that we couldn't handle it.

"I'm sure, buddy."

"Okay, thanks." Brian took two steps before turning back to me. "If we got ten cents for each cart return, I could do this all day, and we wouldn't have to worry about the parking lot getting full."

I let out a small chuckle. Brian made this suggestion every day. "In a perfect world, that would be great. But unfortunately, we need help inside with bagging groceries for our customers and helping them carry their orders to their cars."

"Oh, okay," Brian said, disappointed. It was a good idea, but the company would never approve.

"Take your break," I said. "I'll take care of the carts."

Brian pulled a towel from his pants pocket and wiped his brow before heading to the food service department.

A loud, impatient voice broke through the somewhat silent front end. "Is this register open?" the voice demanded.

I looked up from my task and noticed with a sinking feeling that I had left my light on at my register. "Son of a bitch," I muttered, quickly making my way over to register eight.

"I saw the light was on, but nobody was home," the customer snarked, clearly irritated by the delay.

The cashiers were instructed to remain in the aisle at their designated registers when not actively ringing up orders. Two cashiers were following this protocol, but it was evident that the man could have quickly taken a few more steps to have his order rung up by one of them.

"Sorry about that," I said, trying to maintain a professional demeanor despite my frustration.

I switched off my light, signed in on the register, and scanned the guy's items. Thankfully, he didn't seem like one of those entitled douchebags looking for an opportunity to cause trouble.

As I handed the customer his receipt and thanked him by name, a voice called, "Are you still open?" As I turned to face the source, my eyes landed on a young woman setting her handbasket down on the counter. Mentally, I rolled my eyes and thought about how annoying it was that people kept asking me if I was open when the lane light was off. It happened all the time, and it was frustrating. But I put on a fake smile and replied, "This lane is closed, but I'll be happy to check you out."

She was cute, which was another reason I accepted her order. I rang up her six items and totaled the bill.

Another customer approached me as my current customer searched her purse for her checkbook. "Are you open?"

I wanted to pull my hair out. The guy had one item. I couldn't turn him down. It was just common courtesy. "This lane is closed, but I'll ring up your item."

"Cool, man. Thanks!"

Meanwhile, my current customer was still digging in her purse. She had so many items strewn about the counter. "I can't find my checkbook," she said.

"We gladly accept credit cards or cash," I suggested.

The lady briefly glanced at me before returning to rummaging through her purse.

I sighed, trying to remain patient to finish this transaction. As I looked up at the next customer in line, two more appeared behind him.

Stretching my neck to see over the impulse buy racks, I noticed that the other two cashiers were still standing out in their aisles. "Hey, Dylan!" I called out to the cashier, who was three lanes over. "Can you take these customers so I can manage this front end?"

Dylan whisked over and took the last person in my line instead of the next one.

I slapped a hand over my face. Dylan knew he was supposed to follow the rules and take the next customer in line. What was going on with him today?

This was going to be a long and hectic night. Ron had warned me this was a day from hell, and I could see it was coming true.

3:30 PM

Larry and another cashier, Jessica, couldn't extend their shifts, so I had to let them leave.

Unfortunately, out of three cashiers scheduled for 3:30 PM, only one showed up for their shift. No one had marked their absence on the break sheet before I arrived for my shift. A sinking feeling of dread hit me as I realized we would be severely understaffed for the rest of the evening.

Customers kept pouring in, forming long lines at each register. The rule of a maximum of three customers per lane was utterly disregarded. I could see the desperation in every customer's eyes as they searched for an open register. We wouldn't be able to keep up with the demand. I paged over the intercom for other department managers and a produce clerk to help at the registers. Ron was one of the other managers I paged back to the front end.

This wasn't a holiday, so why was everyone grocery shopping all at once? Was there some major storm coming that I didn't know about?

As the chaos unfolded, Brian arrived at my register and helped me bag a large order. He looked at me with concern and determination, knowing we were in for a rough night ahead. "Where are the other cashiers?" he asked, his voice filled with worry.

"I have no clue," I replied, feeling the weight of responsibility settling on my shoulders. "But we need to hold down the fort until I get off this register and make some calls. This is insane!"

A customer, clearly frustrated, approached me from behind. "Excuse me, is there another register that can be opened?"

I continued scanning the items of the order I was ringing up, purposely avoiding eye contact with the disgruntled individual behind me. "I have all available cashiers working now," I replied calmly. "Unfortunately, we are shorthanded."

"Sounds like someone needs to write a better schedule," the customer said, huffing, dropping his handbasket on the floor, and storming out of the store.

As the front end manager, I created the weekly schedule for the cashiers and baggers. However, the company's policy allowed a software program to generate the schedule based on availability, time-off requests from employees, sales data from the previous year, and projected sales for the current week. I could manually fill in shifts the system missed. Still, the company restricted our ability to override more than ten percent of the schedule. It was a flawed system that often resulted in understaffed shifts during busy times. Plus, the damn thing didn't account for callouts and no-call no-shows. The computer did not understand how to schedule our most reliable employees and give them enough hours. The company needed to go back to the drawing board on this issue.

3:55 PM

Ron switched off his register light and finished ringing up his last order. I had one more customer in my line before I could escape my register. I remembered to turn off my light this time.

After Ron finished his order, he approached me and said, "I'll cover the front end for you. Go take your lunch."

I looked at him like he was crazy. I couldn't leave the front end until it was staffed before five o'clock. Rush hour was between five and seven. Something must've been up his sleeve. I understood he wanted to ensure I ate, and I appreciated it, but in the long run, it wasn't very wise. "I need to make some phone calls first," I said. "We're down two cashiers, and I need to fill the shifts. You're leaving at eight o'clock, and it's only gonna get worse from here."

"Do your thing," Ron agreed. "I'll stay nearby and cover for you. I'm done ordering."

It was rare to find someone like Ron who would go out of their way to help you in this business, and I appreciated it greatly.

4:15 PM

I scanned the contact list, desperately trying to find someone who could work on such short notice. Unfortunately, it was a school night, and most people were unavailable, politely declining, citing the late notice. The rest of the contacts didn't even bother picking up the phone.

Knowing I was shit out of luck, I went ahead and took my meal break.

5:20 PM

As I returned from break, the front end was bustling once again. I saw Jill, the store director, dip out the front door. At least she stayed past her shift long enough for me to finish my break.

It was no surprise to see Ron manning a register; he could never catch a break in his department. Before calling it a day, he had to condition all the shelves in his department.

We were counting on one more cashier to come in at six o'clock before our overnight cashier arrived at ten. I just hoped the six o'clock shift would be covered; it was assigned to Craig, one of my assistant service managers. However, his availability was unpredictable as he was a sophomore in college and could only work one day a week, plus weekends. It would be interesting to see how this would play out.

6:00 PM

With relief, I watched as Craig strode through the front doors. And to my surprise, he was on time! Without hesitation, I sent him to take over for another cashier who needed a meal break.

For the next hour, I ran a register. Ron, two other cashiers, and I controlled the chaos. The rest of the store was operating on autopilot. Long lines of impatient customers snaked from the registers into the food aisles. Everyone was angry and agitated, and I couldn't blame them.

As the closing manager tonight, I monitored high-traffic areas for low stock throughout the evening, like in the dairy department. Milk and eggs were flying off the shelves. In the produce department, bananas were responsible for one percent of our sales, so I also needed to make sure we had an ample supply of those. The closing produce clerk tonight had a good head on his shoulders, so I trusted he would take care of those bananas for me.

My job also entailed protecting the store assets and aggressively chasing sales. This required me to stay vigilant and be on the lookout for potential thefts. I had to be alert for anyone trying to rush out of the store with a handbasket filled with items, sneaking something into their pocket while browsing an aisle, or pretending to shop with a bascart only to abandon it full of goods in a remote part of the store. More often, I caught customers trying the "fake shopping" tactic, especially in the meat department. They would grab a bascart and fill it with various items in the store before heading to the meat section. After selecting expensive packaged steaks, they would push their bascart down an empty aisle, stuff the meat into their clothing, and exit through the front doors without paying. No one on the front end would ever suspect this tactic in progress. A department manager or another employee walking around the store must keep tabs on the suspect without losing sight of them at any time.

But my back was turned, and the store was highly vulnerable to theft.

8:00 PM

"Okay, I'm outta here," Ron said while I jotted notes about today's events at the service desk. "You got this for the next two hours?"

"I'll handle it," I said. "No matter what we go through, we always make it."

"Ain't that the truth," Ron said. "Have a good night, and I'll see you in the morning."

"Thanks for your help!" I said as Ron stepped away from the service desk. He gave me a thumbs-up over his shoulder and then dipped out of the store.

I looked up from the service desk and noted three cashiers. Each had one customer in their lane. I also had two baggers until ten o'clock. One was helping bag a midsize order, and the other one I had assigned to empty the overflowing trashcans outside.

Thankfully, I was able to take a breather and walk the store. I picked up trash on my way to the dairy department. "Don't pass it up, pick it up" was one of our store's mottos. When I got to dairy, it looked like a tornado had blown through. There were so many holes in the shelves where the milk and eggs were located! I quickly burst through the double doors leading to the backroom, slid open the thick cooler door, and restocked the milk. I found a few boxes of eggs, ran them back onto the sales floor, and filled the shelves.

I checked in with the butcher running the meat department, and he was prepping to close the department by hosing down the floors.

When I walked to the produce department, I discovered Blake had already stocked the bananas.

Finally, I headed to the bakery and food service departments. The employees there were already cleaning as well. The store was slowly coming back together again.

9:15 PM

After securing the northeast entrance and barricading it with bas-carts, I went to the service desk to organize the timesheets for the opening manager. Just as I reached the desk, a page came through on the intercom from the customer service booth near the pharmacy. "Tony Phoenix, you have a phone call on line one."

I picked up the receiver and pressed the button for line one. "This is Tony, how may I help you?"

"Hey, Tony. It's Eileen. I won't be able to make it to work to-night. I'm having chest pains, and my husband is about to take me to the ER."

I checked my watch. Eileen was my overnight cashier, scheduled to work at ten o'clock. I had previously exhausted all my contacts to find someone to come in to work earlier. I knew they wouldn't come in for the overnight shift. Once again, I was screwed. My brain felt like it was exploding, and I gripped the phone so tight my knuckles turned white. I remembered I had agreed to work the dairy depart-ment at six o'clock in the morning, which would make this a triple shift for me.

But I remained calm and spoke to Eileen in a friendly and sym-pathetic tone. "Oh no! Thank you for letting me know. Keep me posted, okay? I hope you start feeling better soon."

Although Eileen was in her sixties, she could run circles around the high school kids. She kept her register cleaned, gum and candy stocked, magazine racks straightened, and more. She knew how to keep herself busy when business was slow.

After hanging up the phone, I walked into the restroom and smacked my hand against the wall in frustration. The restroom was trashed and smelled of urine. I picked up some wadded towels on the floor and threw them away.

Walking back to the front end, I counted the cases of plastic bags at each register. We were running low, and I would need to grab a few cases from the backroom.

The customer service booth paged me again over the intercom: "Tony Phoenix, there's a delivery truck at the back door."

I threw my hands in the air. The truck should've been here at seven o'clock. Ron didn't inform me that it had never arrived during his shift. I looked at my watch. I had twenty minutes to unload the truck and return to the front end to run a register. I was about to lose the remaining cashiers at ten o'clock.

I stepped to Craig's register and instructed him to handle the front end until I finished with the truck.

"You got it, boss," Craig said while ringing up an order.

"Thanks, man. I know you leave at ten, but it might be a few minutes later, depending on how many pallets I need to unload. Eileen called in tonight, so I'll have to stay overnight. Unless you can help."

"Nah, man. I've got a class in the morning. But I'll cover you while you get the truck."

Heading to the backroom, I had made it halfway down the store's center aisle when the customer service booth paged me again over the intercom. "Tony Phoenix, you have a phone call on line one."

I detoured to the meat department and picked up the phone there. "This is Tony, how may I help you?"

"Tony, it's Jason. I'm running about forty-five minutes late. The train stopped near my house and blocked the road."

Jason was the manager of the overnight stocking crew. I wanted to hang up on him, walk out the front door, and go home. But that wasn't like me. *No matter what we go through, we always make it.* "Okay. Try and hurry, but be safe. Eileen called out, so I'm having to run the register overnight. The truck is here now, and I need to unload it before everyone leaves."

9:40 PM

I disabled the alarm system on the back door before unlocking it to let the truck driver inside the backroom. Then I pressed a button on the wall that opened the roll-up door where the truck was parked. I cut the ID tag on the back of the semi and waited as the truck driver unlocked the padlock and raised the rear door.

"How many pallets do we have tonight?" I asked.

The truck driver looked at the paperwork on his clipboard. "Seven. But there's another pallet coming later as it was overlooked on this delivery."

"I guess that's not too bad, considering the shitty day I've had," I said. I retrieved an electric pallet jack from its charger and began unloading the truck.

"Oh yeah?" said the truck driver. "Is that why getting to the dock took you a while?"

I inserted the forks into the first pallet, lifted it, and pulled it out of the truck. "Yeah. We've been shorthanded all day since I started

47

my shift this afternoon. I have to work a triple because the overnight cashier called in sick at the last minute. I previously agreed to work the dairy department in the morning, too."

"That sucks!"

"Tell me about it," I replied, carefully placing the first pallet beside some backstock. Then, without wasting time, I returned to the truck with the pallet jack to retrieve the next load. I repeated this process until I had one more pallet to unload. It was a single box shrink-wrapped to the pallet and was noticeably loose and crushed at one corner.

"What's this?" I asked, pulling the final pallet from the truck.

"It looks like a shipper display for a new item." The truck driver skimmed through his paperwork. "This is one of two shippers—the other pallet is arriving later."

"Does it say the description of the product?" I questioned, placing the pallet beside the others I had already unloaded.

"Nope," the truck driver replied, shaking his head.

I parked and plugged in the pallet jack to keep it charged before looking at the paperwork.

"Interesting. All the other items listed have descriptions," I noticed.

"Yep." The truck driver nodded, handing me his pen.

I signed off on the delivery in exchange for a dot matrix printed packet containing the detailed inventory list of delivered items. "Sorry for the wait, but thank you for waiting," I said apologetically.

The truck driver shut the back door of his trailer, locked it with the padlock, and added another identification tag. "It's no trouble," he replied, heading for the exit. "Have a good night, and don't work too hard!"

As the door closed behind him, I locked it and activated the alarm system.

10:05 PM

A voice boomed through the backroom intercom. It was Craig calling my name urgently. "Tony Phoenix, dial station zero-three, please. Tony Phoenix, dial station zero-three . . . please."

I realized I was already five minutes late to return to the front end. Craig was supposed to be going home. Hurrying to the receiving desk, I picked up the phone and dialed his station. "Hey, Craig, sorry for the delay. The truck took longer to unload than expected—"

"Mr. Phoenix, a homeless man just walked into the store and took a shit on the floor in front of the registers!"

I couldn't believe what I was hearing. This had to be a joke. But Craig's tone was serious. "What?!" I exclaimed, waiting for him to reveal it was a prank.

"Some older guy just dropped his pants and crapped on the floor," Craig repeated.

"Are you kidding me?" I asked incredulously. "The bathrooms are *right there!*"

"I'm not joking," Craig replied, struggling to hold back laughter. "He's gone now, but what should I do?"

"Ugh! This night just keeps getting worse," I groaned. "See if Brian is still here and can clean it up. If not, I'll take care of it."

"Brian already went home," Craig informed me.

"Okay, I'll be there in a minute. In the meantime, throw some paper towels over it and block off the area with cones." I slammed down the phone and started back to the front end. But as I rounded the corner to the double doors leading out onto the sales floor, I saw the last box I had unloaded from the truck was discolored. I didn't notice this before. Curiosity sparked, causing me to pause and examine it more closely.

It looked like something was leaking through the side of the box. I knelt to inspect the box and got a whiff of a strange smell. It was a sickly sweet scent, like overripe fruit mixed with something metallic and acrid. With cautious fingers, I pressed on the side of the soggy cardboard box, feeling it give way beneath my touch. The box caved in, and dozens of puffball toys with googly eyes spilled onto the floor, revealing a sight that caused my breath to catch in my throat. The toys were the size of softballs.

The puffballs came in all colors, their fuzzy exteriors adorned with mismatched eyes that seemed to follow me as I moved. They looked like a bunch of balled up hedgehogs with blinking eyes staring at me from the floor. But what truly grabbed my attention was the wormlike creatures crawling all over them. They were slimy and iridescent, their movements quick and erratic as they slithered over and between them. Oddly enough, none of the worms touched the ground.

I wasn't quite sure what to think when I stumbled upon this strange discovery. But one thing was certain: the toys scattered across the floor needed to be picked up.

I quickly went to the storage room and grabbed a box of latex gloves. As I stretched them over my hands, I heard whistling sounds from where the toys were spilled. I figured the night crew had arrived for their shift.

I turned off the light in the storage room and closed the door behind me. When I rounded the corner back into the receiving area, three night crew stockers, who didn't speak English, were throwing the puffball toys at each other. Each time a ball soared through the air, it emitted a distinct whistling sound similar to a dog toy. The crew must not have noticed the worms crawling all over the toys. My second thought was how annoying those sounds were. They varied from high-pitched squeals to low-pitched rumbles and were already driving me insane.

Despite my attempts to get the crew's attention and tell them to stop playing around and help me pick up these stupid toys, they continued their game. Eventually, Hector threw a pink puffball at Jose's crotch, causing him to double over in laughter while Juan pointed and laughed hysterically. Jose kicked a puffball under the box baler machine nearby as he tried to regain his composure.

Finally fed up with their shenanigans, I yelled at them, pointing at the scattered toys and then at the collapsed box, hoping they would understand to clean up their mess.

10:15 PM

As the night crew gathered the scattered toys, I went down the center aisle to the front end. Craig was busy ringing up orders—a constant stream of customers lined up at his checkout lane. The low murmur of voices and beeps from the cash register blended into a symphony of retail chaos. Craig flashed me a tired smile before returning to the never-ending line before him.

Every eye seemed to be fixed on me as I walked past the registers to deal with the issue Craig had called me about. I was relieved to see that he had followed my instructions and gathered a pile of paper towels, surrounded by four bright orange caution cones around the offending turd on the floor. The odor was unbearable, and I couldn't believe no one had complained about the smell yet. As I made my way toward the mess, I half expected someone to stop me and comment on how the store smelled like shit, literally.

Luckily, I was still wearing my latex gloves. I quickly gathered the pile of soiled towels and burst through the bathroom door, holding my breath. With a swift motion, I tossed the towels into the trash can and grabbed a disinfectant spray bottle and a fresh set of towels. In no time, I had wiped away all traces of feces from the floor. Why anyone would have the nerve to crap directly on the floor in a public place was mind-blowing. This was undoubtedly one for the books!

I returned to the bathroom to put away the spray bottle in the cabinet beneath the sinks. Then I disposed of my gloves in the trash can and replaced the liner with a new one. I'd take the trash back to the dumpster in the receiving area later. I needed to help Craig get his line down. So, after thoroughly washing my hands up to my elbows and drying them off, I headed back out to hop on a register.

10:40 PM

Jason, the night manager, finally made it to work. I saw him walk in as I rang up the last customer in my line. Craig, who was four registers up from me, had finished his line of customers a few minutes before me and was wiping down his register.

After totaling my customer's order, I picked up the phone at my register and dialed Craig's register number. "Hey, man, can you stay another twenty minutes?" I asked.

"Yeah, but I can't stay any later than eleven," Craig replied.

"Great! Thank you so much. I just need to get with the night manager and give him the rundown before you leave."

"No problem," Craig said.

10:47 PM

Jason caught up with me as I was walking to the receiving area to check on the mess the crew had left.

"Sorry I'm late," Jason apologized.

In my head, I wanted to strangle him, but I stayed calm. "Shit happens. Thanks for letting me know. You missed all the chaos, though." I recounted the story of the customer pinching a loaf on the floor.

We stopped when we opened the double doors leading to the backroom. The three stockers were sprawled out on the ground near the box baler machine.

51

Glancing down at the floor, I noticed it was no longer littered with the puffball toys they tossed around earlier.

"What the fuck!" Jason shouted.

"What the hell?" I added.

Jason quickly hurried to Hector's side and knelt beside him. I checked on Juan and Jose, who were both unconscious next to each other. First, I felt a pulse on Juan, which was faint but still there. Then I reached for Jose and placed two fingers on his neck. Like Juan, his pulse was faint as well. But as I felt the pulsating movement underneath my fingers, it didn't feel like a regular pulse. Something slithered underneath my fingers.

"Looks like Hector has a weak pulse, but he's breathing," Jason informed me. "Is there a gas leak in here or something?"

"I noticed the same for Juan and Jose," I replied. "I walked in on them throwing around some new toys we got tonight and told them to put them away. I'm unsure about a gas leak, but I'll contact Jill if you want to call 911."

Jason and I maintained our composure despite the fear gnawing at our insides. But as we removed our cell phones from our pockets, Hector and Juan reached and firmly grabbed our wrists.

Juan's grip tightened on my wrist. My phone slipped from my hand like a bar of soap and clattered to the concrete floor. When I looked down in disbelief, Juan's eyes snapped open, and a writhing wormlike creature crawled across his eyeball.

Panicking, I squeezed his wrist with my free hand, hoping it would force him to release his grip on me. But I could feel the constant slithering movements beneath his skin like the worms were swimming inside him.

"Let go!" Jason shouted across from me, mimicking my actions by grabbing Hector's wrist. His phone had slipped out of his hand as well.

Suddenly, Jose's eyes flew open, revealing more of those slimy creatures undulating beneath the skin on his face. Fear coursed through me as I realized these parasites were taking control of the night stockers' bodies.

Juan's grip tightened more, the pressure numbing my hand. My fingers spasmed as I struggled to break free. Frantically searching for a solution, I reached into my pocket and found my trusty box knife, flicking the slider with my thumb to expose the glinting blade.

With a trembling hand, I pressed the sharp edge against the back of Juan's wrist and sliced open a small gash. A sudden rush of warm liquid oozed out, and a swarm of those tiny wormlike creatures spilled forth from the wound, writhing and squirming on the floor like something out of a nightmare.

I scrambled to stand up and ran to where Hector held Jason. I used my box knife to cut into Hector's hand. Like Juan, he had a horde of slimy worms pour out from his wound, scattering across the concrete floor like an army of cockroaches.

Jason didn't waste a second. He grabbed his aching wrist and took off, completely forgetting about his phone lying on the ground behind him.

As I reached down to retrieve my flip phone, I saw Jose slowly sit up and stare at me. His face was covered in writhing worms, and it was as if they controlled his movements and coordinated his actions perfectly. Shortly after, Juan and Hector also sat up simultaneously. I was unsure how to react as the three stockers gawked at me like twisted marionettes from a carnival sideshow.

Then, once more, the unexpected occurred. The fluffy pink toy that had rolled under the box baler machine suddenly began to move on its own, rolling and stopping at the edge of the machine. Its googly eyes shifted in opposite directions as the worms scattered from Hector and Juan. They latched onto the toy as though it were a magnet.

As I watched this strange scene unfold, I jumped back in surprise before quickly regaining my composure and making a beeline for the double doors leading to the sales floor.

11:02 PM

Proceeding down the center aisle, I noticed customers pushing their bascarts around, unaware of the horror unfolding in the back of the store. Spotting Craig at his register, I hurried over to him, my heart pounding.

Craig glanced up as I approached, his expression puzzled. Thankfully, there were no customers in his lane.

"Shut down your register and leave the store right now!" I whispered urgently to Craig, trying to convey the gravity of the situation without causing panic among any nearby customers.

Craig's eyes widened in alarm, but he nodded and quickly closed his register. "I saw Jason run out the front door," he said as he fumbled with the cash drawer.

"I figured he would," I said. "No time to explain. You need to leave, too."

I headed to the cash office booth to call 911.

When I abruptly entered, Cathy, the cash office booth manager, was focused on counting and bundling bills for the next day's pickup by the cash handling company. "What's the matter with you?" she snapped sarcastically. She'd worked for this company for nearly ten years and knew her job well. Cathy was stern and direct with her team operating the cash office booth.

"Something is going on with the night stockers," I said, my hands shaking as I dialed 911 and waited for a dispatcher to answer.

Cathy swiftly strapped a stack of bills, wrote the total amount on the band, and locked them in a small safe. "What do you mean?"

The dispatcher answered my call, and my voice trembled as I explained the strange events happening in the store.

Cathy listened with a look of disbelief on her face. Then she pointed at the glass window in front of us. "Oh my God!"

I looked up from my phone and saw Hector chasing after a customer. The woman was shrieking and throwing items at him from her hand basket. But Hector was too fast, dodging her attacks. He tackled her to the ground, pinning her down on the tiled floor.

Meanwhile, Juan and Jose appeared at the ends of aisles two and three. They were both holding puffball toys in their hands. By this point, other customers had caught on to what was happening and began rushing toward the front of the store in a panic. Thankfully, all the departments in the store had shut down, and the employees had clocked out and gone home for the evening. This would be one hell of an incident report I'd need to complete.

I noticed Juan eyeballing someone in the store like he had picked his target and followed their every move. That's when I saw Craig walking out of the restroom. "Oh no!" I said. My hand holding the phone to my ear relaxed, and I slowly lowered the handset. I could still hear the emergency dispatcher talking, but I couldn't understand what she said. Her words were garbled like the voice of Charlie Brown's mom in the *Peanuts* cartoons.

Cathy stood next to me in shock. "What?"

"Juan's gonna go after Craig!"

Cathy cupped her hand over her mouth.

I placed the dispatcher on hold and then pressed the intercom button on the phone. "Craig, run to the cash office booth!" I spoke through the handset, my voice carrying through the speakers around the store.

Craig made eye contact with me while walking to the cash office booth. Confusion was written all over his face.

"Run!" I raised my voice over the intercom.

Craig glanced behind him and saw Juan running at him at full speed.

Juan jumped over a display of colorful flowers near the store's entrance, determined to take down Craig.

"Craig, run to the office!" I shouted through the intercom, trying to get his attention.

But it was too late. Jose hurled one of the small orange puffballs he had held while standing at the end of aisle three. The ball whistled a high-pitched sound as it flew over all eight cash registers and struck Craig in the back of his head.

Craig fell to his knees, clutching his head. The puffball had pierced through his skull, blood gushing from the wound and pooling around him. The ball disappeared into his brain in seconds, and Craig collapsed onto the floor facedown.

Speechless and horrified by what I had just witnessed, I turned to Cathy, who had fainted on the floor. "Shit," I muttered and depressed the hold button to return to speak to the emergency dispatcher. "Hello? Are you still there? Please send the police to—"

Before I could finish my sentence, another puffball whizzed through the air and smashed against the glass window of the office booth. The window cracked under the impact as I recoiled from the loud noise. And there, staring me in the face with its googly eyes, was a green puffball oozing worms. It was devouring the glass!

11:20 PM

Two customers walked into the store and stopped in their tracks when they saw Craig's body on the floor covered in blood. They were too shocked to notice Juan standing there, glaring at them. They panicked when he walked toward them, and they ran out of the store.

However, Juan didn't stop there. He continued walking to the cash office booth.

I tried desperately to wake Cathy, gently shaking her shoulders. But she remained unconscious, leaving me with a difficult decision: keep trying to wake her or save myself and escape from the office.

I could hear the worms eating away at the window, and I knew it was only a matter of time before they broke through and let the googly-eyed puffball inside. If that happened, I didn't want to think about what would become of Cathy. Despite the danger, I couldn't leave her behind.

I shook Cathy again and called her name, hoping for a response. "Cathy, come on! We need to get out of here!" I pleaded.

Finally, she stirred and opened her eyes slowly, groaning as she touched her forehead. "What's going on?" she asked groggily.

"No time to explain," I replied urgently. "We need to leave now! Can you stand?"

Cathy nodded weakly.

I helped her to her feet and supported her weight as we made our way to the office door. Just as we stepped out and the door closed, I heard the glass shatter inside the booth and knew the puffball had entered the office.

I was left with another decision. We could climb the flight of stairs to the management offices and break room and descend a different set of stairs back onto the sales floor. Or we could enter the door behind us, which led outside the front of the cash office, where Juan was waiting.

I chose to take the stairs, moving slowly and carefully. Once we reached the top, I led Cathy down the hallway. We passed the locked door to Jill's office and entered the break room next door, where we could grab some bottled water.

While Cathy rested at a desk and drank her water, I searched for something to use as a weapon, rummaging through drawers and cabinets, even empty lockers. I only found basic office supplies like pens, pencils, papers, and staplers. I was so furious that my hands were shaking.

I fished my cell phone out of my pocket and flipped it open, redialing 911. The dispatcher answered quickly, and I updated them on the situation. They informed me that the police had been present for five minutes and instructed me to find cover until the threat was eliminated. The dispatcher promised to keep me updated as they communicated with the officers.

I heard a beep on my phone and pulled it away from my ear to look at the screen. A low battery symbol appeared, reminding me of its limited power. No phones were in the break room, and I couldn't access Jill's office. It came as no surprise that I was fucked.

We needed to leave the store and find safety, whether we had a weapon or not. I couldn't wait for that bizarre creature and its worms to come up the stairs and attack us like sitting ducks.

I assisted Cathy from her chair and headed down the hallway to the other staircase. We took our time, carefully descending so as not to trip or fall. Finally, we reached the bottom, and I flipped my phone closed and stuffed it back into my pocket. I couldn't concentrate on my surroundings with the dispatcher yapping in my ear. The battery was going to die soon anyway.

"Let's strategize this for a second," I told Cathy as we stood by the door. "I don't think running for the front doors from here would be wise."

"But what about the police?" Cathy's voice trembled with fear, but she seemed to be regaining some of her energy after resting in the break room. "They could mistake us for those creatures and shoot at us."

"You know what's interesting about that?" I paused, glancing at Cathy's glassy eyes. "I haven't heard any gunshots or shouting from officers. You'd think they would shoot at those stockers since I've seen them go after other people."

Cathy took a deep breath as she processed my words. "Now that you mention it, that's true."

"Exactly." I nodded in agreement. "I think we should take the back aisle of the store, then head down the center aisle and dash for the front door once we get closer to the cash registers."

"If you think that's the best plan, then let's try it," Cathy agreed, for she had no other alternative plan.

"I'm not sure until we get out on the sales floor," I said. "Are you ready?"

Cathy took another deep breath before nodding determinedly. "Let's do this."

12:03 AM

I had already been on the clock for twelve hours and I hadn't felt a hint of exhaustion yet.

I carefully opened the general merchandise sales floor door and peeked out. I scanned left, then right. "It seems safe," I whispered to Cathy, reaching my hand out to her.

Cathy took my hand and wrapped her arm around mine as we

entered the doorway. She stayed close to me, determined we wouldn't get separated as we sauntered down a short aisle filled with various body care products.

We turned down the back aisle and walked to the meat department, which overlooked the store's center aisle—the frozen foods section. This was also where the double doors leading into the receiving area were located, where this nightmare began.

"Where are the police?" Cathy muttered, her body pressing firmly against my back. She was on high alert. Probably more so than me.

I shook my head and quietly said, "I don't know."

We stopped at the meat counter and stared down the center aisle. I could see the cash registers at the end of the aisle. It didn't even occur to me that our backs were turned, facing the double doors leading into the receiving area. Before I could take the first step down the center aisle to the front of the store, a puffball whizzed past us, screaming in midair, and collided with a glass freezer door.

Another puffball shot through the double doors from the receiving area like a baseball pitcher's ninety-mile-per-hour fastball. The thing flew so fast I couldn't tell what color it was. Thankfully, it missed us again by mere inches.

"Run!" I shouted, spinning around and pulling Cathy with me.

We were sprinting through what felt like a warzone, narrowly avoiding puffballs whizzing past us. We stopped at the end of the aisle, just before the cash registers.

To my amazement, there *were* police officers in the store. However, the three visible were lying on the floor, and one was leaning over the counter at a register, covered in worms. Had they yet to call for backup upon discovering the situation inside the store?

My gaze fixed on the northwest exit doors. It was our only escape route. To my left, further down the general merchandise aisles, I noticed the woman whom Hector had taken down was still lying on the ground. Hector's body appeared to have merged with hers, enveloping her and transforming into a protective shell or cocoon around her.

My eyes drifted to the right at the cash office booth. Juan was climbing over the counter. Then he leaped through the shattered window inside the booth, where I initially met up with Cathy.

Scanning the registers, my eyes found Craig's body near the entrance to the restrooms. I could see his legs twitching. Was he still alive?

To my immediate right, Jose stood motionless at the end of aisle three, four rows down from me and Cathy. He stared at us, a puffball gripped in his hand. Worms writhed under his skin, resembling dark veins on his face. His eyes were blazing red.

Cathy's grip tightened on my arm; her voice was filled with panic. "Tony, this is bad. What are we going to do?"

The only solution to the graphic scene before us was to escape. "We have to get out of here," I said urgently. "Head for the front doors, and don't look back."

Suddenly, several colorful puffballs rolled past our feet and stopped before us. Their googly eyes seemed to be staring right at us. A swarm of worms circled each ball, ready to attach themselves to me and Cathy.

"Stay away from those things," I warned Cathy. "As far as I can tell, if even one of those worms attaches itself to you, it'll burrow under your skin and control you like a puppet."

"Can't we just escape through the receiving door?" Cathy's voice trembled.

"That's where this all started," I explained. "And we can't risk being ambushed by those toys lurking back there. Our best bet is to focus on getting out through the front door."

I caught some movement in my peripheral vision and looked to the left. The cocoon on the floor seemed to be bubbling and inflating, with a pus-like substance oozing around it.

Suddenly, the cocoon cracked open, releasing a whiff of heavy steam. A clear slime gushed from the opening, followed by a huge, glistening arm that unfolded onto the floor. Another arm flung out of the crack of the cocoon and landed heavily on the floor beside the other arm. The two grotesque arms stretched up from the floor, supporting the body of an intimidating creature shedding its shell.

"Oh my God…LOOK!" Cathy gasped, pointing at the registers.

My gaze shifted from witnessing the birth of a new creature to following Cathy's finger. I saw the police officer bent over the counter had moved. He struggled to stand up, then rolled off the counter, only to rise to his feet seconds later. His face was covered in worms, just like Jose's. He hadn't noticed us yet but staggered toward the other officers lying on the floor and stood there as if waiting for a reaction.

The other two officers did respond, struggling to their feet and eventually huddling together as if to discuss a plan.

"This is bad," I muttered.

"Now what do we do?" Cathy said, her face drained of color.

The horror was overwhelming, and it was difficult to keep track of everything that was happening. I glanced to my right and realized Jose was no longer standing at the end of aisle three. Where had he gone? I assumed he had turned back down the aisle to surprise us from behind on the frozen foods aisle where Cathy and I were standing.

I was suddenly drawn to the puffballs near our feet and noticed a trail of tiny black worms inching our way.

"Stay back!" I pulled Cathy away from the approaching worms. The googly eyes on each puffball spun in opposite directions, almost hypnotically.

More puffballs whistled past us, narrowly missing our heads. I checked over my shoulder at the double doors leading to the receiving area behind us at the end of the aisle.

Suddenly, the doors burst open, and a dozen or more puffballs flew straight for us.

The police officers at the registers began walking in our direction. I knew we had to change plans.

"Come on!" I exclaimed, grabbing Cathy's arm. She gasped in surprise as we headed for the floral department. When we reached aisle three, I noticed Jose was still gone. But we kept moving.

"Where are we going?" Cathy yelled over the whistling noises of the puffball toys gathering at the front of the store.

I couldn't find the words to respond. Fear for our lives consumed me.

Making it to the floral department, we weaved between floral displays until we reached the bakery department. I looked around and saw no sign of Jose or any puffballs. The only other area of the store that might be safe was the produce department. But I knew it wouldn't be long before the creatures found us, so I had to act fast. My new plan was to lure most of the puffballs away from the receiving area and circle back to escape through there. But first, we needed weapons.

I guided Cathy behind the bakery counter and into the back area where they stored bread knives.

"What are we doing here?" Cathy said.

I opened a drawer under a long wooden table and grabbed two of the largest bread knives. "Protecting ourselves," I said, slipping off the plastic blade covers. I handed a knife to Cathy. "If anything comes near you, stab it. It's better than nothing."

As I glanced at the front of the bakery, I noticed the three police officers approaching like a pack of zombies, their bodies infected by the wormlike creatures.

Distant screams erupted on the front end. I figured more customers must've entered the store. Did the puffballs or the creature that emerged from the cocoon attack them? Or were they fleeing the store screaming like the others before? Hell was being unleashed in this store!

12:40 AM

I remembered the bakery had a telephone on the wall, and it could dial an outside line. But with the impending dead police officers, I wouldn't have time to make the call for help. I'd have to keep moving while trying to talk on the phone.

Reaching into my pocket, I retrieved my cell phone and flipped it open, only to find a blank screen. The battery had died. I pocketed my phone and turned to Cathy. "Do you have your cell phone with you?"

"It's in my purse in the cash office booth," Cathy said.

"Damn! Well, we can't go back there now."

"So, what do we do?" Cathy asked in a rush.

"Let's get to the produce department," I said, grabbing Cathy's hand.

We escaped the bakery before the zombified officers could weave through the floral department and flower displays. I was surprised they didn't attempt to draw their handguns and fire at us. The parasitic worms controlling their minds were probably too dull-witted to consider using weapons. If I could somehow grab one of the officers' holstered firearms, I might be able to shoot our way out of the store. But it would be too dangerous to approach them. I had no idea what might happen if we got too close; the worms burrowed under their skin could potentially devour their way through their flesh and leap onto me before I could even reach for a gun.

A swinging door led to the back room in the produce department, which also connected to the receiving area. My objective was to reach this door without drawing any attention. Instead of making a straight dash toward it, I had to ensure the coast was clear.

As we entered the produce department, I quickly pulled Cathy behind a bin full of bananas and crouched down.

"What did you see?" Cathy whispered as she settled next to me.

I peered around the bin's edge at the back aisle of the store. From my vantage point, I could see more puffballs flying out from the receiving doors, down the frozen foods aisle, and to the front end of the store. How many of those damn things were packed in that shipping box? They seemed never-ending!

I spun to Cathy and said quietly, "We need to make sure none of those balls or the police officers see us." My eyes drifted over her shoulder to the bakery department behind her. Cathy followed my gaze. The officers had just entered the department and left from behind the cake display counter.

"It's a good thing they're slow," Cathy said. "Can't we just outrun them?"

I shook my head. "We risk those toy balls attacking us that are gathering at the front end," I reminded her.

Cathy gasped in horror when she saw something behind me.

My heart raced when Jose loomed over us, his eyes wild and crazed, worms swimming all over his face underneath his skin. He gripped a silver puffball in his hand.

In a panic, I raised my bread knife and stabbed it into Jose's foot, and he doubled over, worms spilling out from his mouth.

Without hesitation, I pulled Cathy away from the banana bin before any worms could touch us. We couldn't waste more time playing hide and seek or waiting things out; we had to get out of here. I sprinted for the exit, with Cathy holding on tightly behind me for dear life.

As I burst through the produce door, the silver puffball Jose had thrown whistled past us and smashed against the back wall of the produce storeroom. The evil toy dropped to the floor, and its googly eyes began to spin in their hypnotic pattern. A gorefest of worms spilled from the puffball's pours and scattered about the floor. How could that toy hold so many worms?

Behind us, I could hear the zombified officers scrambling (slowly) to catch up to us. They must've discovered Cathy and I weren't in the bakery department.

Cathy gasped, her eyes wide with terror. Her face was pale, and her breaths were ragged. I grabbed her hand tightly, urging her not to give up, because we were near the receiving door. I took the bread knife from her so she wouldn't injure herself with it running through the store. From my observation, she didn't want anything to do with the weapon anyway.

"Don't let these tiny creatures touch you," I warned Cathy again, peering down at the wriggling worms inching closer to us. I immediately took a few steps back and glanced over my shoulder through the small window on the produce door.

Jose crouched down and removed the knife from his foot. He held up the bread knife to examine it as if it were a foreign object, turning it over and examining every angle. Funny enough, there was no sign of blood on the blade, just a few worms crawling around it like an army of ants. They made their way onto Jose's hand and began burrowing under his skin until they all disappeared.

"Is he made up of these worms?" I couldn't help but wonder out loud.

Cathy did a double take when she looked at Jose through the produce door window.

Jose caught her stare and faced us, his gaze piercing us from the produce sales floor.

"I'm gonna be sick," Cathy said. She pulled away from me, clutching her stomach, dashed to the corner of the produce storeroom, and vomited.

"Are you okay?" I asked anxiously, worried that Cathy's sickness would slow us down.

Through the produce door window, I could see Jose approaching. And the officers were close behind him.

Cathy spit out remnants of vomit seeds from her mouth. "I should be fine."

Feeling pressed for time with the worms rapidly approaching us and Jose getting closer every second, I grabbed Cathy's hand, determined to keep moving forward. "We have to keep going!"

We leaped over the worms on the floor and turned down a hallway to the receiving area. Upon entering the grocery backroom, I felt a strange sensation on my leg and stopped to look down. A worm!

Cathy sidestepped, heeding my previous warning to avoid the tiny worms.

My panic rose as I reached down with shaking hands and grabbed hold of the tiny creature from my pants leg. It did not squirm or wriggle but instead seemed floppy like a fish out of water pinched between my fingers. Its skin was cold, smooth, and slick.

"How in the hell did this thing get on me?" I said, intrigued by the worm's features. It almost looked like it had a miniature human head, complete with tiny eyes and a mouth opening and closing.

"Get rid of it!" Cathy demanded.

With an awful sense of resignation, I flicked the worm like a booger stuck on my finger across the backroom. Where it landed, I could not tell because it was so small. It did not fulfill its purpose, and that's all I cared about.

Cathy and I were just a short distance from the receiving door when a puffball flew at us unexpectedly. Its high-pitched scream bounced off the backroom walls, sounding almost like a demented banshee. How did they sneak onto the delivery truck in the first place? And who the hell shipped them? It was clear that someone with a grudge had caused this chaos. I couldn't imagine anyone in my workplace being behind it. Perhaps it was a new method of warfare, and this store was the unfortunate testing ground for such aggression.

It was a black puffball that banged against the receiving roll-up door and went splat on the ground, releasing an army of worms. Its googly eyes danced a hypnotic pattern, then paused instantly, the eyes fixed on Cathy.

Then, the unexpected happened. Some of the worms began jumping! They were becoming more intelligent. I dodged a couple of them leaping in my direction. But Cathy wasn't so lucky. Her reflexes were too slow, and one of the worms hopped onto her hand.

Cathy yelped and shook her hand, hoping to fling the worm off. But the black creature quickly slithered down her finger and curled under her fingernail.

"It burns!" Cathy screamed, still trying to shake the worm off. Realizing she could not catch it in time, I watched in horror as the worm burrowed underneath her nail bed and inched back up her finger.

My first thought was the little bastard had a one-way ticket to Cathy's brain, and it was taking the bullet train. The thing was fast. It had already reached her forearm just seconds after digging beneath her skin.

Cathy was frantic. "Get it out of me!" she screamed.

Tightening my grip on the bread knife, I was suddenly determined to help Cathy in any way possible. And if it meant cutting the worm out of her, so be it. So, I ran to her, grabbed her wrist, and scrunched her shirt sleeve. I scanned her arm and located the tiny bulge where the worm was moving in her skin.

"What are you doing?" Cathy's face lit with fear.

"Hold still," I told her. I positioned the sharp blade on her upper arm, targeting the writhing worm that was making its way up her skin. With careful precision, I waited until it was just about to reach where I had the knife positioned before decisively pushing down and pulling, cutting through Cathy's flesh.

Cathy winced in pain, but I was surprised at how well she handled it.

The jagged teeth on the knife made for an uneven cut, and within seconds, blood began gushing out from the wound. The worm escaped with a rush of blood, leaping off Cathy's arm like a flea leaving a dog.

"Put pressure on this," I said, placing Cathy's other hand over the cut on her arm. "You'll probably need stitches after we escape this hellhole." I saw a pallet of paper towels, ripped open a box, and pulled out a roll. Tearing off several squares, I handed them to Cathy to place over her wound.

"Thanks," Cathy sighed.

Our minds preoccupied with first aid, we almost forgot about the worms approaching us from the black puffball. I didn't see any more of them jumping, but the googly eyes were still on Cathy.

"Let's head for the exit door by the receiving desk," I directed, pointing to the door. "It's our only way out."

Another loud shriek came from a flying puffball as it narrowly missed us again. It came from the shipper box I had opened earlier.

"Oh my God! Watch out!" Cathy yelled suddenly.

I saw Jose approaching us from the hallway to the produce storeroom.

"Run!" I said.

But when we tried to make a break for the exit door, Juan burst through the double doors of the backroom and headed straight for us. How did he know we were in the receiving area? He didn't see us escape from the cash office booth. I had assumed he would be stuck there like a windup toy, going back and forth aimlessly until we showed up again.

We were stuck between two zombified stockers and a swarm of flying puffballs. But this time, they weren't targeting us. They were blocking the exit door! They knew we were trying to escape through that door. But how? They were just toys. They couldn't think or strategize, could they?

Fear was evident in Cathy's voice as she pressed against me. "We need better weapons!"

I raised the bread knife but knew it would not match what confronted us. "A blow torch would come in handy right about now," I said, half-jokingly.

Then Cathy pointed a bloodied hand to the fire extinguisher on the wall near the box baler. Streaks of blood trickled down her arm to the tips of her fingers from the knife wound, even though she was keeping pressure on it with the wad of paper towels. "Would that help?" she asked.

We needed any help we could get with this situation, so I dashed to the fire extinguisher. I thought Cathy would've followed me, but she stood defenseless in the center of the receiving area.

I reached for the fire extinguisher and pulled the pin. When I spun around, Jose and Juan had closed in on Cathy. I dashed back to her and bashed the butt of the fire extinguisher against Jose's head, then aimed the hose at Juan's face point-blank and squeezed the handle.

The situation intensified when the three police officers approached us from behind. Their eyes locked on me, and they rushed forward in unison. I couldn't help but feel overwhelmed and helpless against this swarming threat. My heart pounded like a drumbeat, echoing through every fiber of my body.

I aimed the fire extinguisher at the approaching officers and pulled the trigger. A plume of white foam engulfed them, buying more time to devise another escape plan.

I noticed Cathy's face was pale. But I didn't think she was going to be sick again. Nor was it due to blood loss from her wound. Instead, she was rooted to the spot, her eyes fixed on something I didn't see yet.

"Behind you!" Cathy screeched.

I didn't even pause to think before turning around and being confronted by the terrifying creature that was a fusion of Hector and the shopper he'd attacked. It was a repulsive sight, looming over Cathy and me with its massive size. Its body lacked skin, revealing nothing but exposed muscles. Its head was deformed, and its coal-black eyes seemed to stare into our souls. Its jagged teeth jutted out like the tusks of a boar.

My mind raced as I desperately tried to think of a way to distract the creature before it tore us apart. Juan and the officers I sprayed with the fire extinguisher were stumbling around in confusion while Jose was regaining his bearings after I hit him in the head. The foam from the extinguisher confused them, so I hoped it would have the same effect on Jose and the puffballs blocking the exit door.

I handed Cathy the fire extinguisher, even though she was still pressing the bloody wad of paper towels over her wound. "Spray Jose and those demon balls at the door," I instructed her. "I'll catch up to you. Go!"

Cathy was speechless. Her expression screamed, "Fuck that," as I spun around and hurled the bread knife at the creature before sprinting past it, hoping it would give chase. I could tell by the sound of the knife bouncing and sliding on the floor that it hadn't stuck into the creature.

1:06 AM

The creature got pissed when I chunked the knife at it.

But my plan succeeded (although I wasn't sure if Cathy followed my instructions since I fled the grocery backroom). The grotesque creature was hot on my heels. As it ran after me, it crashed into pallets of backstock lining the walls, causing boxes to topple and spill their contents all over the floor.

I sprinted down the hallway where the freezer and dairy coolers were located. I passed them, whipped around the corner, and entered the general merchandise backroom. A swinging door with a window like the one in the produce storeroom was only a few yards ahead, which led out to the dairy department sales floor.

The creature charged around the corner and skidded into a backstock shelf, scattering bottles of hairspray, rubbing alcohol, nail polish remover, and shaving cream all over the floor.

I raced through the swinging door onto the sales floor, nearly slipping on the tiled surface as I turned toward the meat department. After navigating past the dairy products, I cautiously made my way to the center aisle, where puffballs had flown out from the double doors that led to the receiving area.

Glancing over my shoulder, I saw the creature slide across the floor and smash into the glass doors stocked with milk and orange juice. The impact caused a loud crash as glass shattered and liquids spilled everywhere. This creature had no control when it came to turning corners.

Despite my hesitation, I entered through the double doors and into the receiving area, where this chaos had started. I assumed Cathy had escaped the receiving area because the alarm to the exit door was blaring.

To my right was the pallet with the puffball shipper I had opened. The box was flattened.

To my left, the zombified officers and Juan and Jose walked around the backroom aimlessly. They bumped into each other in the open area with foam covering their faces, resembling a scene from a Saturday morning cartoon.

My eyes immediately went to the exit door near the receiving desk. Foam from the fire extinguisher was splattered around the door frame and the floor, covering the puffballs blocking the exit.

I heard the monster roar on the sales floor and looked behind me. Through the windows in the double doors, I saw the creature slide into a turn and charge at me once again.

Without wasting a second, I ran for the exit door, deftly dodging between the roaming zombies, and forced myself against the heavy door's push bar.

1:11 AM

I stumbled out onto the truck docking area, and the exit door shut behind me and locked as a truck driver and Cathy dodged out of my way. I narrowly collided with a box truck parked at the dock.

Catching my breath, I leaned against the side of the truck.

"What in bloody hell is going on in there?" the truck driver said. "And what's with all the cops scattered in the front parking lot?"

I breathed some more before answering. "She hasn't told you?" I said, pointing at Cathy.

Cathy shook her head. She was still holding the wad of paper towels soaked in blood on her arm. "He just pulled up shortly before you came out," she said, moving away from the door.

I noticed the fire extinguisher I gave her was on the ground.

The truck driver, a short and stocky man, walked toward me with a clipboard, an invoice flapping in the breeze.

Under the full moon, the store was a terrifying sight. Muffled roars escalated from inside the receiving area. I prepared for the creature to burst through the receiving door at any moment.

"What was that?" The truck driver glanced at the door.

"There's a demon in there," I said. I started moving away from the door, my shoulder gliding against the side of the box truck.

The truck driver looked at me like I was insane. "Right. Look, I just need you to sign for this delivery."

"I'm quitting this job," I declared. "The store will most likely be closed for a while."

Suddenly, a barrage of bullets erupted from inside the store, and the creature's cries filled the air before falling silent.

"Holy shit!" the truck driver screamed, diving for cover behind the front of his truck.

I glanced at Cathy, who stood off to the side in the grass. "Great timing for more police to finally show up, huh?"

I sensed Cathy's frustration with law enforcement for not handling the situation earlier.

The truck driver crept back out from cover. "Sounds like a warzone in there," he said, hesitating to approach any closer from where he stood at the front of the truck.

"Yeah, well, that should've happened long ago," I said, moving away from the truck and standing beside Cathy.

"Thank you for leading us out of there alive," Cathy said, choking on her words. Her teary eyes locked with mine. "And saving me from turning into one of those . . . things." She threw her arms around my neck.

"So, whose signature should I get for this delivery?" the truck driver said from afar.

I turned to him. "What is it? We got a delivery earlier last night."

The truck driver pointed at the side of his truck. "They're called Crazy Whistling Balls," he replied. "It's the second of two pallets. This is the other half of what was delivered earlier."

I forgot another half of those puffball toys were being delivered. I looked at the graphic on the side of the truck and saw an enlarged print of colorful puffballs with googly eyes. But these looked different from the ones I encountered. They had wings sprouting from them.

My eyes grew as I glanced at Cathy in disbelief. Then, back on the truck driver, I said, "Oh, screw that, I'm not signing anything! Those evil things are what started this shit. Do you know where they came from?"

"Made in China and shipped from California," said the truck driver. "I only started working for the company a couple of weeks ago, but they're supposed to be the hot toy this holiday season."

"Are all the stores supposed to be getting them?" I asked, hoping the guy would say there was only a limited supply.

To my dismay, he replied, "Every major retailer and the larger grocery chains are getting them."

Suddenly, the receiving door burst open, and a SWAT team surrounded us.

"Hands on your heads and face down on the ground!" the SWAT commander yelled.

Before hitting the deck, I ensured their faces weren't infested with worms. They all appeared human.

The truck driver flung his clipboard in the air, and he hit the ground.

Cathy and I followed the commander's instructions, but I couldn't resist speaking up.

"We know how to stop these creatures!" I said, the side of my face kissing the ground.

The SWAT commander approached with his assault rifle pointed at my head while his team circled me. "You're human?" he asked.

"Yes. I'm not one of those things," I replied. I wasn't intimidated by the SWAT team. I'd already experienced a hell of a lot more fear than the weapons drawn on me.

The commander inspected my face up close before backing away. "Stand him up. He appears clean."

Two SWAT officers helped me up, and the SWAT commander and I squared up.

"There's more of these things," I warned him.

"Where and how do you know?"

I pointed behind him at the truck. "There's a truckload, and apparently at other major retailers."

The commander looked at the truck before stepping close to me again. "You said you know how to eliminate them. How?"

"Fire extinguishers," I explained over the loud noise of helicopters flying overhead. "It stuns the puffballs with the googly eyes and confuses those infected by the worms from the toys."

The commander studied me briefly before instructing his team to help Cathy and the truck driver to their feet.

"You may want to inform someone how to kill these things," I suggested. "Anyone who opens the shipment will release these evil toys and spread the infection."

The commander immediately radioed his incident commander and shared the information about using fire extinguishers to stun the creatures. "And send a medic around the back of the store at the dock stat," he added.

I was thankful he ordered EMS to attend to Cathy's arm. I felt terrible for what I did to her, but it was definitely better than having her turn into one of those wandering zombies.

The commander returned to me, asking how many were inside the truck.

I glanced over his shoulder at the truck driver standing up from lying on the ground. "Ask him," I said.

"I have a shipment of ten pallets," the truck driver confirmed.

I checked on Cathy, but instead of finding her standing there, she had picked up the fire extinguisher and handed it to one of the SWAT members.

"You sure this does the trick?" the SWAT officer asked.

Cathy nodded confidently. "Yes, but you'll need more than one."

January 21, 1999 / Revised December 16, 2024

I remember writing this story in college. The professor edited it in pencil. When I reread the story to include in this collection, a laugh escaped me before being replaced by an eye roll. The pacing was slow, and the dialogue felt forced and not authentic to the characters.

Later, I submitted the story to a magazine editor in hopes it would be selected for publication. But two months later, I received a response via snail mail that the company had gone out of business.

Now, with a fresh perspective, I completely overhauled the story while retaining some key elements from the original version.

A GRAVE MATTER

Two lovers strolled through the cemetery, unaware of the groundskeeper lurking behind an old monument.

It was Chris and Stacey's first anniversary as sweethearts. They could have opted for a fancy dinner or a fun game of putt-putt golf. Instead, they chose this unorthodox location for their celebration.

The couple walked hand in hand, wearing goth clothing, Chris in his ripped black skinny jeans and Stacey going for that emo princess look. The crunch of fall leaves echoed through the silent grounds as they admired the atmosphere.

They walked along the winding, narrow pathway between headstones, looking at the dates. Some markers were recent, some were from many years past, and some ancient ones dated back to the 1800s. Tonight, on their anniversary, they searched for the oldest tombstone together.

Chris and Stacy were artists with distinct careers in stone rubbing. Their passion for this art began when they stumbled upon an ancient graveyard during a road trip through the countryside. The history etched in the stones throughout the cemetery called out to them, whispering stories of lives long past and forgotten. Placing paper over a tombstone and gently rubbing charcoal or wax to reveal its details was like uncovering hidden secrets preserved in time. Every tombstone was a work of art waiting to be discovered and brought to life through their craft. The textures, patterns, and designs captured in stone held a mesmerizing allure that eventually transposed their dedication to the craft into careers.

The groundskeeper moved stealthily between monuments, unseen in the distance. He was a tall and slender older man and could pass for a limo driver or a butler answering the door for his employer. His breath came in rapid bursts. His shoulder-length silver hair was slicked back against his scalp as if tamed with paste. The old man maintained a watchful yet creepy eye on the couple wandering the grounds.

Chris and Stacey continued through the old cemetery, still unaware of the man who secretly kept tabs on them.

A gentle breeze swept through the cemetery and toyed with Chris's choppy layered hair, causing it to fall over his eyes. He withdrew his hand from Stacey's grasp and smoothed back his locks.

With Stacey's hand now free, she could adjust the bow in her jet-black hair. She secured it tighter against the wind, her bracelets jingling as they slid down her forearm. She wanted to look pretty for Chris during this special occasion, but it wasn't going her way.

With heavy eyeliner bringing out the intensity of his gaze, Chris noticed Stacey's frustration. "You need me to fix that for you?" he offered.

Stacey sighed and admitted defeat. "I'm taking this damn thing off!" she declared, unclipping the cheap bow and realizing she would have no use for it ever again.

"Are you okay?" Chris asked, worried Stacey's short outburst might ruin their night.

Stacey turned to him and smiled. "Sorry. I just wanted to dress the occasion for our special day."

"Stacey, you've been beautiful since the day I met you," Chris reassured her. "No need to go all out for me."

A warm smile spread across Stacey's face, and she leaned in, initiating the first kiss of the evening.

The groundskeeper continued following their every move. He skillfully navigated around fallen leaves and carefully trod upon the freshly trimmed grass. Finally, he positioned himself behind a towering monument, spying on them from the side.

As Chris and Stacey wandered deeper into the heart of the cemetery, Stacey's eyes fell upon a delicate bloom peeking out from behind an ancient gravestone. The flower was a vibrant crimson, starkly contrasting with the somber surroundings. With a gleam in her eye, she tugged on Chris's hand and led him to the grave.

"Look at this, Chris," Stacey said softly, her voice filled with wonder. "It's as if nature is trying to bring life to this place."

Chris gazed at the flower and then Stacey, his heart swelling with love. Without a word, he reached out and plucked the flower from its resting place, careful not to damage its fragile petals. Turning to Stacey,

Chris presented her with the crimson blossom. "For you, my love," he said.

Stacey's eyes widened as she accepted the flower, her lips, heavy in dark lipstick, parting in awe.

With overwhelming emotion, Chris dropped to one knee and took Stacey's delicate hand in his trembling fingers. Their painted black fingernails overlapped each other's. As he gazed into her eyes, he reached into the front pocket of his jeans with his free hand and pulled out a small, red velvet box. His fingers fumbled nervously to pry it open, revealing a sparkling diamond ring nestled between soft foam padding. He held the open box up to Stacey.

Stacey gasped, and her eyes filled with tears.

"Stacey," Chris said, his voice thick with emotion and a lump forming in his throat, "from the moment I saw you, I knew you were the one I wanted to spend the rest of my life with. Will you do me the honor of being my bride and marry me?"

The words hung between them. The surrounding sounds of nature seemed to fade away as Chris waited anxiously for Stacey's answer, his heart beating wildly. The rustling leaves and chirping birds were replaced with the sound of blood pounding in his ears. All that mattered to him was Stacey's response.

Stacey squeezed tears from her eyes and placed her fingertips to her lips, the flower in her hand swaying with the gentle breeze. "Yes!" she said, her breathing quick and nervous.

Chris's smile broadened. He released Stacey's hand and stood up, pinching the ring from its cushioned box. Then he slipped the ring onto her finger, sealing their love forever.

A soft gasp escaped Stacey's lips, and she threw her arms around Chris in a tight embrace.

Watching them, the groundskeeper's jaw dropped. The site of the two lovers vandalizing the grounds he kept well-manicured and then making out onsite was appalling. A fiery rage flooded his eyes, and he stormed out from behind the old monument and speed-walked across the grounds. He cared not about stomping on cemetery plots. He'd tend to them later.

A harsh, distant voice slicing through the air abruptly interrupted Chris and Stacey's tender moment. They jumped apart, startled by the sudden intrusion.

"What do you think you're doing?!" The groundskeeper approached from afar, his voice echoing among the ancient tombs. He pumped his fist in the air, and his gray hair bounced with every step. "This is a place of rest and reverence, not for your petty theft and frivolity!"

Stacey's cheeks flushed with embarrassment as she clutched the stolen flower tighter, her eyes wide with guilt.

Chris closed the lid to the ring box and slipped it back into his pocket. Then he stepped forward to try and defuse the tension.

The groundskeeper's dark eyes bored into the couple as he finally caught up to them. "How dare you desecrate this sacred ground with your selfish display of affection."

Chris glanced around his surroundings. Seeing no one else was visiting the cemetery, he didn't understand the old man's problem. "Sir, we meant no disrespect," he said. "And who are you to come over here and get up all in our business?"

"I'm the groundskeeper here," the old man replied, scowling. His eyes met the flower in Stacey's hand. "The flower. I saw you pluck it from the vase."

Stacey held the flower against her chest as a means of safekeeping.

"And the display of desire for one another," the groundskeeper added, his attention back on Chris.

"What's the big deal?" Chris said. If this old man was about to get cockier with him, he'd fire back with a hateful attitude of his own. "There are flowers all around here. And there's a reason I picked this one."

"Is this grave a relative of yours?" the groundskeeper asked, glaring at them.

"No. But we are—"

"Then you have no business disturbing this deceased's place of rest!" the old man snapped.

Chris rose on the tips of his toes, then down again, forcing himself to hold back from decking the guy. But he kept his cool. "If you'd let me finish, I'll explain."

The groundskeeper, impatient and angry, slumped to one side. Although he had no desire to hear the young man speak, he allowed Chris an opportunity to continue. He gestured a hand to signal for him to proceed.

"We are stone rubbers," Chris explained. "We do this for a living, and it's perfectly legal. But it's our anniversary today, and we thought it'd be a good idea to find the oldest gravestone here since we've never been to this cemetery. We don't have our materials for the rubbings;

we're just looking, and then we will return another day to do our work.

"Anyway, I wanted to surprise my girlfriend with an engagement ring during our stroll. So, I picked the flower she noticed and proposed to her."

Stacey extended her arm and tilted down her wrist to show the old man her ring, but the mood had been spoiled. She wasn't excited anymore.

"Everything was romantic between us until you interrupted," Chris added.

The groundskeeper looked at the ring and smiled a mouthful of crooked teeth. It was only a glimpse before his lips closed, and his face contorted back into disgust. "Well, isn't that something special," he said sarcastically. His eyes glared into Chris's. "But it's still not your property. The flower does not belong to you or her."

A nervous knot twisted in Chris's stomach as the old man's words dripped with menace, sinking into his mind. The groundskeeper's tone grew darker, filling the air with an oppressive fear that settled over Chris and Stacey like a heavy blanket.

As they stood before this grumpy old man, Chris couldn't help but think that maybe the guy was right. Perhaps it was wrong to have unwittingly stolen from the dead.

"You want something better to give your bride-to-be?" the groundskeeper suggested. He spun on his heel and pointed a gnarled finger toward a crumbling gravestone at the far end of the cemetery. It was sheltered beneath the twisted branches of a deformed tree, adding to its eerie presence. He turned back to the young couple, his voice low and commanding. "Follow me."

Chris exchanged a hesitant glance with Stacey, uncertainty clouding their minds. But when he looked back at the groundskeeper, he saw something in the man's eyes that made him trust him. Was it a secret? A promise? But he still felt uneasy, sensing an ultimatum looming before them. "What's over there?" he asked.

The groundskeeper gave a slight wink. His tone had shifted in a snap. His anger seemed to have faltered. "You say you are stone rubbers. Come see for yourself."

Chris and Stacey shrugged at one another and accepted the stranger's offer. They followed him, each step seeming to echo in the heavy silence of the graveyard. The air was thick with unspoken secrets and hidden intentions, only increasing the sense of unease within them. But they continued, wondering what awaited them at the end of this mysterious journey.

They approached the old gravestone, its surface covered in moss and barely readable. This was undoubtedly a perfect place to perform a stone rubbing.

The groundskeeper ran his fingers over the worn engraving, and a chill shot through Stacey's body. Suddenly, she could sense an ancient presence below them. Desperately seeking comfort, she reached out to Chris, grasping his hand tightly.

"This is the resting place of Florence Blackwood, the oldest gravesite in this cemetery," the old man explained in a low, ominous voice. "Her life was plagued with mystery and tragedy. Legend has it she was buried with a valuable possession, an item worth killing for."

The groundskeeper's words piqued Chris's interest. He leaned in closer to examine the engravings on the headstone. His eyes scanned the moss-covered surface as if trying to decipher a hidden message. The etchings in the stone were barely legible. It would have been the perfect stone to transfer onto paper had he brought his rendering materials. "Why should we care about your ghost story?" he asked curiously. "A moment ago, you were trying to throw us out of the cemetery."

"The Locket of Eternity is a rare black diamond, a stone of immense value and power," the groundskeeper intoned solemnly. "Many have sought it, but none have returned to tell the tale."

Stacey turned to Chris. "He's just trying to scare us," she whispered.

Chris wrinkled his brow at the old man. "Wait. Are you a graverobber? You're a damn hypocrite! Who are you?"

The old man lowered his long arms and clasped his hands together. Shadows from the wilted tree near the gravesite filled his face. "I'm Willard, in charge of these grounds, and I'm giving you a choice," he said. The tone in his voice was deeper, adding to the eeriness of the surroundings. "Return the flower you plucked to its rightful owner or help me dig up this grave for the item of value."

"We're not robbing someone's grave!" Chris snapped.

"Ah, but you already have," Willard reminded him, gesturing to the flower.

Chris and Stacey exchanged a puzzled look, unsure what to make of the strange proposition. However, the mention of a valuable black diamond tugged at Stacey's heart.

"What if we don't do either?" Chris tried to gauge the old man's intentions.

A sly smile crept across Willard's face, his eyes glittering within the shadows. "Ah, that is the gamble you'll have to risk. This cemetery holds more secrets and dangers than meets the eye."

With fear settling over them, Chris and Stacey stood before the crumbling gravestone and the old man, contemplating if they should flee the cemetery. Willard was too old to outrun them, and they could easily escape this place. But curiosity burned bright within them. The Locket of Eternity sounded intriguing.

"If we find this necklace, is it ours to keep?" Chris asked. "What's the catch?"

Willard gave a slight grin. "The Locket of Eternity has never been claimed. But if you dig it up, I would like half the value as my share."

Stacey's jaw dropped as she turned to Chris. "What are you doing? I'm not stealing from someone's grave!"

"Oh, but you have," Willard reminded them. "The flower is not yours. Return it and leave or set your eye on the real prize, something worth more than you would imagine."

"No," Stacey said sternly. "The flower is mine. We've stolen nothing of value from this place."

Chris felt torn between the allure of a valuable black diamond and Stacey's unwavering sense of morality. He knew disturbing a grave crossed a line he never thought he would approach. Yet, the promise of riches whispered seductively in his ear.

Willard's gaze pierced through them, his patience wearing thin. "Make your decision quickly," he urged. "The night is unforgiving, and the darkness holds secrets you cannot fathom."

Stacey stood her ground, her eyes blazing with defiance. "We're leaving," she declared, stepping back from the grave.

But Chris hesitated. The thought of what could lie beneath the soil tantalized him, filling his mind with visions of grandeur and wealth beyond measure.

As if he sensed Chris's internal conflict, Willard's expression softened. The cheer in his voice resembled something out of a cautionary fairy tale. "Remember, young man, every choice has consequences. The flower may be innocent, but the Locket of Eternity is a different enchantment altogether."

Chris felt the weight of Willard's words pressing down on him. His heart raced with conflicting desires. The temptation of the pendant loomed over him like a shadow. What if he gave Stacey the locket to further seal his love for her? Then again, what if this was just a mere grave robbery, and the old man wanted to use them as accomplices for his dirty crime?

But as Chris looked into Stacey's eyes, filled with unwavering morality and a deep-rooted sense of right and wrong, Chris knew what he had to do.

With a smirk, Willard raised his head slightly, anticipating the young man's decision.

With renewed resolve, Chris turned to Willard and said firmly, "We're leaving. We want no part in this madness."

Willard's head leveled with Chris's, his gaze boring into his soul. "You're making a mistake, boy," he cautioned.

Chris squeezed Stacey's hand. "C'mon, babe. Let's get out of here."

The two lovers retraced their steps quickly along the dirt path leading them back to the cemetery entrance. But when they approached the spiked, arched gates, they were shut and sealed with a chain and padlock.

"You gotta be kidding me!" Chris fumed. He grabbed the gates and shook them madly. He looked at his watch. "How is a cemetery closed to the public? It's only six o'clock."

"The old man!" Stacey said, her voice shaky. "We are the only ones here, and he was probably watching us the whole time from when we arrived."

"And locked the gates," Chris added.

Stacey fiddled impatiently with the flower she held against her chest as if it were a teddy bear offering her solace.

Chris paced back and forth, brainstorming ways to escape. He could see his car parked in the lot on the other side, just a short distance away.

"I warned you every choice has consequences," a voice called from afar.

Stacey turned like a haunting specter.

Chris ceased his pacing and stood petrified as if turned to stone.

Willard emerged along the worn path between plots, his sinister figure casting an elongated shadow upon the cemetery's forsaken grounds.

Stacey spun back to Chris. "He's creeping me out! What do we do?"

"Stay calm," Chris said. "I'll handle this guy."

Stacey slowly retreated against the cemetery gates, her breath tinged with icy fear. "Don't do anything stupid."

With a tender caress, Chris brushed his lips against Stacey's cheek. "I'll get us out of here, my love. Don't worry." Slipping his hand behind her neck, he pulled her closer, pressing his forehead against hers and sealing his assurance with a smile. Then he hastened toward the groundskeeper, who stood motionless in the distance.

Upon meeting Willard in the desolate expanse of the cemetery, Chris's voice thundered with rage. "Open those gates or give me the keys and I'll do it!" he demanded. "You can't hold us hostage here."

Willard's silence hung thick in the air, his hands clasped before him as if praying for some untimely demise.

The more Chris observed the old man, the more Willard resembled a sinister undertaker rather than a mere groundskeeper.

"You cannot deny fate," Willard intoned, his words swirling like mist around them. "The Locket of Eternity holds the key to your escape."

"What is your problem, old man!" Chris fumed. He clenched his fists, his lips pursed in stubborn determination. He was ready to knock this guy out with a swift uppercut to the jaw.

Yet Willard stood unthreatened by Chris's outrage, allowing him to expel the steam out of his system. Then, as if the Reaper himself whispered in his ear, Willard replied with a single word. "Dig."

"What?" Chris gasped.

"Dig," Willard repeated. "This is not a game. Do as I say, and we all leave unscathed."

"No!" Chris's howl shattered through the cemetery.

Still gripping her flower, Stacey heard her lover's scream echo amongst the tombstones. Dread enveloped her heart. Her desperate eyes watched as Chris's confrontation with the groundskeeper intensified. She was scared for Chris and herself. What began as an enchanted evening had descended into an unholy nightmare.

Stacey thought there must be a way to escape this place other than through these gates. Perhaps she and Chris could scale the towering fence that encircled the cemetery. Chris could hoist her over its sharpened pinnacles and then vault over himself.

She couldn't withstand being alone in this unwelcoming environment any longer, so she approached her new fiancé to reveal her plan.

Chris stared into Willard's eyes, which gleamed with an other-worldly light. He sensed mystery and malice behind those dark orbs—an omen of his damned fate. He contemplated what the old man would threaten next.

Stacey approached Chris from behind, Willard's attention still fixed on Chris. She reached out to touch his shoulder, but a bone-chilling scream pierced the air, making her freeze in her tracks. The terrifying sound seemed to be coming from deep within the heart of the cemetery, echoing off the gravestones and filling the atmosphere with an ominous energy.

Chris and Willard turned their heads in the direction of the scream. For Willard, the scream was all too familiar. He turned back to Chris, now finding Stacey by his side, and ripped a grin across his face. "That would be Florence Blackwood—her spirit risen from the grave. Again, I warned you about the consequences of your failed decision."

Stacey leaned toward Chris, her lips close to his ear. "I think I know how we can get out of here," she whispered.

Willard must have had fantastic hearing, for he understood what Stacey had whispered. He furrowed his brow, listening intently to her words, then announced with a stern tone in his voice, "The only way out, young lady, is with the locket."

Chris turned to Stacey, who looked at him with hope in her eyes despite the dread that lingered around them. He could sense she was confident about her plan of escape. And Chris saw the anticipation building up inside her. "I trust you," he said softly.

The stern look on Willard's face slowly transposed to a look of disappointment, knowing the couple was about to deny him once again. "Don't make the same mistake twice," he warned harshly.

"We'll take our chances," Chris asserted, his voice unwavering.

With a quick nod to Stacey, they both turned and sprinted to the cemetery's fence. The wrought iron spikes loomed over them like menacing guardians, their shadows stretching out as if trying to en-trap the fleeing couple.

Chris attempted to find a foothold, searching for any sign of weakness in the towering obstacle. But the iron fence was too tall, too foreboding for them to overcome on their own.

Panic clawed at Stacey's heart as she realized their predicament. She shouted for help through the bars. But on the other side was a never-ending field without any foot traffic.

The shrills from Florence Blackwood grew louder through the cemetery.

With a heavy heart and trembling hands, Chris faced Stacey. They shared a silent exchange filled with unspoken understanding—there was no choice but to turn back to Willard.

Resigned, they reluctantly retraced their steps to where Willard stood. His figure was stoic and unmoving, a silent witness to their fate as soon as they had fled from him.

"You have seen for yourselves twice now that there is no escape," Willard's gravelly voice rang out. "Do you wish to take one last chance and proceed with my solution?" His words hung like a warning, daring them to defy him.

Chris and Stacey stood before the old man, their breaths heavy. After a tense moment of silence, Chris finally caught his breath and answered, "Yes. What do we need to do?"

Willard nodded at the young couple. "Very well. Follow me."

The groundskeeper spun and led Chris and Stacey back down the winding dirt path between headstones. The sky was darkening, adding an ominous feel to their journey.

Chris and Stacey walked hand in hand, close behind the old man, each lost in their thoughts. Chris still contemplated a way to escape this nightmare. At the same time, Stacey clutched the flower close to her as if it were a lifeline.

Florence Blackwood's gravesite loomed ahead.

* * *

The lovers neared Florence Blackwood's grave, the air growing thick and heavy. An unnatural chill crept over them. The twisted tree looming over the ancient headstone seemed to groan and creak, its gnarled branches reaching out like skeletal fingers.

Willard stopped before the moss-covered gravestone and stood before Chris and Stacey, his eyes glinting in the fading light. "This is where your journey truly begins," he intoned ominously.

Chris swallowed, his gaze darting between Willard and the grave. "What exactly do you want us to do?"

A slow, unsettling smile spread across Willard's weathered face before he produced two shovels from behind a nearby headstone. He thrust them toward Chris and Stacey. "Dig. Unearth Florence's final resting place and claim the Locket of Eternity."

"Where's *your* shovel?" Chris asked the groundskeeper.

Stacey remained motionless, mirroring Chris's stance. She wasn't going to lift a finger if Chris wasn't.

Willard's grin collapsed. "These old bones can't handle digging like they used to," he said, gesturing to himself.

Chris stared back at the old man, his gut telling him this was not a good idea. He stood silently, unmoving as a statue, determined not to give in. He refused to dig, no matter what Willard said or did.

Chris's resistance abruptly shifted when the elderly man pulled out a flashlight from his back pocket and switched it on, shining it directly in Chris's face. But it wasn't the light that alarmed him; it was what the groundskeeper revealed next.

Reaching behind himself again, Willard produced a 9mm gun and aimed it directly at Chris's forehead. "You'll dig," he growled, "or I'll make your girlfriend dig your grave next to Florence Blackwood's."

Chris's heart raced as he stared down the barrel of the gun. He glanced at Stacey, her eyes wide with fear. The flower she clutched fell from her trembling hands, landing softly on the disturbed earth. "Alright, we'll dig," Chris said, his voice barely above a whisper.

Stacey, realizing the gravity of the situation, plunged her shovel into the ground.

The earth was hard and unyielding, as if the very soil was trying to protect its secrets. Each thrust of the shovels sent shivers through Chris's and Stacey's bodies, the act of disturbing a final resting place weighing heavily on their consciences.

As the young couple dug deeper, the air grew thick and oppressive, and an unnatural fog began to roll in. The mist curled around their ankles, obscuring the surrounding tombstones. The twisted tree above them creaked and groaned, its branches reaching down toward them with each gust of wind.

With every scoop of dirt that Chris and Stacey flung over their shoulders, Willard's excitement grew more vigorous. He gripped his flashlight tightly, illuminating the deepening hole Chris and Stacey dug above Florence Blackwood's grave. With the flick of a wrist, he'd shine the light upon the dirt-covered faces of the two lovers turned unexpected grave diggers. His gun remained steady, aimed directly at them as they worked. The earthy scent of freshly dug soil mingled with the faint smell of decay as the hole deepened, creating an eerie atmosphere in the still night air.

They stood knee-deep in the grave when Chris paused to wipe his face. Stacey could barely put effort into digging; her body was exhausted and weak.

"Why are you stopping?" Willard asked, suddenly on high alert.

"We need a break," Chris said, gasping for air.

"And some water," Stacey added, collapsing onto the ground. She struggled to catch her breath.

Willard grumbled angrily. "I'll get you some water," he said, stepping closer to Chris and pressing the tip of his gun against his temple. "Don't even think about trying anything while I'm gone. If you do, I'll put a bullet in your brain without hesitation. And if I return and you're not here, I'll track you down like a wild hog."

"We won't leave," Chris replied through heavy breaths and gritted teeth.

The old groundskeeper studied Chris for a moment longer before pulling the gun away from his head. He then pointed the flashlight at Stacey's face, giving her a menacing look.

Stacey refused to meet the old man's gaze and sat with her hands in her lap, struggling to catch her breath.

Willard kept a watchful eye as he slowly walked away, occasionally glancing back at Chris and Stacey to ensure they took his threat seriously.

Stacey burst into tears when the groundskeeper had gained some distance from them. "I want to go home!" she sobbed, her emotions overwhelming her. "Why is this happening to us?"

Chris shuffled over to Stacey and sat beside her, wrapping his arms around her to offer comfort as she rested her head on his shoulder.

The air was getting colder, and the sky was dark. The only source of light was the moon above them. The old tree's branches looming over them provided shelter from the chilly winds blowing through the cemetery.

"We need to devise a plan," Chris suggested, rubbing Stacey's arm. It was all he could do to help keep her warm. He observed their hole and realized they had barely scratched the surface. Six feet was a long way down. How long would it take them to reach the casket? With their current pace and the hardened soil, Chris figured it would take them until sunrise to finish.

Chris considered the possibility of the old man falling asleep during the night. If that happened, he and Stacey could use their shovels to attack him while he slept. It seemed like a viable option. After all, it was unlikely someone as old as Willard could stay awake all night.

"Isn't there a phone somewhere we could use?" Stacey sniffled. "We can run faster than that guy, find the administration building, and break in to use the phone."

Chris shook his head at Stacey's theory. "We can't outrun a bullet."

"Oh, I forgot about the gun," Stacey said in disappointment with a hushed voice.

"I say we bash his head in when he dozes off," Chris said, sticking to his plan.

Stacey looked up at Chris, her eyes filled with tears and her makeup streaking her face. "But I'm so tired. He'll pester me to keep digging."

Chris took in a deep breath and released it slowly. He knew Stacey was right. But the old man couldn't pester her constantly. He'd eventually lose focus, which would be another opportunity for Chris to bash him upside the head. "Just try and do as much as you can," he told Stacey. "I'll whack the guy when I see the chance."

* * *

As he approached, Willard's footsteps crunched through the fallen leaves, his figure emerging from the shadows. He carried two plastic water bottles between his fingers, the condensation glistening in the moonlight, as did the gun clutched in his other hand. He also brought a folding metal chair, which he had hung by its frame on his forearm. He must've taken it from the administration office where he got the water.

"Here," Willard growled, tossing the bottles at Chris's and Stacey's feet. "Drink up and get back to work." He pried open the metal chair and set it down near the gravesite. Before plopping down, he pulled the flashlight he had stuffed in his back pocket and clicked it on.

Chris unscrewed the cap of his water bottle and took a long gulp. The cool liquid was a blessed relief to his parched throat. Beside him, Stacey drank greedily, water dribbling down her chin.

"That's enough," Willard barked after a few moments, gesturing his gun toward the partially dug grave. "Back to digging. We've wasted enough time already."

Chris hauled himself to his feet with a weary sigh and picked up his shovel. Stacey followed suit, only her movements were sluggish and weak.

It seemed like an eternity as the young couple dug deeper into the grave. The way Stacey was barely thrusting her shovel in the dirt made it seem like she had been digging for another hour, but only ten minutes had elapsed.

"Slowing down won't get you anywhere," Willard scowled.

"Leave her alone!" Chris roared. "We don't dig graves for a living, asshole."

Willard sat on the edge of his chair, his gun and flashlight pointing directly at Chris. His eyes narrowed as he spoke. "Tonight will be your first time experiencing this, won't it?"

Stacey's frustration boiled over, and she thrust her shovel into the ground with a loud thud. It stood upright in the dirt as she let out a growl of annoyance and turned her hands over to reveal blisters forming on her palms.

Suddenly, a muffled scream erupted from beneath their feet.

Willard leaped from his chair, shining the flashlight down into the grave. "We're getting close."

"We?" Chris said, looking down where a strange mist rose from the earth. Then he glared back at the old groundskeeper. "You're not doing anything except sitting there watching us like we're your slaves."

Another scream bellowed from beneath the grave, followed by a gasp from Stacey as she quickly climbed out of the hole.

"Is someone down there?" Stacey asked, panting.

Willard tracked her movements. "You can't give up now," he grumbled. "Get back in there and finish digging."

Stacey looked at Chris, who was standing knee-deep in the grave. Chris was speechless, but Stacey's eyes spoke to him.

"No." Stacey shook her head nervously, stepping away from the hole. "I won't be part of this crime of yours any longer."

Willard stood and pointed his gun and flashlight at Stacey. "I'll count to three, and you better get back in that hole and finish digging," he snarled. "One…"

Willard's back was turned to Chris while he was focused on Stacey. Chris grabbed his shovel and swiftly scrambled out of the grave. He crept behind Willard, raising his shovel.

"Two…" Willard continued counting slowly.

Chris swung the shovel, the sharp metal striking Willard in the back of the head with a loud *ping*.

The groundskeeper stumbled and fell to one knee.

Chris approached the old man and took another swing with all his strength, hitting the guy on the head again and knocking him unconscious.

Willard dropped his gun and flashlight as he collapsed to the ground.

"Get the gun!" Chris urged Stacey.

Stacey grabbed the gun from the ground and placed it on Willard's chair. She didn't want anything to do with the weapon.

"Help me drag him into the grave," Chris said, looking at Stacey.

"What?" Stacey said. "We can't bury him. That's murder!"

Chris struggled, but he finally turned Willard onto his back. "We're not going to kill him," he assured her, repositioning the man's limbs and clearing away any obstacles on the ground to make it easier to drag the body. "Just help me get him over to the hole and roll him in. It'll give us some time to escape."

"Okay," Stacey complied. "Let me get my shovel out first." She returned to the hole, pulled her shovel out of the dirt, and tossed it aside.

"Grab his other leg," Chris said when Stacey returned.

Stacey reached down and grasped the old man's ankle, waiting for Chris's signal.

"Let's drag him over to the edge of the hole," Chris said.

Stacey nodded.

"Go!" Chris commanded.

The couple pulled on the old man's legs and slowly dragged him toward the grave. When they reached the edge, they stopped momentarily to catch their breath.

"Now push him in," Chris said.

Stacey looked down at her blistered palms. "My hands hurt," she complained.

"We're almost done," Chris reassured her.

Stacey glanced down at the old man's face. "Is he still breathing?"

"I don't know," Chris replied, not looking at the man's face. "But it doesn't matter now. He was planning to kill us. Why else would we be digging this hole? I'm sure he wanted us to dig our own graves!"

"What if he dies?" Stacey fretted. "My fingerprints are on that gun!"

Chris glanced over at the gun that Stacey had set on Willard's chair. He grabbed it and wiped it clean with his shirt before tossing it into the grave. "Now he has possession of it again. Let's finish this so we can get out of here."

They positioned themselves on one side of the old man and pushed him into the hole. But his body was too big to fit entirely inside since Chris and Stacey had not dug a large enough hole. The groundskeeper's legs and head stuck out from either end.

"The hole isn't deep enough," Chris grunted, wiping sweat from his brow.

"Let's just go!" Stacey urged, tugging on Chris's arm. "We can call the cops after we're far away from here."

"Wait!" Chris said suddenly, looking down into the grave.

"Now what?" Stacey asked anxiously.

Chris pointed to something inside the hole. "Do you see it?"

"See what?" Stacey leaned in closer to try to see what Chris was pointing at.

Chris stepped around her and picked up the flashlight that had rolled from the old man's hand when he collapsed. He returned to the grave and shined the light inside.

A chain glistening in the light hung from the old man's front pants pocket.

"That!" Chris pointed into the grave.

"Who cares? It's just his watch or something." Stacey shrugged.

"No," Chris said, reaching down, grabbing the chain, and giving it a yank. A large black jewel tumbled out of the groundskeeper's pocket at the end of the chain.

Chris stood dangling the black gem before Stacey's eyes.

"The Locket of Eternity?" Stacie gasped in awe.

A sly grin appeared on Chris's face. "That old man had this all along! I knew it was a trick to have us digging our own graves."

"Oh my!" Stacey's expression shifted from fear and anxiety to satisfaction and greed.

After carefully examining the black gem, Chris unlocked the chain. But as he tried to place it around Stacey's neck, a hand shot up from the grave and grabbed his ankle.

Willard sat up in the hole, his face pale beneath the long silver hair that fell over his eyes. "Don't!" his gurgled voice pleaded. "Help me out of this grave and bury the locket!"

But Chris wasn't swayed. He kicked his leg out, forcing the groundskeeper's grip loose. "Over my dead body!" he exclaimed before delivering a blow to the old man's chest with his foot, causing him to sink further into the hole.

Willard exhaled the breath from his lungs and muttered an obscure word before losing consciousness again.

"Now, where were we?" Chris turned back to Stacey. He placed the chain around her neck and secured it.

Stepping back to admire how the jewel looked on her, he suddenly remembered something. "Hang on," he said while quickly picking up the flower he had given Stacey in the cemetery. He placed it behind her ear. "There we go—gorgeous!"

A tear trickled down Stacey's cheek as she said, "I love you, Chris."

Chris held the black gem in his palm, gazing at it in wonder. "I love you, too," he said softly, curious how to unlock its mystery.

Stacey observed Chris struggling to open the locket and took matters into her own hands. With a slight twist, she clicked it open.

Inside was a tiny old photograph of a young woman.

Chris plucked the photo from the frame without hesitation and tossed it into the grave. He closed the locket and suggested, "Let's fill this with a new photo of us. What do you think?"

Stacey's face lit with excitement, and she threw her arms around Chris in joy.

But before they could share a passionate kiss, a piercing scream erupted from the depths of the grave.

Chris and Stacey parted, gazing at the elderly man lying awkwardly in the hole.

Suddenly, a black light emitted from the gem hanging around Stacey's neck, gradually growing brighter.

"Whoa!" Chris exclaimed in shock.

Stacey held the locket delicately between her fingers, mesmerized by its beauty. As they stood under the glow of the black light, their clothes seemed to come alive as if on a dark carnival ride.

The light continued to intensify, revealing the twisted tree branches above them.

"What's going on?" Chris asked, bewildered.

Stacey looked back at him, shaking her head. "I have no idea. Help me get it off!"

As Chris reached for the chain around Stacey's neck, the light from the gem became blindingly bright. And before they knew it, they were engulfed in its power and transported through a mysterious time portal.

***

Stacey flinched, pushing herself away from the gravestone. She could feel her heart racing in her chest. "Oh my God!"

"What happened?" Chris gasped, trying to comfort her.

Stacey pressed a hand to her chest, her fingertips black with charcoal. "That was a trippy one."

"The vision?" Chris asked.

"More like an experience," Stacey clarified. "It felt so real."

Chris wrinkled his brow, confused. "Did you come in contact with the dead woman?"

"Not exactly. At least I hadn't yet before the drug wore off."

"What does the inscription read on your paper?" Chris said, kneeling next to Stacey.

Stacey held up the parchment paper. "Florence Blackwood," she read aloud, concentrating on each word. The etchings transferred on her paper from the stone were nearly illegible but easier to read than from the stone itself. "1790 to 1825. A bride and mother-to-be."

"This is the oldest stone found since we've been doing this, right?" Chris asked.

Stacey breathed rapidly, recovering from the effects of the pill that had caused her to hallucinate. "I think so," she said faintly. "You should see if you can figure out Florence's life. I discovered it involves a black locket—the Locket of Eternity."

Chris pulled an unlabeled pill bottle from his pocket and opened the lid. He popped a pill in his mouth, swallowed it with a wad of saliva, tightened the cap, and slipped the bottle back into his pocket. Grabbing a sheet of parchment paper from a stack on the ground that was weighted down with a rock and some masking tape, Chris secured the paper over the gravestone. Then he borrowed the stick of charcoal Stacey used to rub on her paper.

Sitting comfortably on the ground before the ancient stone, he worked on transferring the stone's etchings onto the paper.

Moments later, Chris's eyes rolled back into his head, and his hand motions slowed as he moved the charcoal back and forth on the paper like something else was in control. The drug he swallowed worked fast in connection with the stone rubbing.

Stacey scooched a few feet over from Chris, knowing he'd convulse from this gravestone's history at any moment once the drug wore off.

Behind Chris and Stacey, near a towering monument in the cemetery, a tall, slender older man watched the couple's every move near Florence Blackwood's grave. With a nervous hand in his pocket, he partially removed a black gem and glanced at it discreetly. Then he slid the jewel back into his pocket and traversed the cemetery grounds to confront the couple.

December 14, 1995 / Revised December 18, 2024

Controversy and sex are surefire ways to grab attention. Strangely, people's thoughts often gravitate toward these behaviors, causing them to become viral sensations.

I wanted to push the boundaries and write a provocative story to see how far I could go. I felt compelled to do so but was almost too scared to revisit this story.

Originally titled "Jack's Terrible Mistake," I rewrote this piece, holding nothing back. Now, I bid farewell to this story again as it's out of my hands, my eyes peeking through my fingers to witness readers' reactions or any backlash that would come of it.

ONLY AFTER DARK

The sound of rain tapping against the windows filled the room. Each drop traced a unique path, creating a melody that echoed off the glass. A bright flash of lightning tore through the night sky, followed by a deep rumble of thunder. The rhythmic one-one thousand, two-one thousand, three-one thousand counting game began in Lindsey Merrill's head as the storm rolled on. The only element missing from this somber evening was an eerie wail of wind.

Settled in her creaking rocking chair in the den, Lindsey fixed her attention on the front door. The dark bags under her eyes looked like the rings around a raccoon's face. Ten PM was well past her bedtime, but she couldn't sleep.

Her nightgown hugged her curves. Her breasts lifted prominently, areolas peeking through the thin fabric. Across her lap lay her husband's rifle, its polished barrel reflecting the light from the floor lamp behind her. Her fingers traced the cold metal, nails clicking softly against the barrel.

Lindsey's auburn hair cascaded over her shoulders in loose waves, framing her face in the dim lamplight. With each slow rock of her chair, the satin nightgown shifted across her skin, clinging to her curves.

The thin fabric left little to the imagination, outlining the swell of Lindsey's hips. Her nipples stood prominently against the silky material, hardened by the chill in the room. As she leaned forward, the garment's neckline gaped open, revealing the soft valley between her breasts.

Beside her on the end table, the condensation from a glass of water puddled the coaster, and a crumpled printout of her husband's itinerary hung over the edge.

Lindsey eagerly awaited her husband's return.

She swayed back and forth in the chair like a mental patient in a psychiatric ward. Her gaze was unblinking. Her full lips barely moved as she repeatedly chanted the same rhyme to herself: "As the clock winds down, your life is bound. When the rifle sings, goodbye to your dreams."

With a faint sigh, her monotonous words trailed off into the air. But deep inside, the pain and disrespect she had endured from her husband the morning of his departure lingered like a venomous snake coiled around her thoughts. The memory of his harsh words and abuse replayed in her head, cutting deeper with each repeat. Despite her attempts to push away the thoughts, the hurt remained.

Lindsey thought her marriage to Ralph had been a happy one for the past seven years. Ralph used to take her places she'd never been before and showed her the natural wonders of the world she hadn't seen—something she would never have experienced on her own. He made love to her more often than she would have liked, but afterward, she always wanted more. Like a drug, the lust inside her was a constant thought, an intense urge to satisfy her desires.

Lindsey and Ralph both had a reserved demeanor. They were often shy around confined crowds like at parties, and were consistently polite in the public eye. But their most prominent features were being warm and welcoming toward others.

Ralph worked as a senior software engineer at an expanding aerospace corporation. His duties included creating intricate software systems and seeing them through to completion. "Long hours" was an inadequate description of his hectic schedule. However, his high-paying salary allowed him to travel with Lindsey at least twice a year, staying at lavish hotels in various countries.

And every August Ralph packed his bags and left the country for two weeks to attend tradeshows.

Lindsey thought about that morning two weeks ago when Ralph left for England. His routine differed from when he usually headed out for work each morning. The scent of his cologne lingered in the air, which generally comforted Lindsey but now only served to twist the knife in her heart.

The bedroom was dimly lit with the soft glow of the moon. But dawn was slowly approaching. Ralph leaned over the bedside and pressed his lips against Lindsey's, her mouth dry like cotton. She tried to keep her morning breath to herself, inhaling as she spoke. But it never helped, and Ralph didn't seem to mind. It was more of a self-conscious habit.

Ralph's kiss deepened, his tongue seeking entry, and Lindsey parted her lips, allowing him access as a gentle moan escaped her. His hand slid up her thigh, pushing her nightgown higher. Lindsey arched into his touch, her body responding eagerly. Fully awake now, she lashed her tongue in Ralph's minty fresh mouth, and his fingers found the hem of her nightgown and slowly inched it upward.

Lindsey lifted her hips and removed her garment entirely with Ralph's help, the cool air pebbling her smooth skin.

Ralph tossed her garment to the side of the bed and returned to her, cupping her breast.

Lindsey gasped with pleasure, her fingers tangling his hair, urging him closer where his mouth replaced his hand.

A few heated breaths later, Ralph's mouth trailed lower, leaving a path of tingling kisses down Lindsey's stomach. His stubble grazed her inner thighs. When his tongue finally made contact, Lindsey arched off the bed. He worked her skillfully, alternating between broad strokes and focusing on her most sensitive spots.

Lindsey's fingers clenched the sheets as waves of pleasure washed over her. Her breath came in short pants, transitioning into soft moans. And just as she neared her peak, she felt Ralph's fingers inside her, tongue still lashing. The added stimulation pushed her over the edge, ecstasy coursing through her body as orgasmic squirts misted Ralph's face.

Ralph wiped his mouth with the back of his hand and climbed back up to her, then positioned himself between her thighs. With a single thrust, he entered her, and they both let out a satisfied groan.

Their bodies moved in a familiar rhythm, their breathing synchronized, and their shadows dancing in the bed.

Then, it happened. As Ralph continued thrusting harder and faster, Lindsey opened an eye and noticed his face hovering close to hers. Meaning to caress his face, she reached up and scratched his cheek with her fingernail.

"Ouch!" Ralph stopped abruptly and pressed his hand against his face.

"I'm so sorry!" Lindsey shrunk back. "Did I hurt you?"

Ralph examined his hand, where a thin line of blood dribbled from his finger into his palm. Feeling embarrassed that he stopped before his climax, he pulled out of her.

Lindsey sat upright against the headboard, the mood completely shattered.

Ralph got off the bed and reached behind the dresser for the light switch.

Lindsey's eyes met Ralph's manhood when the room lit, and her worst fear during sex came true. She cupped her hands over her mouth in shock. Streaks of blood covered Ralph's deflating erection. Lindsey glanced down at the sheets, now stained with a ring of blood between her legs.

Ralph's reflection in the dresser's mirror caught his attention. Blood had soaked through the stubble around his mouth. In shock, he turned to Lindsey, who was busy flipping the sheets over the blood on the bed. "What the fuck, Lindsey!" he said, touching his fingers to his lips and looking at them. Fresh blood moistened his fingertips.

"I'm sorry!" Lindsey apologized again, grabbing her garment from the bed and rushing into the bathroom.

Ralph barged into the bathroom after her, turning the faucet knob harshly. He cupped his hands underneath the faucet, splashed warm water on his face, then pumped some hand soap and scrubbed it around his mouth.

Lindsey continued apologizing as she sat on the toilet, wiping herself clean.

"A warning would have been nice." Ralph spat out water with traces of blood.

"I said I was sorry," Lindsey sobbed. "I didn't know that was going to happen. It started earlier than usual."

"Don't you know your own body? You've been having monthly periods for what, almost fifteen years now? Geez."

Lindsey glared at Ralph with a mix of anger and hurt. How could he say such cruel things to her? It was an accident.

Ralph grabbed a towel from the rack on the wall and patted his face dry. As he leaned closer to the mirror, he noticed a faint red ring still visible on the stubble around his mouth. "You've got to be kidding me!"

"What?" Lindsey said, flushing the toilet. She slipped her nightgown over her head, pulled it down, and walked past Ralph to wash her hands at the sink beside him.

"Your bloody fluid won't come off my face!" Ralph exclaimed.

"Oh my God, Ralph! What is wrong with you? IT WAS AN ACCIDENT."

Ralph rewet the towel and wiped himself down. "I need to shower again, but I have a flight to catch. Ugh. I smell like dead fish."

Lindsey's jaw dropped in shock. "That's so rude! You're the one who woke me up to have sex. What would you have done if I had a tampon inside me overnight? Would you have pulled it out for me?"

"So, you *did* know about your period," Ralph sneered.

Lindsey slammed her hands down on the counter. "Stop saying that! I didn't know. It must have started when you were inside me."

"Well, don't count on me being inside you again for a while," Ralph said coldly. "You've always warned me——"

"Shut up!" Lindsey cried out. "You're such an…asshole!"

Without thinking, Ralph backhanded Lindsey across the face. "Don't ever call me that again."

Lindsey stumbled back and crashed against the wall. "Ralph!" she wailed, her hand pressed against her cheek. Tears streamed down her face.

Ralph shook his head in disgust, not looking ashamed at all. "Stop the crying!" he yelled, backhanding her once more. "You brought this on yourself."

Lindsey slumped against the wall and crumpled to the floor.

"Don't wait up for me when I return from this trip," Ralph declared angrily. "I need time to think. Hell, I might not even come back."

Lindsey curled into a ball, crying harder as Ralph stormed out of the bathroom and into the bedroom. She could hear him getting dressed, banging dresser drawers shut and jingling keys. He didn't say another word before slamming the front door on his way out. It felt like he had just walked out of her life.

Over the next two weeks, while Lindsey recovered from the blows to her face with cold compresses, painkillers, and covering bruises with makeup, she conducted some research around the house. She spent days going through closets, dresser drawers, shelves in the garage, and boxes in the attic. She couldn't understand why Ralph suddenly became abusive, both verbally and physically. Had he been seeing someone behind her back?

Lindsey didn't find anything hidden in the house that could have explained Ralph's sudden change in behavior. At least not while she was looking for evidence. But she accidentally stumbled on something later the following week, two days before Ralph's flight home.

She did her hair and applied makeup on the fading bruises on her face. Then she stepped into the walk-in closet to pick out a blouse to wear that day. She was meeting a friend for lunch to talk about Ralph.

Browsing through the clothes hanging on her side of the closet, Lindsey selected the blouse she had in mind, removed it from the hanger, and turned around to allow herself enough space to slip it on. As she turned back to select a pair of slacks, her eye caught the corner of a crumpled piece of paper jutting from underneath a box on the shelf above Ralph's clothing.

Lindsey reached for the paper and slipped it out from underneath the box. She smoothed it out and read it. It was Ralph's flight itinerary. As she was already aware, his flight was scheduled to land in two days at 11:00 AM. Lindsey kept the paper handy to check Ralph's flight number for updates. But it wasn't the itinerary that explained her husband's unusual behavior from two weeks ago. She glanced up at the box the itinerary was under and pulled it from the shelf.

Lindsey opened the box and discovered a pink slip of paper inside. She unfolded it and read it, her eyes widening. Ralph had been laid off from work over six months ago.

What had he been doing for the past six months? Lindsey wondered. Why was he traveling to England for a tradeshow if he no longer worked for the company? The first thought that came to Lindsey's mind was her husband meeting up with someone with whom he was in a long-distance relationship.

Lindsey felt her heart sink and her stomach churn. She was confident Ralph was cheating on her. That would explain his sudden behavioral change. And the way he aroused her the morning of his flight was something he had never done to her before. It was great, but it wasn't Ralph. Where did he pick up that experience from? Lindsey didn't think pornography would've made him a better lover in bed. She knew he watched it, but the sexual pleasures he performed with her were always the same. He very seldomly changed the ways he made love to her. Someone else had to be giving him explicit ideas in bed.

And with that thought, she dashed to the toilet and threw up.

Lindsey canceled her lunch plans with her friend. She was too emotionally drained for small talk while worrying about the state of her marriage. The thoughts swirling in her head became more distressing as the day went on. By evening, Lindsey was consumed with so much rage she was throwing things around the house.

Every reminder of Ralph had to be eliminated. She shattered the glass on picture frames, tore apart any photos of them together, and destroyed the china dishes they had collected from their travels. She even discarded Ralph's frequently used tools in the trash bin outside.

Lindsey entered the walk-in closet and tore Ralph's clothes off hangers, tossing them into a pile on the floor. As she reached for his pants, she noticed his rifles standing upright against the wall in their soft cases. She picked one up and unzipped the case, removing a Winchester Big Boy 44 Magnum. Feeling around the top shelf, Lindsey found boxes of ammo.

The steady rhythm of the rocking chair filled the silence as Lindsey waited, her nerves frayed and her patience wearing thin. The rain continued its relentless assault on the windows, each drop a ticking clock counting down to Ralph's return. She glanced at the clock on the wall for what felt like the hundredth time. 10:37 PM. Still no sign of Ralph. No phone call. Her fingers tightened around the cool metal of the rifle. She had called the airlines earlier and knew his flight landed on time. Her mind raced with other possibilities, like Ralph was probably at some extravagant hotel, or worse, with his mistress.

She imagined him out in the storm, watching the house, waiting for the perfect moment to slink back home like a guilty dog. Probably hoping she'd be asleep so he could avoid a confrontation.

Her lips barely moved as she continued her repetitive chant to herself: "As the clock winds down, your life is bound. When the rifle sings, say goodbye to your dreams. As the clock winds down, your life is bound. When the rifle sings, say goodbye to your dreams . . ."

CLICK! The deadbolt on the front door slid back from the strike plate.

Lindsey stopped rocking and cocked the lever on the rifle, instantly loading a cartridge into the chamber. She pointed the gun toward the door, ready to defend herself.

The doorknob turned slowly, and the door creaked open as the sound of heavy rain grew louder.

Lindsey kept her eye through the scope, her finger hovering over the trigger. This was the moment she had been preparing for. But she still couldn't decide whether to end his life or just scare him with the rifle. Her gut was torn between the two options, causing her breaths to become rapid and making it difficult to keep the gun steady in her hands.

What if she went through with it? Did she have a plan for what would happen next? And if she didn't shoot him, would he become enraged and turn the gun on her instead? So many thoughts, so many decisions, and so many nerves running through her body.

Ralph entered the house and set his suitcase down by the door. He hadn't noticed Lindsey sitting in the rocking chair yet; his back was turned as he shut and secured the door. But when Ralph turned to reach for his suitcase, his eyes locked on the barrel of the rifle aimed right at him. He hadn't noticed Lindsey wearing her see-through gown. Only the gun glistened in the soft light of the floor lamp behind her, casting a shadow over her figure in the rocking chair. "Lindsey, what are you—"

BLAM! The gun barked simultaneously with a thunderclap outside.

Lindsey felt the strong recoil as the butt of the gun punched into her shoulder, causing the rocking chair to slide across the floor. In the same instant, she saw Ralph's body fly backward and crash into the front door with a loud thud.

Lindsey stood from the rocking chair, the rifle still smoking, and approached Ralph's body sprawled face down on the floor. A thin line of blood flowed along the grooves of the wood flooring from his chest.

Tears streamed down her face as she again pointed the rifle at Ralph. "You're still breathing, so I know you can hear me. My words are the last you will hear. I know you've been cheating on me. Was I not satisfying your needs enough? You've ruined my life, Ralph!"

Lindsey flicked the gun's action lever, sending the empty casing flying through the air and loading the next cartridge into the chamber. The metallic clink echoed in the quiet room, punctuated only by Ralph's soft murmurs of distress.

Lindsey cocked her head to catch Ralph's words. "What?" Her voice was low and steady.

Ralph took a shallow breath, wincing in pain as he spoke louder. "It's all part of the plan," he gasped out.

Lindsey's eyes widened in confusion. "What plan?" Her grip loosened on the rifle as she pondered what Ralph meant.

Suddenly, Ralph's hand shot up and grasped the gun barrel. With a strength that defied his apparent injury, he pulled the weapon from Lindsey's grasp. He flung it across the room, where it clattered against the far wall and discharged.

Lindsey stumbled backward. She watched in horror as Ralph slowly rose to his feet, his movements fluid and graceful despite the bullet wound in his chest. Blood stained his shirt, but he no longer showed any sign of pain or weakness.

As Ralph straightened to his full height, Lindsey noticed a change coming over him. His skin seemed to pale, taking on an otherworldly sheen. Once a warm brown, his eyes gleamed a deep crimson, reflecting the dim lamplight like polished rubies.

"What… what are you?" Lindsey's voice trembled.

Ralph moved with inhuman speed, his form blurring as he crossed the room in the blink of an eye. Before Lindsey could react, he slammed into her with such force that it sent her flying backward, the impact knocking the breath from her lungs. Time seemed to slow as she flew across the room, glimpses of the walls blurring past her. Her nightgown billowed around her when she soared through the air.

The rocking chair loomed closer, its wooden frame awaiting her collision. She crashed into the chair, which skidded across the polished floor, leaving faint scratches.

Lindsey's head snapped back, her hair whipping around her face as she struggled to process what had just happened. The room spun, and she blinked rapidly, trying to focus on Ralph's face mere inches from hers.

Ralph's crimson eyes bored into hers, holding her gaze with a hypnotic intensity. His lips curled into a wicked grin as he leaned in closer, revealing elongated canines that glinted in the soft light. He glided his tongue across his teeth, a low growl rumbling in his chest. The sound reverberated through Lindsey's body, awakening a primal fear within her. His breath was cool against her skin as he leaned in closer, his lips barely brushing her ear.

"My dear Lindsey," he purred, his voice silky. "Did you really think I'd leave you? That I'd throw away the memories we experienced together?"

Lindsey's heart raced as she struggled to comprehend the situation. She realized the familiar scent of Ralph's cologne was mingled with something metallic. Blood.

Ralph pulled back slightly, his crimson eyes locking on hers. "No, my love. I've been planning this for months. The layoff and the trip were all part of the plan—my transformation. I've been reborn, Lindsey. And now I want you to join me."

Lindsey sank back into the rocking chair as Ralph expressed his love for her.

Ralph's eyes blazed with hunger as he gazed down at Lindsey. In a fluid motion, he tore open her nightgown, exposing her perky breasts to the cool air. His icy hands roamed her body, leaving trails of goosebumps in their wake.

Lindsey's breath caught in her throat as Ralph's cold hands caressed her skin. Despite her fear, she felt a familiar heat building within her. Ralph lowered his head to her chest, his tongue flicking out to tease her nipple. The contrast between his icy breath and warm tongue sent shivers through her body.

Lindsey arched her back in the rocking chair, pressing herself closer. Soft moans escaped her lips as Ralph lavished attention on each breast. Then his hands roamed her curves as he kissed a trail down her stomach, pausing to dip his tongue into her navel.

Settling lower still, Lindsey felt Ralph's fingers trace delicate patterns along her inner thighs. His touch was feather-light yet electrifying. Then Lindsey's hips bucked involuntarily as Ralph slid a finger inside her.

Moaning with pleasure, Lindsey threw her arms around Ralph's neck. But before she could climax, Ralph lifted her and impaled her on his rigid length. She cried out at the sudden fullness, her body instinctively clenching around him as he balanced skillfully in the chair.

The chair rocked violently as Ralph set a punishing pace, driving into her with inhuman force. And upon release, he leaned close to Lindsey, his lips barely stroking her ear. "Will you be mine beyond mortality?" he whispered. "The pleasures are sensational. No more worries. No more lies or deceit. What do you say, my love? Do you accept?"

Lindsey closed her eyes and exhaled deeply, feeling a sense of calm wash over her. The thought of shooting her husband and facing the possibility of spending the rest of her life in prison did not sit well with her. And the mounting debt and unpaid bills also crossed her mind. All she desired was to escape from it all. "Can you make it all go away?" she murmured.

"I promise," Ralph replied confidently. "I can give you everything you've ever wanted."

Lindsey opened her eyes to meet Ralph's intense gaze. She reached out and touched his face tenderly. "Then take all my stress away." She smiled.

Ralph's lips parted, his canines growing longer as he leaned closer.

He gently brushed Lindsey's hair away from her neck. Then he slowly grazed his tongue along her jugular, savoring the rapid pulse beneath. With a low growl, he sank his teeth into the soft flesh of her neck.

Lindsey gasped, her body tensing at the sharp pain. But as Ralph began to drink, waves of euphoria washed over her. Her vision swam, the room fading in and out of focus as Ralph drained her life force. Her heartbeat slowed, each pulse pushing more of her essence into her husband. As darkness crept in at the edges of her consciousness, Ralph finally withdrew.

With a swift motion, Ralph sliced open his wrist with a sharpened fingernail and dark crimson blood welled up from the wound. He pressed the fresh wound to Lindsey's pale lips. "Drink," he commanded.

Lindsey struggled to resist the urge, but her weakened strength was no match for the hunger that consumed her. Her mouth clung to the wound like a desperate lover, drinking in the rich, metallic blood. Her fears and concerns faded with each gulp, replaced by a primal satisfaction coursing through her veins. The darkness around her melted away, leaving only the warm glow of satisfaction and contentment. When the last drops of blood slid down her throat, Lindsey's body relaxed.

She wiped the blood trickling down the sides of her mouth, a searing pain coursing through her body. Every cell seemed to ignite, her flesh burning from the inside out. She writhed in agony, clawing at her skin as the transformation took hold.

Ralph held her close, whispering soothing words as her body convulsed. "It will pass, my love. The pain is temporary, but the rewards are eternal."

Lindsey's vision blurred, the room spinning around her. Colors became more vibrant and the sounds more intense. She could hear the faintest whisper of wind outside and the scurrying of a mouse in the walls. Her senses were overwhelmed.

Then, she felt a new strength coursing through her veins as the pain subsided. She flexed her fingers, marveling at the power. Then she cried out. But the sound that emerged was inhuman—a feral growl reverberating in the room.

Looking deep into Ralph's eyes, Lindsey dove in for an arousing kiss, which led to another round of intense pleasure.

Lindsey Merrill was in love again. This time forever.

April 23, 1996 / Rewritten January 6, 2025

I was excited about essay writing, except for one assignment in my high school creative writing course. The task was to write a full-page essay comparing two unlikely objects using metaphors. Our teacher, Mrs. Morrison, referred to the assignment as the "fruit basket experiment."

She walked around the classroom with a wicker basket filled with clipped pieces of paper. On each piece was written the name of an object. We had to reach in blindly and pull out two pieces of paper, then spend the next thirty minutes comparing them in our essays.

The two objects I drew were *brain* and *dynamite*.

Spoiler alert: This may sound familiar if you've read my previous book, *Jack Stinger and the Haunting of Whitlock Manor*. My character, Daisy, also experienced the fruit basket experiment at school. I included a few sentences from my essay as her take on the comparison between brain and dynamite.

The following essay can be read in its entirety from Daisy's scene. This was certainly an interesting exercise to update and revise.

Word of advice: If you're a fellow writer struggling with a particular scene or feeling stuck on your project, I recommend taking a break and focusing on writing a short piece comparing two random objects. Even if you initially don't like the words you draw, push through and finish the assignment. When returning to your project, you'll be surprised how this simple exercise can stimulate your brain and give you a fresh perspective.

BRAIN AND DYNAMITE

The brain is a ticking time bomb.

Dynamite is an idle memory.

Comparing the brain to dynamite holds immense power, and it's the precision and timing involved in harnessing that power. The brain's intricate design and billions of neurons are the delicate lumpia wrapper of a stick of dynamite. Each neuron is a fuse, igniting a spark to send it through the nervous tissue and deliver messages to control reactions.

The brain and dynamite are explosives. Each must maintain balance to function properly. When the temperature rises, coordination becomes more crucial. It's a simple process: reach from point A to point B with one fluid motion and achieve the desired outcome.

The pressure is on.

Emotions add to the escalating anticipation building within the brain and surrounding [stick of] dynamite. Is there a pattern or rhythm between the two? A heartbeat and gunpowder are certainly factors.

There are only two possible outcomes between the brain and dynamite: success or failure.

Looking at the explosion factor—the moment of contraction before a release—the passage of time within us determines what we become on the outside. Male or female, black or white, it makes no difference. It all boils down to whether the brain is recycled or reunited with a physical form. We must pick up the pieces (or particles) from exploded dynamite, and it's up to us to choose to recycle them.

The complexity of the brain and the simplicity of dynamite are emotions controlled through the senses. The spinal cord and the detonating cord serve as central systems, powerful organs guiding the [re]actions.

To further compare, the brain is a chock-full of memories responsible for learning. Dynamite is a compact material soaking up nitroglycerin, such as clay. Both the brain and dynamite contain stabilized mixtures of substances. Therefore, by actively participating in various activities and focusing on specific tasks, the connections between neurons in the brain become stronger, creating a robust network of explosive potential.

Next, to understand the relationship between the brain and a stick of dynamite, let's delve into their anatomy. Both are composed of essential parts working together to perform their functions. Brain parts consist of the parietal lobe, the frontal lobe, the temporal lobe, the occipital lobe, the spinal cord, and the cerebellum. The anatomy of a stick of dynamite includes a fuse, a preload, a wooden case containing the igniter, a black gunpowder load of the igniter, surrounding rock or clay, and a cardboard casing.

Furthermore, the brain is divided, creating multiple functions on the left and right sides. The left brain controls analytical, logical, precise, repetitive, organized, detailed, scientific, detached, literal, and sequential functions. The right brain controls creative, imaginative, general, intuitive, conceptual, big-picture, heuristic, empathetic, figurative, and irregular functions.

Dynamite serves many purposes and is used in construction, mining, military, and social movements. Invented by Alfred Nobel (also founder of the Nobel Prizes) in 1867, dynamite was used to control a safer explosion yet was a more powerful alternative to only using black powder.

By throwing beliefs into the mix, many are strong, and others are weak or nonexistent. According to some religious views, God gave humans a brain to understand creation, use reason, make decisions, express God, and fulfill God's plan. Nonreligious or nonexistent beliefs follow the trail from actual results—millions of years of evolution that affected other primates.

In conclusion, contrasting the intricate, explosive nature of human emotions and cognitive faculties (the brain) with physical dynamite emphasizes tension, balance, and potentially uncontrollable outcomes. The tension is tight. The brain and dynamite require material to remain in existence. However, natural reverse reactions lead to their demise. The explosion of emotions in the brain mirrors the controlled chaos of dynamite igniting, which becomes an energy-coiled serpent ready to strike.

No blood and no oxygen? BLOCKAGE! The brain is dead.
A wick and blasting cap? BOOM! Dynamite explodes.

January 22, 1992 / Revised November 6, 2024

In the early 1990s, as a budding writer hungry for knowledge and guidance, I subscribed to *Writer's Digest* magazine. The pages of each issue were filled with tips on writing and manuscript formats, articles, short stories, and more, providing me with valuable insight and inspiration. And every year, without fail, I purchased the latest edition of the *Literary Guide to Agents and Publishers* from *Writer's Digest*, devouring its contents in search of my dream publishing deal.

One day, while flipping through the pages, I stumbled upon an ad that would change my writing journey forever. It introduced me to *Writer's Digest School*—a unique program where writers were paired with a published author who served as a one-on-one instructor and mentor. Without hesitation, I signed up for the course, "How to Write and Sell Short Stories," and chose to explore the horror genre.

Over the next few months, I poured my heart and soul into completing the assignments: crafting the perfect opening, building tension in the middle, and delivering a satisfying end to my short story. With the help of my professional instructor—who provided invaluable critique and editing assistance—I emerged from the course with a sense of fulfillment and pride in my work.

This gory tale still stands out as one of my best pieces. It's also the closest I've come to being published in *Worlds of Fantasy & Horror* (formerly *Weird Tales*), a magazine I've always dreamed of being featured in. The editor had read my previous submissions and provided constructive criticism for this story, motivating me to keep writing and never give up. Despite the rejection, I was content knowing it was a step toward improvement.

Interestingly, this story sparked a pivotal scene in my book, *Jack Stinger and the Haunting of Whitlock Manor*. Suppose you've had the chance to read it. In that case, you'll know exactly which scene I'm referring to—a testament to the power of inspiration and how it can shape our creative pursuits.

But fair warning: this story is not for the faint of heart. Brace yourself for gruesome details.

PREY FOR ESCAPE

Bobby Eastland's face contorted with frustration as he repeatedly squeezed the trigger to the gas pump handle. Nothing was coming out of the nozzle. He had inserted his credit card and selected the fuel grade, so what was the deal?

I-10 stretched a lonely path behind him, winding through a vast expanse of red rock and dry, cracked earth. The bony landscape stretched out endlessly, with no signs of life or civilization in any direction. The sun cast a harsh glow and intensified the feeling of isolation and emptiness. It was as if Bobby were standing at the world's edge, with nothing but this barren wasteland before him . . . and a lonely gas station.

Bobby's idea was to drive from New Mexico to the yearly Frightmare Weekend in Texas. He loved horror films, and when he heard about the event, he had to attend the horror-oriented media gathering. The event was created for horror genre fans to connect with other horror enthusiasts, meet celebrities, discover new films, purchase merchandise, and have items signed by actors who portray monsters in movies.

In the passenger seat of his '69 Mustang, Bobby's childhood friend, Daniel Blake, sat idly playing with a Rubik's Cube. He had no trouble filling one side of the cube with a solid color but struggled to complete the rest. Sighing in defeat, he rolled the puzzle off his fingertips, where it landed on the floorboard between his legs. Hearing the repetitive clicks from the trigger to the gas pump, he leaned over the driver's side seat and called at Bobby through the open window. "What's going on?"

"This damn thing isn't working!" Bobby fumed, gesturing wildly. "We're in the middle of fucking nowhere! We won't have enough gas to make it to the next town."

Daniel stepped out of the car, shutting the door. "Relax, dude," he said, leaning over the car's roof. "I'm sure there's another station not too far up the road." His eyes scanned past Bobby at the pump behind him, giving a quick nod. "Why don't we check that one out?"

Bobby turned and let out an exasperated sigh. "There's a bag over the handle," he muttered, returning to priming the pump.

"How about we go inside and ask the attendant if there's even gas here?" Daniel suggested.

Bobby yanked the handle from the tank, slamming it back to its place on the pump. "I better not be charged for this!" he grumbled as he secured the gas cap.

"What's up with the short fuse, man?" Daniel said as they made their way to the small convenience store.

"I've been getting shit on with bad luck lately," Bobby griped. "First, with Kelly dumping me last week, to the damn grease fire I created in the kitchen at home that scorched the walls, and now this crap—no gas when I need it. I knew I should've stopped in that other town back there. It wasn't quite so much of a hell hole as this place!"

The building resembled something out of a horror film. The sign hung precariously from the roof. "Fill 'N Go," it read. The "G" swung in slow, haunting rhythms.

"Looks like the sign reads Fill No," Daniel laughed.

"Should have known there'd be no gas here," Bobby added. "It clearly says it on the sign!"

They stepped onto the covered porch, their footsteps echoing off the wooden floorboards. The porch was lined with a couple of old rocking chairs, their paint peeling and their joints creaking as they swayed back and forth in the breeze. The scent of freshly cut grass mingled with the musty smell of old wood. The atmosphere was suffocating and unrelenting.

A screen door with a rusty handle awaited ahead, inviting Bobby and Daniel inside. A radio faintly played catchy tunes from decades past, a relic from another era beckoning them to step inside and explore.

The static-filled sound from the outdated radio inside the convenience store sent waves of nostalgia through Daniel's mind. The familiar tunes reminded him of his childhood spent playing Chiptune 8-bit video games on his home console. And although he still indulged in those nostalgic games, his passion had shifted to sketching characters inspired by them. He recreated creatures from the *Final Fantasy*

RPGs and heroes like Link from *The Legend of Zelda*. Each line and curve of his drawings reflected the passion and nostalgia contained in his heart.

Bobby was not a video game geek like Daniel. His repertoire was horror films. He could recite just about any '70s or '80s horror flick and name the actors who portrayed the evil characters in each movie. Actors like Kane Hodder and Gunnar Hansen were his all-time favorites; their portrayals of Jason Voorhees and Leatherface convinced Bobby as a kid that these madmen were real. And despite being far from talkative, these guys remained true to their form in Bobby's eyes.

With a calm gesture, Daniel reached for the screen door handle and opened the door for Bobby. He knew his friend was still on edge after their encounter at the gas pump, so he tried to be extra nice.

As they entered, the hydraulic tube controlling the force of the door's closure caught Daniel's eye. It was broken, dangling precariously at the top and banging against the inside of the door.

The malfunctioning door was the least of their observations when the two college boys entered the convenience store. They were greeted by a dimly lit interior with thickened air and a stale scent of cigarette smoke and spilled beer. The fluorescent lights flickered ominously overhead, casting eerie shadows that danced across the scuffed linoleum floor.

Behind the sales counter slouched the convenience store clerk, his presence imposing and unsettling like a backwoods hillbilly. He wore a stained ballcap over his greasy hair with a receding hairline and a forehead creased with deep lines. His belly strained against his discolored T-shirt, and his leering grin revealed yellowed teeth. It was as if he had been waiting awhile for someone to walk in. He seemed to be relishing the power and authority granted by his position behind the counter. And the shotgun resting on the counter in front of him made the grotesque man's character more unsettling and unlikable.

Despite his grin, the man's bloodshot eyes darted at the two boys nervously, one hand polishing the break-action double-barreled shotgun. The tension in the air was palpable.

Daniel felt a chill run down his spine as he took in the unsettling scene. *Is this guy selling guns?* he thought.

Bobby was just as shocked as Daniel.

With the clerk's gaze settled on his two customers, a wicked glint flashed in his eyes before he let out a low chuckle. A sneer was permanently etched on his face. His eyes narrowed as he glared at Daniel as if he were the target he longed for. He slowly raised the shotgun, finger poised on the trigger. Then, without hesitation, he pointed the barrel of the gun right at Daniel.

Before Bobby or Daniel could react, a deafening blast echoed through the store as the shotgun fired.

BLAM!

The blast knocked Daniel backward, and he fell into a paperback spinner rack. A searing pain exploded in his chest as he clutched at the spreading warmth of blood seeping through his shirt. Books that had scattered on the dirty floor were soaking up the blood like sponges.

Bobby's eyes widened in shock as he watched his friend collapse. His first thought was that the guy was holding up the store, and the actual clerk was lying on the floor, dead behind the counter. Perhaps Bobby and Daniel happened to enter the store at the wrong time. But this was not the case, as Bobby soon discovered.

"You crazy son of a bitch!" Bobby gasped. Rage boiled within him like a fierce inferno when he glanced from Daniel lying motionless on the floor to the scum of the earth standing behind the sales counter. Shockwaves of horror zipped through him, and his hands clenched into trembling fists. Every fiber of his being screamed with raw emotion as his eyes locked with the clerk's. He could sense a mixture of malice and amusement deep within the man's eyes. But why? Bobby and Daniel hadn't done a single thing to provoke the guy to shoot Daniel.

The monster panned the shotgun toward Bobby.

With a sudden surge of adrenaline, Bobby lunged toward the counter, his movements fueled by a primal need for justice. But his heel slipped on the pool of blood on the floor, and he fell backward, landing on his hip.

The shotgun fired the second round.

BLAM!

Good fortune was in Bobby's favor. The shot had missed him when he fell.

Realizing the guy had to reload, Bobby quickly sprang from the floor and lunged again toward the counter.

By this time, the clerk had opened the break of the shotgun and removed the spent casings. In a sloppy panic at Bobby's approach, he fumbled with two fresh shells from underneath the counter to insert into the chambers. Before he could load the first shell, the college boy was already leaping over the counter at him.

Bobby slid over the top of the counter and reached out to grasp the hot metal clutched in the hands of the clerk, whose grin faltered for a split second. Bobby's strength overpowered the lunatic, and he wrestled the weapon from the clerk.

The acrid stench of burnt gunpowder hung heavy in the air, assaulting Bobby's senses and fueling his adrenaline. He closed the shotgun break with a *click* and kept the double barrel pointing at the man, who was now pressed against the far corner behind the counter.

The clerk gazed upon the young college boy gone mad, holding a deadly weapon aimed directly at him. But the worry on his face quickly turned to sly satisfaction as he revealed the two shotgun shells still clutched in his hand before releasing them to bounce on the ground.

Bobby's attention was momentarily diverted by the sound of the shells hitting the floor.

In that split second, the clerk took advantage of the boy's distraction and reached for the weapon, repossessing the shotgun from Bobby's grasp.

Before Bobby could register what had happened, a sharp blow from the stock of the gun sent him reeling to the floor, unconscious.

The eerie echo of footsteps crunching in the dirt, followed by the ominous clanking of chains and metal against metal, permeated the silence and darkness within Bobby's mind. As he drifted in and out of consciousness, his eyes struggled to adjust to the dim light in the room. Soon, he would fully awaken to the nightmare unfolding around him.

Sounds from a set of gears creaked and groaned as they turned, their rusty hinges protesting with every revolution. More chains dragging and rattling added to the macabre symphony filling Bobby's ears. It was a soundtrack fit for a horror film or a chilling recording on vinyl.

Bobby's numbness gradually gave way to tingling sensations as he regained awareness. The unsettling feeling of weightlessness was replaced with a dull pain in his hip, aggravated by even the slightest movement of his legs.

Suddenly, a voice pierced through the darkness with its subtle yet haunting tone. "What fun Lezabel will have," it whispered. And just as quickly as he had awakened, Bobby slipped back unconscious, unsure if what he heard was real or merely a product of his feverish mind.

Bobby slowly opened his eyes again, feeling disoriented as if he had just woken up from surgery. He found himself sitting on the floor, trapped within the confines of a cage. As he took in his surroundings, he noticed everything felt unfamiliar and foreign. A single lightbulb dangled from the dirt ceiling above him.

Suddenly, he felt a sharp pain in his temple and reached up to find a large bump. Groaning at its tenderness, he took a moment to catch his breath and assess the situation. The cage was small, only about five square feet, with thick bars that isolated him from the room he was trapped in. It appeared to be a cave or a root cellar of some sort. The walls were nothing but dirt. "Where am I?" he grumbled, feeling a dry lump in his throat.

Looking at his legs stretched out on the floor, he noticed a pile of bones near the corner of the cage. Pieces of meat and flesh dangled loosely from them. Had an animal been trapped in the cage before Bobby?

Bobby took a deep breath and tried to ignore the pain radiating from his hip due to the slip and fall on Daniel's blood in the gas station's convenience store. He struggled to stand up, hoping it would alleviate the pressure on his injured side. But as he looked up and saw the low ceiling of the cage, barely three feet above him, he realized it wouldn't make much of a difference.

A rattling chain echoed from the corner of the room, catching Bobby's attention like a siren's call. His eyes strained to see behind him, but the sharp pain in his hip intensified with any movement, preventing him from looking back between the bars. Catching a glimpse of what was creating the noise would make him feel a little better about who was in the room with him. But no matter how hard he tried, he couldn't locate the source, even in his peripherals.

When the rattling noise finally ceased, Bobby breathed a sigh. An eerie silence filled the room.

"Who's there? Let me out of here!" Bobby broke the quiet. Assuming a human voice would respond, he was shocked when he heard a low, guttural growl reverberating from within the room. The sound grew louder and closer as if the source was approaching from behind.

Still, Bobby could not find the strength to see what advanced from behind him. Fear gripped his heart when he realized something that wasn't human accompanied him in this mysterious, dimly lit room.

From somewhere in this underground, a door creaked open.

Bobby darted his gaze toward a wall that curved out of sight. He could see a shadow moving into the room.

"How's that head of yours?" a voice called out.

Moments later, the lunatic clerk from the gas station stepped around the corner and into the room. He was still dressed in his dirty white shirt, ballcap pulled low over his eyes. But now, he was holding a rusted set of keys jingling on a ring that swung back and forth like a hypnotist's pocket watch. In his other hand, he twirled the shotgun he used to knock Bobby unconscious. His face, smeared with grease and dirt, split into a malicious grin at the sight of Bobby struggling against the bars.

"Lezabel's been waitin' for ya," the clerk drawled, his voice sending chills down Bobby's spine.

"Who's Lezabel—your whore wife? And where am I?" Bobby bellowed. "What have you done with my friend?"

The clerk didn't answer immediately. Instead, he circled the cage like a predator stalking its prey, the weight of his gaze making Bobby shudder. He stopped at the corner of the cage and pointed a dislocated finger at the pile of bones near Bobby's feet. "Right there."

Bobby winced, his face contorting in agony as he drew his knees to his chest. The pain in his hip was nearly unbearable, but he pushed it aside as thoughts of escaping this hellhole consumed him. "No!" he cried out. "How could you? You're a sick fuck!"

The clerk knelt and placed the set of keys on the ground. He reached between the rusted bars of the cage and rummaged through the pile of bones, searching for something buried within. With a triumphant grin, he retrieved a skull and brought it closer to his face as if admiring his handiwork. Then, with a flick of his wrist, he let it fall back onto the mound of bones, and his malevolent eyes shifted to Bobby. "Your friend had a lot on his mind," he said with a disturbing, maniacal laugh.

A single bead of sweat dripped down Bobby's face as he cringed at the sound of the clerk's laughter. "Why have you locked me in here?" he demanded, trying to keep his voice steady despite the fear that threatened to consume him. "You gonna chop me into pieces like you did with Daniel? Just wait until I get my hands on you! You'll be dead meat. Do you hear me? *Dead meat!"*

The clerk leaned forward, the menacing grin stretching across his face revealing his mouth full of yellowed, rotting teeth. "The name's Stephen," he spat out.

Bobby couldn't shake the image of Jack Torrance from *The Shining* sticking his face through the axed hole in the bathroom door. "That's not what I asked you," he spat back. "Why have you locked me in here?"

"The low price of gas is hard to come by these days," Stephen smirked. "You took the bait, and I followed through. Lezabel needs her feeding monthly. And it's that time of the month."

As Bobby listened to Stephen's sinister words, he couldn't help but feel a chill run down his spine. He understood this madman was feeding some twisted being named Lezabel. But what horrifying creature could Stephen be referring to?

Bobby struggled to maintain his composure. "What kind of name is Lezabel?" he asked, his voice shaky.

Stephen chuckled darkly. "It's not the name that matters," he replied, gesturing to the pile of bones with a twisted satisfaction. "It's what she does. She's a very special girl."

Bobby recoiled at the overpowering stench of Stephen's rotten breath, which seeped through the bars of the cage and into every fiber of his being. His heart raced with adrenaline when Stephen mentioned the unseen creature that lurked in the shadows, its presence unknown but feared. Every instinct in Bobby screamed to escape this prison and be free from this hellish situation.

A cold dread settled in his stomach at the sudden thought of never seeing his family again. And the weight of the truth he would have to tell Daniel's family hung heavy on his shoulders like a boulder crushing him into the ground. Daniel butchered at a run-down gas station in the middle of nowhere was a gruesome image he dreaded explaining. But worse yet, he had to stare at his friend's remains up close and in person. Thoughts of Daniel's family's reactions of shock and grief only added to his already unbearable anxiety.

Bobby couldn't stand being trapped with Stephen the backwoods hillbilly any longer. Yet, as much as he despised him, he also knew the smelly guy was not the sharpest tool in the shed. He thought if he could work together with Stephen and use his wits, Bobby could figure a way out.

"What's on your mind, sonny boy?" Stephen noticed a shift in Bobby's demeanor. Instead of fear and desperation, there was now a determined look in the college boy's eyes.

A chain rattled from somewhere in the room, and Bobby turned his head just in time to witness two red eyes in his peripherals fade into the shadows. "What was that?" He jolted, the sharp pain in his hip surging down his leg.

Stephen's smile stretched wide as he backed away from the cage, his eyes fixed on the shadow behind the cage. "That would be Lezabel," he announced with a devilish grin. Then, with a cruel chuckle, he called out to his pet, "C'mon out. Don't be shy."

A slow, guttural growl filled the room.

Bobby's heart threatened to burst out of his chest. The sound shook him to his core.

Slowly, yet laboriously, Lezabel crawled out of the shadows, moving on all fours to the side of the cage where Bobby could catch sight of her. Her muscles and spine ripped through her grotesque, slimy skin. She had the rugged appearance of a savage beast yet moved with the grace of something more humanlike. From Bobby's perspective, she would easily loom over him if she stood upright. A chain of unknown length was shackled to one of her bony ankles, reminiscent of a dog tethered to a tree. Bobby's blood ran cold as the grotesque creature came into view. Its eyes blazed like twin infernos, searing into his soul. Its lips curled back, revealing a mouth full of jagged, bloodstained teeth. Thick drool oozed from its mouth and splattered onto the ground in glistening pools. The creature's drooping breasts resembled two over-medium eggs hanging by rusted nails. Lezabel's massive hands, with their long, razor-sharp nails, were caked with what appeared to be shreds of human flesh. Could it have been Daniel's? The stench of decay and death emanated from her twisted form.

Stephen's lips curved into a wide smirk. He took a few steps backward from the cage and watched his pet examine its prize, ready to unleash chaos and terror upon his command.

"What the fuck is that thing!" Bobby cried in sheer terror. If it entered the cage with him, death would be instant.

The creature slunk toward the cage, its lithe body pressing against the metal bars like a cat marking its territory. Its movements were fluid and graceful, betraying the primal instincts lurking beneath its humanlike form.

"I found Lezabel several years ago wanderin' along the side of the road 'bout six miles from here," Stephen explained, his body tense as he kept a safe distance from the cage. He knew the chain around Lezabel's leg would prevent her from reaching him, but he didn't want to take any chances. He kept the shotgun aimed toward the creature for extra precaution. "I could've sworn she was a dog because she was so tiny when I found her. But when I picked her up, she clawed and bit at my arms. That's when I reckoned what she longed for in life. And she sure grows fast!"

Lezabel continued to rub herself against the cage, drawn in by the scent of the injured human trapped inside. Her elongated tongue flicked out, splitting at the tip and slithering in and out of her mouth in a hypnotic rhythm.

Bobby instinctively backed away from the creature, wary of its sharp claws and unpredictable behavior. He could sense its eyes on him, calculating and predatory, ready to reach through the bars at any moment. He winced as he placed a hand on his hip, trying to suppress the pain in his leg.

"You see, Bobby, Lezabel must eat to stay alive," Stephen explained. "Just like us. But she's only fed once a month, from what I discovered. And guess what? It's feedin' time! She devours flesh. Not just any meat but the salty taste of human flesh. It's her favorite, just like your friend there." He clasped a hand on his hip, thinking. Then he continued softly, "I still need to do somethin' with them bones."

Bobby cringed at Stephen's disturbing words." You're a sick son of a bitch!"

"Thank you kindly," Stephen replied with a twisted grin.

"I bet you mate with this disgusting creature, don't you?" Bobby couldn't believe the thought even crossed his mind, much less passed through his lips.

Stephen remained silent, and his focus returned to the creature.

Lezabel appeared to be growing more anxious about breaking into the cage.

"I think I'm gonna leave you two alone," Stephen said. "I ain't gotta be here to witness the devouring. It ain't for my eyes."

Stephen slung the shotgun over his shoulder, spun on his heel in resemblance of a Nazi soldier, and exited the room with a loud slam of the creaky door. The echoes reverberated through the room, causing the single lightbulb hanging from the ceiling above the cage to sway back and forth.

The shifting shadows danced across Bobby's face as he sat frozen in the cage, watching in horror as the creature pressed its body against the bars as if trying to squeeze through.

Sweat stung Bobby's eyes as he desperately scrabbled for a plan. He knew he had to act fast. Lezabel's growling grew louder and more impatient with each passing moment outside the cage.

If Bobby didn't come up with a solution soon, he would be a delicious snack for the monstrous beast.

Bobby's eyes darted toward the front of the cage. The dim, flickering lightbulb above cast shadows on the ground, revealing something glistening with each passing swing.

As Bobby squinted at the object, a memory flooded back to him. Stephen had forgotten to retrieve the keys he placed on the ground while examining . . . Daniel's . . . skull! If he could somehow lure Lezabel away from the cage for just long enough, he could grab the keys and make his daring escape.

But how could he distract the ferocious creature? It showed no signs of relenting, constantly bunting against the bars and emitting vicious growls.

With determination, Bobby pushed himself forward onto his stomach, gritting his teeth against the searing pain in his hip and leg. Every inch closer to freedom was both exhilarating and excruciating at the same time. He paused briefly to swallow the sweltering pain.

And when Bobby paused, the creature also halted its movements.

Bobby could feel its eyes boring into him, waiting for any sign of weakness or vulnerability. He dared to meet Lezabel's gaze, feeling the fear bubbling inside him. His peripheral vision caught glimpses of its sharp claws and jagged teeth.

Then, as if it had a short attention span, Lezabel hunched back into the shadows.

Taking advantage of the distraction, Bobby brushed the pile of (Daniel's) bones to one side, nearly retching from the feel of their texture especially knowing they were his friend's remains. He stretched out an arm through the bars. His fingertips grazed the keys just out of reach. But Bobby didn't give up. He took a breath and reached out further. Feeling the jagged edge of the keys, he pressed down on them gently and dragged them closer until he could grasp them with his other hand.

With jittering nerves, he gingerly inserted the key into the lock of the cage door. Making too much noise could startle the creature, and Bobby would probably lose more than just an arm.

He held his breath as he turned the key, praying the key would pop the lock.

CLICK! The sound of success echoed through the room.

But before Bobby could open the cage door, a low growl erupted from deep within the shadows.

Shit! Bobby swore in his mind. *I've startled it.*

Lezabel's shadowy figure emerged from the darkness, her grotesque face contorting in rage.

Her mouth twisted into a menacing grimace, once again revealing her sharp teeth coated in dried blood and remnants of raw meat. Her eyes glowed like hot embers.

This is it, Bobby thought, forcing open the cage door despite the pain in his hip.

As he stumbled out into the room, the sound of rattling chains closed in on him from behind.

Trembling with fear, Bobby approached the center of the room. Each step felt heavy, like he was carrying an extra hundred pounds on his back.

Suddenly, his foot slammed against something on the ground, causing him to trip and fall to the cold, rough floor with a thud. Scrambling to his feet, he watched in horror as Lezabel approached with all her terrifying fury.

But then, as if by some twist of fate, his eyes caught a glimmer on the ground where he had tripped—an egg-like object the size of a watermelon. And without a second thought, Bobby lunged for the egg and cradled it. A spark of hope ignited as he held onto the smooth, round object.

Lezabel's long, slender arms reached out toward Bobby, but the chain attached to her ankle reached its entire length and viciously yanked her back. She stood there, her arms flailing in a rage while her piercing gaze remained fixed on the egg in Bobby's grasp.

The air filled with tension as the creature and the college boy stood their ground, locked in a battle for control over the mysterious object.

Lezabel swiped at Bobby and let out an ear-piercing scream.

"Get back!" Bobby demanded. "I'll crush this thing!"

To Bobby's surprise, the creature seemed to understand his words. She lowered her head in what could be seen as a display of submission or worship toward him as he held her precious egg hostage. The moment hung in the air, both parties testing each other's strength.

Behind Bobby, a door crept open.

Bobby spun around, his eyes locking on Stephen stepping through the doorway, shotgun resting over his shoulder and a human head clasped in his hand.

Stephen's movements halted abruptly as his eyes caught sight of Bobby's escape from the cage. He dropped the severed head on the ground and swiftly brought down the shotgun, pointing it directly at Bobby. "Set the egg down gently," Stephen warned through gritted teeth.

Bobby's body tensed, his mind racing for a solution. He was trapped between a loaded shotgun and a vicious creature eagerly waiting to tear him apart.

With his face contorting into pure rage, Stephen advanced toward Bobby. "I said set it down before I blast your brains out into Lezabel's mouth."

Fear and desperation pulsed through Bobby's veins as he tried to find a way out. But with no options in sight, he resigned himself to his fate. "What's the use? I'm dead anyway."

Stephen's cold eyes bored into Bobby's, his finger hovering over the shotgun's trigger. He spat a wad of chewing tobacco juice on the ground. "Don't be a fool. If you don't set that egg down by the count of three, you're—"

But before Stephen could finish his threat, Bobby made a daring move. He threw the egg at Stephen in a sudden burst of adrenaline-fueled bravery before limping toward him.

Stephen's reflexes were swift; he dropped the shotgun and caught the egg just inches from splatting on the ground. He cradled it protectively against his chest. And when the gun hit the ground surprisingly without discharge, Bobby was already there to retrieve it.

With an unblinking eye and a ferocious roar, Lezabel let out another deafening scream as loud as an Aztec death whistle. Her massive form reared back, then leaped forward with a swift kick, breaking free from the shackle around her ankle. Like Bobby, Lezabel could now roam free from the room's dark corners. In a flash of instinct, Lezabel rushed toward Stephen and the egg, her claws extended in anticipation.

Stephen attempted to dodge the creature's sudden attack but was not quick enough, and the egg slipped from his grasp onto the floor, miraculously not shattering.

Lezabel scooped Stephen off the ground and tore into him in a savage fury, limbs and clothes shredding and flesh ripping from bones.

Bobby aimed the shotgun at Lezabel. He knew what must be done before escaping this vault of horror. But first, as a witness to justification, he watched Lezabel continue mauling Stephen, tearing his body to pieces and popping his head off like a rag doll in a bloody finale. Then she reached down and picked up the egg. Her curiosity was stimulated as she watched cracks form along the surface of the soft shell, followed by a thick green substance oozing from within.

Bobby waited for the perfect moment to discharge the firearm. And it happened when Lezabel's gaze was transfixed on the hatching egg.

He squeezed the trigger.

BLAM! The deafening blast rang throughout the room.

Lezabel's occipital burst like a pimple under the impact of the buckshot. Blood and brain matter exploded from her skull in a grotesque display. After a stumble, she collapsed, the cracked egg rolling across the ground.

Bobby stood in shock, panting as his body limped to one side from the surging pain in his leg. Then he noticed movement again, and his attention diverted to the egg. It was hatching.

A tiny creature pushed away a piece of the shell and stretched its clawed hand into the air.

Bobby cringed at this new life emerging before him, oddly fascinated by its strange features and vulnerability. But Bobby had seen enough when the creature poked its humanlike head out from the top of the egg and took its first breath. The little monster had facial features similar to Stephen's.

"Oh, that's fucked up," Bobby said, aiming the shotgun down toward the hatching egg. Then, before the humanoid could wriggle free from its shell, he squeezed the trigger.

Bobby burst through the door Stephen had barreled through moments before. He entered the convenience store, a front for the underground where he had been trapped. The door leading to the underground had been disguised as a wall.

The pain in Bobby's hip continued to flare, a constant reminder of the brutal attack he endured. He moved forward, knowing he needed to escape before some other horrible thing happened to him.

Navigating through the cramped aisles beneath the flickering fluorescent lighting, he passed rows of candy bars and chips. He paused halfway down an aisle when he noticed a trail of blood leading to the end cap. His eyes followed the blood until they landed on a pair of brown cowboy boots pointing toward the ceiling. Steeling himself, Bobby crept closer and peered around the corner. The headless body of a man lay on the floor, surrounded by various packaged food items from a collapsed display.

Tears blurred his vision as Bobby wiped them away, trying to keep his composure. Shaking his head in disbelief, he continued to the front of the store and out the screen door.

Relief flooded over him when he saw his Mustang still parked at the gas pump, illuminated by the eerie orange glow of the setting sun. An abandoned pickup truck was parked behind it, adding to the desolate atmosphere.

With shaking hands, Bobby fumbled for his keys in his pocket, relieved that Stephen was dumb enough not to have taken them. He slid into the driver's seat of his beloved car and revved its powerful engine. It roared to life, symbolizing freedom and escaping this horrific ordeal.

Without looking back, Bobby shifted into gear and peeled out of the gas station, drifting into a U-turn and heading home. But this time, it would be a lonely ride without his friend by his side.

Bobby's stomach dropped as he glanced at the fuel gauge and realized how close he was to running on empty. He prayed he could make it to the gas station in the other town he had passed on the way up earlier.

Through tear-stained eyes, he spotted a road sign up ahead: "Gas 10 Miles." And with a desperate grip on the steering wheel, Bobby pushed forward toward hope and safety.

November 29, 1995 / Revised November 2, 2024

"When the Clock Strikes" was inspired by a 3D puzzle of a medieval grandfather clock I purchased at an arts and crafts store in 1998. It was fun putting it together because when I finished it, the thing actually functioned! The idea for the story struck me as I pieced together the battle-axe pendulum (no pun intended).

In 2003, *Fangoria* created a short-form horror film contest called "Fangoria Blood Drive." The winners had their films released in 2004 on a DVD compilation hosted by Rob Zombie. I wanted to enter the competition but needed to write a script first. My story for "When the Clock Strikes" immediately came to mind.

With my first movie script completed, I enlisted the help of friends, family, and colleagues to help me film it using a borrowed digital consumer camcorder. It was a fun project, but unfortunately, the result was shit, primarily due to my lack of proper equipment and microphones at the time. We had to use the camera's built-in microphone for the audio recording. Blah!

The best part of the film was when we created the practical effects to shoot my brother in the head. My co-worker at the time, when I was working retail, tossed a measuring cup filled with two cups of fake blood against the inside of my friend's garage door as my brother was on his knees and threw his head back. It looked like a bullet blew his brains out onto the roll-up door.

Alas, the film wasn't chosen to be included in *Fangoria*'s DVD package. But looking back on the film project today, I think it would be fun to recreate it now that I know what I'm doing.

WHEN THE CLOCK STRIKES

Dressed in sturdy overalls and boots, Charles Dream collected a bundle of wood and made his way to a quaint cottage hidden deep within the woods. Upon entering, he neatly arranged the wood on a rustic table at the center of the room and cleared away surrounding debris and clutter.

Next, Charles retrieved a hand ax, chisel, hammer, nails, and paintbrush from a toolbox behind him. He returned to the table with the tools and began his work. His work routine was tedious and repetitive, working tirelessly until sunset before covering the worktable with a sheet and heading upstairs to rest before returning back downstairs the next morning and continuing to create his masterpiece.

On the fifth day, Charles removed a black cloth hiding his secret formulas on a mangled shelf near his worktable. Each liquid was displayed in various-sized bottles.

Charles reached for the clear bottle filled with green liquid. He set the bottle on the table and pulled a pair of latex gloves over his hands. Then he poured the serum from the bottle into the hollowed-out clock frame and smeared it around the inside edges with his gloved hand.

Charles was interrupted by the telephone ringing as he continued pouring more green liquid into the clock. He hated to be interrupted during his work, especially when creating this masterpiece.

Setting down the serum bottle and removing his gloves, Charles stepped to the corner of the room and picked up the phone. "Hello?"

"Dad, it's Stephanie."

Charles's eyes widened with joy. "Hi, darlin'!"

"Is the clock ready yet? She called *again*, reminding me to tell you she's already paid."

"The construction is complete, hon," Charles replied with a grin.

"All I have left to do is paint it. Then I'll have it shipped."

"Well, try to ship it to the office by the weekend. That's four days from now, Dad."

Charles did not like his work rushed, but he didn't often get to hear his daughter's voice, so he made an exception. "Okay. It'll be ready by this weekend. Don't worry. Now, let me get back to work."

Charles hung up the phone and returned to the table. He peered inside the clock where he had spread the green liquid. "That should be enough," he said.

He stepped to the cabinet with the mangled shelf and removed a few paint cans and a paintbrush. Charles set the items on the table and dipped the brush into the first color of paint. "Yeah, this is definitely my best work."

* * *

The stately three-story mansion towered above a steel, arrow-tipped fence surrounding a vast acreage of lush, manicured lawn and garden. Within the gate, magnificent maples enriched the extended awning above the manor's doorway.

The property had been passed down from generations of statesmen and worldly political bluebloods. The estate was so vast that the true worth of its magnificent treasures was unknown.

Kristi Jackson, a descendent of the world's wealthiest and most traveled textile king, lived in the mansion with her fourteen-year-old son, Frederick.

Divorced and alone with bitter memories of days long past, Kristi had a razor-sharp tongue and a quick temper that left poor Fred a sniveling love-starved boy with fantasies of a warm and loving mother.

Though she loved her son, Kristi had never known the love of her parents or the feel of a gentle touch, so she didn't know how to display her love to Frederick.

Kristi dressed for bed in her silk pinafore, which flowed loosely down her curvaceous body. She absentmindedly chased down a handful of prescription medication with a glass of red wine. Gazing at her reflection in the crystal glass, she thought of the countless nights she lay awake in bed.

"Ugh! I can't bear another sleepless night," Kristi cried, dreading going to her bedroom. She slept upstairs because it was quieter—something to do with the insulation in the house when it was initially built. The upstairs bedroom was designed differently, with sound-absorbing panels and heavy curtains over the window that looked out into the vast backyard.

As she walked through the sitting room, her attention was drawn to her mail and a sizeable package that Fred had retrieved earlier. Envelopes were haphazardly piled on the delicate antique tea table near the front entrance. A large, tall box sat near the doorway.

"Oh. It's finally here!" Kristi trembled with anticipation. She grabbed the large parcel and sat on her favorite crimson onyx sofa. Kristi flung her long, dark hair out of her face before carelessly throwing wadded newspaper and Styrofoam peanuts from the box onto the floor.

Finally digging up the instruction booklet, Kristi flipped through the pages before carelessly tossing the pamphlet aside. She had no intention of reading it. She hated to read, thinking it was a waste of her time.

Feeling her hand against the smooth, intricately carved wood inside the shipping box, Kristi pulled at the object's edges and slowly wiggled it free. But her excitement quickly faded as she placed the item onto the floor to observe.

"This is it?" Kristi snickered at the three-foot-tall medieval-style clock. "Considering how much it cost, you'd think it was made of gold!"

Fred peered around the corner from the hallway to investigate what stirred his mother's excitement. Then he stepped into the sitting room and leaned over his mother's shoulder. He gazed at the gothic pendulum and miniature gargoyles, which mesmerized him with thoughts of knights in shining armor and damsels in distress.

But to Kristi, she only saw cheap pine wood and tin. She rose from the sofa and stepped to the dining room table, where the crumpled flyer advertising the clock she ordered hung over the edge. She snatched the paper and scowled at the words.

DREAM MAKER'S ONE-OF-A-KIND HAND-CRAFTED ELEVENTH-CENTURY CLOCK. WOOD SATURATED WITH A SECRET FORMULA. GUARANTEED TO HELP YOU SLEEP OR YOUR MONEY BACK. CALL NOW FOR YOUR PERSONAL HEIRLOOM QUALITY MASTERPIECE IF MONEY IS NO OBJECT. 1-800-TIC-TOC1.

The clock gleamed with a glossy finish, its hands resembling daggers as they marked the minutes, hours, and seconds. A pendulum shaped like a two-headed battle-axe swung below while a large gear peeked through the top of the clock.

"Wow!" Fred praised.

"You're just like your father," Kristi snapped.

Sad and small, Fred took a backward step. "I think it's neat!"

Kristi returned a scornful look at her son. "If I want your opinion, I'll ask for it!"

Fred cringed. His mother had tormented him since the age of ten, and he hated it when she ran his life like a conservator. He pointed a shaky finger at her and said nervously, "I'm tired of your attitude, Mom," and stomped to his bedroom.

"Idiot!" Kristi exclaimed, her voice filled with frustration and anger as she crumpled the advertisement and flung it across the room. "He's *too* much like his father," she muttered bitterly.

Feeling exhausted, Kristi gazed intently at the clock. "As long as you can help me sleep," she murmured, then picked up the clock, which was surprisingly lightweight.

With quickened steps, Kristi entered the kitchen and pulled open a junk drawer, where she grabbed a small hammer and box of nails. Then she slammed the drawer closed and headed upstairs, her gown fluttering as she rounded the corner in the hallway and into the quiet solitude of her bedroom.

The clock was narrow enough to sit beside the mobile phone on her nightstand while she studied the wall. She estimated where the center would be, then hammered a nail into place. Once secured, she picked up the clock and hung it on the nail.

Stepping back with her arms crossed, Kristi admired her room with the new addition. It seemed perfectly centered, but she couldn't shake off the loneliness weighing on her lately. A deep sigh escaped her lips as she gazed at the clock on the wall.

After a moment to herself, Kristi glanced at her diamond wristwatch, which read 10:15 PM. She stood on her tippy toes and adjusted the medieval clock's hands to match the time on her watch, winding the clock by turning the gear protruding from the top of the frame. Then she swung the battle-axe pendulum and let it go, but it slowed to a stop.

"Hmm," Kristi hummed quizzically. She swung the pendulum again.

The pendulum slowed to a stop.

"Hey!" Kristi barked, unsure why the clock wasn't working. The advertisement mentioned it would work right out of the box.

Frustrated yet again, Kristi stormed out of the bedroom and back down the stairs to the sitting room. She remembered tossing the instruction booklet aside, thinking there was no reason to read it.

Kristi discovered the booklet lying on the sofa and settled herself down, flipping through the pages. She began skimming for information about the clock's functions in the troubleshooting section. Her finger glided down the page until she found a solution to the issue she was experiencing. "The clock does not function when the pendulum is set in motion," Kristi read out loud. "Wind the clock and then gently swing the pendulum."

"I've already done that!" Kristi's voice rose in frustration. She flipped to the next page. "For customer service, call 1-800-TIC-TOC1." Without a second thought, she rushed to grab the phone from her bedroom and dialed the number.

"Dream Maker's Sleepy Tic-Toc Clocks. This is Stephanie speaking. How may I help you?"

"I received a purchase today with model number 84711B," Kristi said. "Your product doesn't work. Help me before I lose my mind!"

"I'm sorry for the inconvenience. Give me a moment while I look up the model number. Can you please repeat it?"

"84711B," Kristi snarled, pacing the bedroom.

"Thank you. May I have your name so I can verify the product?"

"How long is this going to take?" Kristi said.

"If I can't verify your name with the name in our system, I won't be able to help you. Each of our products is unique."

Kristi facepalmed herself. "Kristi Jackson!"

After a brief pause, the operator returned. "Our records indicate you've purchased one of our insomnia clocks. For the clock to function properly, wind the gear protruding from the top of the clock and swing the pendulum manually until you hear a thump. Don't let it stop swinging."

"A thump?" Kristi repeated back to the operator. "Why is this not stated in the troubleshooting? This is ridiculous!"

"This will make sense soon," the operator replied. "For me to help you get some rest, you'll need to bear with me. Okay?"

"I'm listening," she said impatiently.

"When you hear the thumping noise, stop swinging the pendulum.

Let it swing on its own. But please be watchful of your fingers when you hear the noise. This is all I can tell you. Also, please call me *only* when your clock is malfunctioning."

Click.

A dial tone buzzed in Kristi's ear. "Hello?"

Kristi ended the call on her landline and slammed the cordless phone onto its charger. She glared at the clock on the wall, dreading troubleshooting it again.

If she wanted a peaceful night's sleep, she had no choice but to try and fix the clock. So, she reached for the clock to remove it from the wall for easier access to the gear on top. However, her efforts were in vain; the clock seemed stuck in place, impossible to remove. It was as if it had been glued to the wall.

Kristi flung her arms up in defeat and collapsed onto her bed, burying her face in her hands as she wept. Then, after composing herself, she rose from the bed. She entered the luxurious bathroom, boasting an open walk-in shower and oversized whirlpool tub. Gazing at herself in the mirror, framed with solid gold and lined with fancy bright bulbs, she noticed her hair was a tangled mess.

Memories of Kristi's failed marriage flooded her mind as she inspected her reflection. She believed she could have been a better mother if only her ex-husband had treated her with respect. As she stared in the mirror, she saw a woman plagued by constant lies and deceit from her past.

Kristi pushed away the lingering memories and turned off the bathroom light. In her bedroom, she made another attempt to fix the clock. Since she could not reach the gear at the top and had no desire to go all the way back downstairs to get the stepstool in the kitchen pantry, she settled for swinging the pendulum back and forth.

She strained her ears for the thumping sound that the operator with the clock company had described to her on the phone.

It was a faint sound, but she heard it and let go of the pendulum. The noise grew louder until it was impossible to ignore. Kristi had assumed the sound would come from the clock, but the thumping emanated from another room downstairs.

"Fred? Is that you?" Kristi yelled from her bedroom.

There was no response.

Curiosity getting the best of her, Kristi leaned through the bedroom doorway and out into the hall, straining to hear where the noise was coming from. It sounded like someone tapping on a drum, but she didn't allow Fred to have a drum kit in the house.

Slowly descending the spiral staircase, the polished brass railing gleaming under the giant chandelier above, Kristi made her way to the foyer. "Fred?" she called out again, hoping for a reply.

The thumping noise had ceased.

Once again, Fred remained silent, causing frustration to bubble up inside Kristi. "He's got another think coming," she grumbled as she stomped through the house to Fred's bedroom.

But before she reached his door, the shattering of glass echoed through the hall.

Kristi froze for a moment, thinking someone had broken into the house. Then she quickly made the rest of the way to Fred's room and banged on the door.

"Fred. Wake up!" she called out urgently. "There's someone in the house."

With no response from inside the room, Kristi pushed open the door. "Fred," she whispered as she stepped into the darkened room.

Still no response.

Kristi reached and flicked on the light switch. To her relief, Fred was asleep with headphones over his ears, blasting rock music through the small speakers.

"No wonder he couldn't hear me," she sighed. She bent over the bed and grasped his headphones, pulling them away from his ears.

Fred's eyes flew open, and he sat up, confused. "What's happening? Am I late for school?"

Kristi placed a finger to her lips. "Shhhh! Listen."

"Listen to what?" Fred asked, annoyed that his mother woke him in the middle of the night.

"Lower your voice," Kristi whispered urgently. "If you shut up, you'll hear it."

Fred glared at his mother. "I think those pills are messing with your head."

"I'm not crazy!" Kristi snapped, looking out into the empty hallway. Then she turned back to Fred. "Go check around the house for me."

Fred sat baffled. "What? Why?"

"There's someone here!" Kristi pointed a shaky hand outside the doorway. "Go!"

"This is insane!" Fred muttered angrily, tossing his headphones aside.

Kristi trailed behind her son but discreetly dipped into the kitchen to pour herself a glass of red wine. With her nerves on end, she gulped down the wine, thinking it would help her relax. A Valium would've done the trick instead of an alcoholic drink.

She poured herself another glass.

Moments later, Fred entered the kitchen. He paused and watched as his mother pulled a knife from the block on the counter while holding a glass of wine in her other hand. He frowned, seeing that she was drinking again. And to show how upset he was with her, not only drinking but waking him up for something completely unnecessary, he raised his voice at her. "There's no one in the house!"

Kristi jumped, spilling red wine onto her gown. "Frederick Bentley Jackson!" she yelled. She hadn't called him by his full name in years. "Look at what you've done!" She slammed the wineglass on the counter, gesturing at the large stain.

"What the hell, Mom? Why do you have a knife?"

Kristi set down the knife, grabbed a wad of paper towels, wet it with water from the kitchen sink, and dabbed at the stain. "I'll never get this out!"

"I didn't know you dipped in here for a stupid drink." Fred felt ashamed for ruining his mother's gown.

"Well, I didn't think you'd finish looking around the house so soon," Kristi said, still dabbing at her nightgown. She pulled several more squares of paper towels from the roll.

"Why are you acting so strange tonight?" Fred asked with concern.

"I can't sleep," Kristi confessed.

"Still? Maybe you should take another sleeping pill or something to calm your nerves."

Kristi paused from dabbing the clean towels on her gown and sighed miserably. The feeling of self-reproach warmed over her. "I don't want more drugs. That's all the doctor ever prescribes." She glanced back at Fred and added, "But there's one more thing I need your help with."

"What is it?" Fred asked.

"I need you to walk me back to my room," Kristi requested.

Fred chuckled. "Are you still afraid someone is in the house? I told you I already checked, and no one is here."

"I just want to make sure it's safe," Kristi replied. "I heard strange noises earlier, and I thought it was you, but you were asleep.

What if someone broke in and is hiding somewhere—sorry, I'm paranoid."

"You definitely are," Fred agreed. He left the kitchen but stopped and turned back to his mother. "Do you want me to escort you back to your room or not?"

Kristi poured the remaining wine in her glass down the sink drain and grabbed the knife off the counter. Then, she followed Fred upstairs to her room.

* * *

Lingering outside the doorway, Kristi reached out and touched her son's face and smiled at him. "I'm sorry for how I've been behaving toward you lately," she apologized. "I'll do better, I promise. Just give me some time."

Fred pulled away from his mother's touch and snickered. He knew she was incapable of change. She'd been married three times in ten years, and he accepted his mother was beyond help. And the men she dated were nothing more than douchebags in his eyes. "Try to get some rest, Mom," he said before returning downstairs to his room.

Kristi closed the bedroom door, placed the knife on the nightstand beside her bed, and crawled underneath the covers. She sighed with satisfaction, feeling better for apologizing to her son. It was something she should have done a long time ago. She switched off the lamp beside her, hoping to finish the night with some much-needed rest.

3:45 AM

Kristi's eyes sprang open, and she sat up and switched on the lamp. The thumping sound had returned. She listened intently; this time, the noise seemed to be right outside in the hall.

Panicked, Kristi reached for the mobile phone on the nightstand.

"Nine-one-one. What's your emergency?"

"This is Kristi Jackson. There's someone in my house!"

"Where is the intruder located, ma'am?" the dispatcher asked calmly.

"I don't know. Send someone over here! 3421 Cemetery Hill. It's the mansion on the cul-de-sac."

"A unit has been notified of your call. Try to remain calm. Please don't hang up until the police arrive."

Kristi flinched from another thump outside her bedroom. "Hurry!" she shouted into the phone.

Static crackled through the phone.

"Hello? Are you there?"

More static.

Kristi set the phone down and swiped the knife off the nightstand. She stood from the bed and faced the door, clenching the knife tighter.

Suddenly, the bedroom door vibrated like someone was banging on it from the other side.

Kristi slowly approached the door. She reached out and grasped the doorknob, giving it a slow twist, then swung open the door as she raised the knife over her head.

To her relief, no one stood outside the doorway. "I must be losing my mind," Kristi muttered. She lowered the knife and peeked into the hallway, looking left then right.

"Fred?" Her voice carried through the hall.

But Fred did not reply.

"The clock!" Kristi suddenly remembered and turned back into the bedroom. Her eyes were immediately drawn to the medieval clock she'd hung above the nightstand.

With her attention focused on the clock, Kristi's mind played tricks on her. She thought she saw the clock banging against the wall like it was possessed. She held her hands to her ears, the knife nearly grazing her earlobe. "Shut up!" she yelled, closing her eyes tightly and wishing the vision away. But when she opened her eyes again, she saw the clock was still bouncing against the wall. This wasn't her imagination.

Determined to get rid of the clock, Kristi tossed the knife onto the bed and approached the clock. She grabbed the sides and paused from pulling it away from the nail. The minute and hour hands transcendentally took the shape of real daggers and were spinning out of control!

Kristi leaped back before the daggers sliced off her fingers. She looked at her hands, thankful she still had all ten fingers. She recalled the operator with the clock company telling her to watch her fingers when she heard the thumping sound. This was what she must have meant.

Kristi stepped back and looked at the clock quizzically. Another transformation was happening. The pendulum started swaying.

Grabbing the mobile phone, she speed-dialed the number of the clock company.

"Dream Maker's Sleepy Tic-Toc Clocks. Stephanie speaking. How may I—"

"This clock is alive!" Kristi raged. "How do I stop it?"

"Who is this?" the operator responded.

"Kristi Jackson. Help me!"

There was a brief silence before the operator finally said, "Are you calling me when your clock is functioning properly?"

Kristi glanced at the clock. The second hand was ticking, and the daggers representing the minute and hour hands had ceased spinning and were pointing at the correct time. The pendulum was swaying. "Yes," she confirmed.

The line filled with silence again.

"Hello?" Kristi said.

Out of nowhere, a loud, high-pitched scream pierced Kristi's ears, followed by gurgling sounds akin to drowning. A deep, demonic voice bellowed through the phone. "They have been summoned," it declared.

Kristi flung the phone onto the bed, shaking off the unnerving call.

The bedroom suddenly filled with the sound of wood splitting, and Kristi glanced at the clock in disbelief. The pendulum had transformed into a real battle-axe!

Hitting the palm of her hand repeatedly against her forehead, Kristi tried to rid this vision from her mind. "It's not real," she said. But it was real. And she didn't know what to do. Who would believe her that a cheap clock she ordered through a catalog would come to life? A schizophrenic, maybe.

Unable to resist its alluring new feature, Kristi reached out and stopped the swaying pendulum, feeling the smooth texture of its intricate handle.

Suddenly, a loud and jarring clanging noise shattered the silence, causing Kristi to spin around in surprise. In the doorway stood a formidable figure—a knight in shining armor from head to toe, his sword at the ready. The metallic sheen reflected the soft light of the room.

Kristi's heart raced as she took in the sight before her, feeling both fear and admiration for this valiant warrior who had appeared out of nowhere. She took a step back. And with each backward step, the knight stomped forward.

Remembering she'd tossed the knife on the bed, Kristi quickly grabbed it. "Get out of my house!" she cried. She clutched the knife in both hands, the tip pointed toward the knight.

"The summoner must be terminated by order of King Richard," the knight declared, taking another step.

Confused and terrified, Kristi shut her eyes tightly once again, hoping to wish away the intruder before her. But the knight was still in the room when she opened her eyes again. "Those damn pills the doctor ordered are making me hallucinate!"

The knight chuckled at her disbelief. "Nice clock," said the man inside the metal suit. But was there truly a person inside the armor? If so, whoever was inside was looking at the medieval clock on the wall.

Kristi followed the knight's stare to the clock behind her. The pendulum, a two-headed battle-axe, glinted dangerously. On instinct, Kristi dropped the knife and sidestepped to the clock, reaching out to grab the pendulum with unexpected strength. She wrenched it forcefully from its frame. The weight of the weapon-like object felt heavy in her hands, starkly contrasting its delicate appearance. She held up the weapon, feeling a surge of adrenaline course through her.

Facing the knight, Kristi cried fiercely and swung the battle-axe.

The knight swiftly parried her attack with his sword, metal clanging in a melodic rhythm. With a quick movement, the knight used his heavy boot to shove her across the carpeted floor, leaving deep imprints in its soft fibers.

Despite the surprise of her strength, Kristi managed to stay on her feet. She quickly regathered herself and charged at the knight again, bringing the axe down upon his chest.

The blade sliced through his breastplate effortlessly and plunged deep into his sternum. The knight stumbled backward into the hallway and crashed against the wall, collapsing to the floor as blood seeped from the wound in the breastplate.

Kristi fell to her knees, sobbing. "What is happening!"

Her head swirled as the room spun in a chaotic dance, twisting and bending reality. The walls pulsated like giant lungs, expanding and contracting. The constant ticking of the medieval clock became almost unbearable, merging with the faint whispers of unseen voices.

Suddenly, the air grew heavy, and Kristi curled up in a fetal position as she slipped into unconsciousness.

* * *

"Wow, that's an interesting clock," a voice proclaimed.

"Don't touch it," another voice warned. "It's evidence!"

Kristi tried to move her hands to touch her face, but they wouldn't budge. She opened her eyes and realized she was sitting in the corner of her bedroom against the wall.

A detective and a police officer stood before a body on the floor, a knife handle sticking out of the victim's chest. Blood pooled around the body.

Kristi groaned and shifted her head against the wall, feeling a migraine coming on. She took deep breaths as her eyes focused on Fred's twisted and mangled body lying on the floor in front of her.

"That punk kid probably deserved it," the detective remarked. He turned to the officer, who was staring at the medieval clock on the wall. "Hey, snap out of it! You have work to do."

The police officer, mesmerized by the swinging pendulum shaped like a battle-axe, had never seen anything like it.

"Forget about that damn clock," the detective ordered. "Focus on your job."

The officer suddenly turned to the detective and drew his service pistol.

"Hey!" The detective reached for his gun in his shoulder holster, but before he could grab it, the officer fired once, the bullet wounding the detective in the stomach.

The officer squeezed the trigger again, and the detective fell backward from the bullet piercing his forehead.

Kristi screamed, trying to break free from the handcuffs that bound her hands behind her back.

The officer's gun slipped from his hand, and he collapsed onto the floor.

Finally managing to get to her feet, Kristi stepped through the blood pooling on the floor as she approached the clock. Its intricate design and ticking sounds drew her in closer, where she watched the pendulum swing back and forth. Its movements were hypnotic. A numbness encompassed her body. It was a familiar feeling she'd sensed recently.

Behind her, another figure dressed as a knight in armor appeared in the bedroom doorway. Footsteps echoed as more knights marched up the stairs and gathered outside the room.

The first knight drew his sword. "The summoner must be destroyed!" he roared as he charged into the bedroom. And with one swift motion, the knight plunged his sword into Kristi's abdomen.

Kristi's jaw gaped as the knight pulled the blade out slowly. She fell onto the bed, her head hitting the nightstand. Before the darkness swallowed her, Stephanie's voice erupted through the mobile phone beside her ear. The Sleepy Tic-Toc Clocks operator somehow controlled Kristi's phone remotely, as if she had been listening to Kristi's struggle with the clock and her hallucinations. "What a masterpiece!" she announced victoriously. "Dad's surely gonna want to make more of these clocks!"

The cordless phone clicked off with a sharp snap, followed by the low hum of a dial tone buzzing through the bedroom. The sound filled the room with an eerie sense of emptiness. It was as if the room held its breath, waiting for someone to fill it with life again. But for now, all that remained was the distant buzz of a disconnected line, several homicide detectives investigating the scene, and the steady ticking of a medieval clock.

February 11, 1998 / Revised December 19, 2024

I only wrote one poem as a kid that genuinely resonated with me. The words came to me in a dark fantasy haze, conjured from a place deep within my imagination. My love for fantasy didn't blossom until I was fifteen, when I enjoyed reading *Dragonlance* books. From that moment on, I was hooked on the fantastical worlds and mystical creatures that filled the pages of those books.

But my attempt at writing a fantasy saga, *The Dragon's Layer: Quest of the Golden Armor*, never saw the light of day. It was meant to be a grand trilogy, but as I sat down to write the second installment, I lacked fresh ideas to continue the story.

My interest in fantasy novels began to wane, and I returned to my first love—horror. It has always been my preferred genre, and nothing compares to the thrill of creating terrifying tales. However, many years later, I felt a pullback toward fantasy. This time, it was for a short story I wrote for my children called "Entrance to the Dragon's Den." I saw it as one last chance to delve into the magic and wonder of fantasy, and perhaps my kids would enjoy it, too, especially since my youngest was obsessed with Harry Potter at the time.

The following poem is written like a story—free verse in its purest form. Whether it will satisfy your taste or only mine, I can't say.

DARK

The dark is night. The knight is dark.

A mighty wind howls through the castle at dusk.
Its structure is erect, reaching high into the star-studded sky.

Behold! The moon is yellow and shaped like a lemon pie.

Beneath the cloak of night, shadows dance,
and within the ancient courtyard, time still stands.

Silhouettes of armies are etched against the moonlight,
while the kingdom falls victim to the secrets of the old.
The commotion begins with the clash of steel filling the air,
and the enemy approaches with malice in their eyes.

Debris from trebuchets soars, crashes, and burns,
launched through the night to explode and destroy.
But once the flames extinguish,
all that returns is the dark . . . and a golden-armored boy.

The dark is night. The knight is dark.

The wind whispers secrets of a battle now past,
carrying echoes of warriors brave and true.
But it's at this moment that the boy stands steadfast.
He's a beacon of hope in a world askew.

He defends the realm from impending wrath.
The moon watches over him, silently glowing upon his path.

As he ventures forth with courage and love,
the dark knight stands atop a hill and is enraged from above.

A sea of forest stretches between them,
and a silver river winds through the valley below.
It's a temporary barrier between the two knights,
for they've faced challenges of what lurks within from long ago.

Black as day, light as a knight;
black as night, light as day.
The dark knight must pay!

Whisking through the forest, the enemies anticipate a final fight
as the night comes for the light.
The golden-armored boy trembles with fear as the cold wind blows,
for the night is a bellows.

The dark is night. The knight is dark.

With their breaths quick and their hearts pounding,
the knights prepare to put their skills to the test.
Through the twisted trees and shadows deep,
The foes clamor through the forest to meet.

Their eyes gleam with an unholy light,
and their swords clash in a symphony of steel.
It's a battle of wills that only one shall feel.

Sparks fly as they dance under the stars,
each strike a testament to their battle scars.

The golden-armored boy fights with all his might,
determined to vanquish the darkness before him with the coming
light.

As the duel rages on in the silent wood,
the dark knight's malice is clearly understood.

But the boy fights not just for victory or land,
but for the people and his kingdom, he aims to withstand.

THE REAL WOLF MAN

The dark is night. The knight is dark.

From a final blow, the dark knight falls to his knees,
defeated by the golden-armored boy who fought without ease.

The shadows retreat and are chased away by dawn.

Now, the golden-armored boy can rest,
and the town can sleep,
for the dark has passed through the night.

May 5, 1992 / Revised September 30, 2024

In 2017, I found myself drawn back to the world of fantasy stories and films. With Christmas approaching, I wanted to write a tale for my kids; not only were they interested in fantasy at the time, but they'd always enjoyed the horror genre. So, I decided to blend both genres in a short story, and this is what I came up with.

ENTRANCE TO THE DRAGON'S DEN

Drackonwulf broke through the water's surface, gasping for air. His mind reeled from shock after waking up. As he struggled to clear his head, a sense of unease settled over him, mixing with his confusion. All around him was darkness, a void that seemed to swallow him whole. The only sound was the water lapping softly against his skin. It was as if he had been cast into another world.

The burly barbarian stood tall and imposing, his muscular frame on full display as he wore nothing but a loose-fitting loincloth. He struggled to piece together his memories—his location, the clothes or armor he once wore, even the time of day—all he could not recall. His mind was a foggy mess, with only his name remaining clear. "I am Drackonwulf the Kind!" he bellowed into the emptiness around him, hoping for a response. "Who is responsible for my downfall? I challenge the coward to face me!"

But the void remained silent, betraying no secrets of Drackonwulf's existence in this mysterious place. As he took hesitant steps forward, his bare feet sinking into the softness beneath, he felt a chill creep up his spine.

His name echoed in his mind, stirring whispers of fear and awe wherever it was spoken. But who was he, indeed? Memories flickered like distant torchlights in the fog of his mind, offering glimpses of battles fought and victories won. Yet a shadow lurked at the edge of his thoughts, a darkness that hinted at a past shrouded in mystery and blood. He protected the weak, a beacon of hope in troubled times. As he delved deeper into his memories, he realized his downfall was brought about by treacherous betrayals. But the plot to rid him of this world forever was foiled. He'd find his way out of here and face the one responsible. And his thoughts pointed to someone he knew for sure would have dumped him into this filth—Clive Salisbury. Soon, justice would be in his own hands.

A putrid stench filled the air, interrupting Drackonwulf's thoughts. It made his senses reel, like an allergy attacking every inch of his body. He clawed at his arms and legs, desperate to alleviate a sudden itching and burning sensation that consumed him. "What is this filth?" he said disgustedly.

Sloshing through the liquid, Drackonwulf felt his feet sinking into the soft and squishy ground. He stumbled a few times, but his arms thrusting against the narrow walls on either side kept him from falling. Confused by the textured walls, he found that they, too, were of the same substance as the material he walked on beneath the water.

If only he could find a torch or a light at the end of this tunnel, he'd see what he was dealing with. However, the more time that passed, the more his eyes adjusted to the dark. And up ahead, silhouettes of figures were slowly coming into view.

Limbs nearby extended from the water's surface, indicating the water was thinning. Was Drackonwulf finally approaching dry land? Although his vision was clearing, his lungs were still struggling. The air was thick.

He pressed on with his mighty strength and willpower, picking up the pace and stomping through the water.

At a young age, Drackonwulf left his hometown of Rosenbarrel to live in the kingdom of Kindora. But he never imagined the events that would later unfold in Kindora under King Clive Salisbury's reign. Despite rumors of the king's cruel intentions and thirst for chaos, Drackonwulf remained loyal. However, as tales spread of Clive capturing and subduing a fierce dragon to assist in his wicked plans, Drackonwulf's attention shifted toward this newfound threat.

The dragon was imprisoned deep beneath Castle Filmar's dungeons, guarding the king's immense hoard of stolen treasure—all for his greedy gain. One had to navigate a complex maze of traps and obstacles to reach the dragon's lair. Some stories even mentioned a treacherous pit that led to the entrance of the dragon's den, where prisoners were thrown in and left helpless against the beast below.

King Grinyard Salisbury of Rosenbarrel ordered Drackonwulf to secretly investigate and confirm Clive's crimes; Clive was Grinyard's sinful younger brother. But his strategy was risky.

Grinyard chose Drackonwulf to carry out his plan because of his loyalty, intelligence, and keen ability to thwart the danger of the keep.

Townsmen of Rosenbarrel referred to the barbarian as a gentle giant, for he had a passionate side like no other warrior before him.

Drackonwulf's task was to command a group of soldiers traveling to Kindora and stage an attack on the gates of Castle Filmar. Serving as a distraction, three other soldiers would sneak in through the less guarded southern entrance, which led into the kitchen. This area of the castle was often overlooked and vulnerable to attacks.

Clive's deep-seated resentment toward his and Grinyard's father, the former and now deceased king of Kindora, puzzled many. Perhaps jealousy played a key role. However, suspicion naturally fell on Clive when the king was poisoned during a dinner and entertainment event featuring jesters and magicians. But with his cleverness and knack for manipulation, he cleared himself of all accusations. He claimed the throne as the new ruler of the Kingdom of Kindora.

On the day his brother was coronated, Grinyard declared, "I'll have you punished for your murderous tendencies! Your deceitful ways and violent pleasures will catch up to you. I am disgusted by your lack of honor!"

Disguising himself as a clergyman, Drackonwulf's mission was to infiltrate the castle with his comrades posing as peasants. Once inside, they would send a messenger to inform Grinyard of their findings so he could strategize on how to overtake the castle. It was common knowledge that Castle Filmar had been fortified without proper authorization. This was Grinyard's chance to exact revenge for Clive's unlawful actions.

Despite their best efforts, Drackonwulf and his infantry were only able to evade detection for just under a fortnight before being caught by the garrison. That same day, a messenger set off on horseback toward Rosenbarrel to deliver the news to Grinyard.

Unfortunately, it was Derek, one of Drackonwulf's soldiers, who was driven by his desire for a beautiful baroness, who ironically was having disgruntled relations with Clive, who ultimately led to their exposure and imprisonment. The soldier had walked in on Jessica weeping at the foot of her bed. Derek kindly offered her his hand.

Drackonwulf noticed the developing relationship between Derek and Jessica, leading to increased tension and arguments between him and Derek. This caught the attention of the garrison, who quickly took them into custody and began searching for the other soldiers in disguise. Then, when Clive was notified of the potential siege of the castle, he declared Jessica guilty on two counts: treason against the castle and being an accomplice to a raid. He showed no leniency and handed down the sentence of beheading.

Drackonwulf and his companions were stripped of their clothing, leaving them vulnerable and exposed to the cold stone walls. Their bodies were subjected to pressing, a form of torture where heavy weights were placed on top of them. They added more weights every few hours, crushing them further with each passing moment.

Despite the brutal conditions, the prisoners were given enough sustenance to keep their weakened bodies alive, prolonging their suffering.

Clive stormed into the chamber, his eyes burning with fury. He needed answers, and he wanted them now.

Drackonwulf lay there, battered but not broken, with only a couple of his comrades still alive.

The silence in the chamber was intense as Clive towered over Drackonwulf. Then the king's voice shook the very foundations of the room as he barked out questions, each one more desperate than the last. "Who sent you?" he roared, spittle flying from his mouth like venomous darts.

But Drackonwulf remained silent, his cold, unblinking eyes staring back at the evil before him, daring him to do his worst.

After several days in the torture chamber, Drackonwulf became the only surviving prisoner. He felt he had failed his men and mission. A deep sorrow filled his heart. Each soldier had been a brother to him, and their deaths weighed heavily on his soul. He thought about how they'd fought bravely and fiercely against the tortures inflicted upon them. Their screams echoed in his mind, a symphony of pain and defeat.

Drackonwulf was released from the torture chamber and transferred to the pit above the dragon's den. Exhausted and drained from days of agony, he stood on a large wooden platform and peered down into the gaping black hole. His bruised body trembled, struggling to support his weight. Defeat weighed more heavily on him now.

Despite his desire to end the pain and let go, a sudden kick to his lower back propelled him over the edge and into the unknown depths below, his fate in the hands (or claws) of the legendary dragon that awaited him.

The pit was a death trap. The stench of blood and decay filled the air. The ground was littered with gruesome remains of soldiers and criminals, their bodies torn apart by the relentless attacks of the dragon. Drackonwulf's memory was refreshing. He could still feel the force that sent him tumbling over the edge and into this dark pit. He recalled Clive's ruthless interrogation. Above all, he knew his mission was far from finished, for Clive was solely responsible for him waking from a stupor and gasping for breath in this pit. Drackonwulf remembered, and he wanted revenge.

Making his way through the carnage, Drackonwulf stepped over a decapitated body before coming across a girdle that belonged to a soldier in heavy armor. He picked it up, and with a determined look, he unsheathed a bastard sword. He felt the odds were turning in his favor and was ready to defend himself against potential threats lurking in the shadows.

Drackonwulf jolted from a sharp thump on his shoulder, causing him to whirl around just in time to see a large rat tumble into the shallow, murky water. More splashing echoed around him, and he quickly turned to witness an unexpected shower of rodents falling from the ceiling. Some landed on him whole, while others fell in pieces. "How is this possible?" Drackonwulf muttered. It must have been a massive nest above him that collapsed.

He stepped back, watching as dead rats rained down before him. When the influx of rodents eventually slowed, Drackonwulf took a battle stance, anticipating a potential threat. Sure enough, a deep groan echoed ahead, and the barbarian said under his breath, "Dragon!"

Shortly after, an immense roar shook the underground, knocking Drackonwulf off his feet and against a nearby wall. He lay in the damp puddle until the reverberation subsided. As he lifted his gaze from where he had fallen, Drackonwulf caught sight of a glimmering light from high above in the ceiling. Perhaps the rats had been dropping from that opening.

His gaze was further drawn to a skeletal figure on the other side of the treacherous mire hanging over a ledge. The corpse was practically skin and bones, wearing a tattered tunic and fauld that barely clung to its frame. "What a pitiful sight," Drackonwulf murmured, rising to his feet and approaching the body. With careful hands, he removed the tunic and wrapped it around his waist. Despite being too small for him, it brought a sense of comfort and completeness. He could feel his strength returning at last.

Drackonwulf's eyes followed the speck of light from above. The climb to the top seemed impossibly long. Clutching his sword, he wondered if it could help him scale the walls and escape this dreadful place.

A water droplet landed on his cheek as another deafening roar vibrated the walls. The creature was getting closer; the ravenous beast must have caught his scent.

Strangely, a thick slime oozed in masses down the walls as Drackonwulf prepared to make his ascent. Time was of the essence!

Studying the walls, a bizarre blend of organic and solid matter that he'd never encountered before, Drackonwulf devised a plan. He would cut small slits in the walls and use them as footholds and hand-holds to hoist himself up. After each successful attempt, he would re-peat the process until he reached the top.

As his sword pierced through the wall, thick red slime oozed from the wound. Drackonwulf wedged his foot into the cut without hesita-tion and raised his sword to create another anchor point. Strangely, the walls swayed slightly as he continued climbing.

The sound of boiling water grew louder as Drackonwulf climbed higher, and more discolored, slimy substances gushed from the gashes he made with his sword.

Suddenly, he lost his foothold, but his reflexes were quick. He caught himself by clinging onto the sword lodged in the wall. "Bloody hell!" Drackonwulf cried out, struggling to hold on.

The dragon's cry echoed through the thick air again, followed by heavy footsteps like it was stomping toward its prey. But the roar transposed into a pitiful groan, as if the creature had become weak or injured.

Drackonwulf shifted his footing, finding a new sturdy spot before he made another lunge up the wall. Sweat dripped into his eyes. He couldn't shake the fear of losing his grip again and falling back into the pit, like all the other unsuccessful climbers whose bodies lay below and eroded over time. The thought constantly gnawed at him as he scaled these seemingly endless walls.

Another roar.

"Come and get me if you dare!" Drackonwulf challenged the creature.

As fate would have it, the light above brightened, revealing a larger opening. Drackonwulf knew he was almost there and couldn't afford to stop now. He thrust his sword into the wall and pulled him-self up with all his might. His veins were pumping with adrenaline like never before, giving him a newfound confidence.

The creature let out another bloodcurdling cry. But Drackonwulf tuned out the distraction.

He was only a few feet away from reaching the top when something peculiar caught his attention, much like the rain of rats that had bombarded him earlier.

"Teeth?" Drackonwulf gasped, unable to believe what he was seeing. Then he realized he was never climbing a wall; he was scaling the dragon's throat! He had been trapped in the beast's stomach all along, ever since he woke up from his initial stupor. It was then he realized, too, that the goop oozing from the walls was a mixture of mucus and blood, and it matched the shallow water he had emerged from—stomach acid. His skin still stung and itched from constant contact with the dragon's bodily fluids.

Maneuvering between the beast's sharp teeth and dodging its lashing tongue, Drackonwulf finally made it to the top. He quickly threw his sword through the opening before pulling himself out. He retrieved the weapon where it had landed outside the pit and, drenched in dragon mucus, prepared to defend himself against potential attacks.

Seeing there was no one else in the room with him, he stepped toward the edge of the pit, looking back down to where he had been kicked. The dragon's jaws were wedged open, some of its teeth stuck in a wooden platform with a hole cut in the center. Clive had imprisoned this creature for his own purposes—using it to dispose of enemies and keep the dragon fed and alive.

Drackonwulf's heart softened toward the dragon. He looked down at the creature, trapped in a dark pit, and he finally understood that every time he had stabbed it while climbing up its throat, the ferocious beast had screeched in agony. It wasn't growling out of anger or confrontation but in pain!

He couldn't look at this disgusting sight anymore.

The room was empty, except for a torch that burned a weak flame on the far wall. Drackonwulf suddenly stumbled backward on the platform. The floor trembled as if amid a powerful earthquake. He looked for something to grab onto, but he lost his balance and fell. The support beams holding the platform over the dragon's gaping mouth buckled. Then they snapped, and Drackonwulf crashed to another level below, narrowly avoiding being swallowed by the beast again.

Returning to his senses, Drackonwulf opened his eyes to a room filled with bright light. And when he got his bearings, he realized where he had landed—Clive's jewel chamber!

Looking around the treasure room, Drackonwulf's eyes widened, and his mouth fell open in awe. He was surrounded by mountains of the most valuable treasures one could only dream of: piles of gold, silver, diamonds, sapphires, rubies, emeralds, and pearls. Despite being swallowed by a dragon moments before, he couldn't help but think that perhaps this wasn't a bad experience.

Drackonwulf staggered to his feet. His sword lay several yards away. His body ached, but being trapped inside the tower of royal treasures eased his mind off the pain. His eyes wandered across the jewels and metals, his thoughts drifting back to the dragon. And there, he saw it. The black dragon! Its head was secured with ropes tied to anchors at the upper level's stone walls from which Drackonwulf fell.

The beast's chest heaved, its breaths coming out in rapid bursts. It thrashed about violently, writhing like a caged animal desperate to break free. As the colossal creature continued its struggle, its movements were so powerful that they eventually ripped the steel rings anchoring it to the stone walls above.

Free from its months-long imprisonment and torture, the dragon roared triumphantly before turning away from the rubble and lowering its massive head to meet Drackonwulf at eye level. It taunted him with a piercing yellow gaze.

Drackonwulf stood frozen just inches from the dragon, its size easily surpassing that of a Roman warship and its horned tail longer than a Greek galley. Massive horns protruded from its cheeks, and the stench of decay emanated from its body. Its nostrils flared in furious intervals.

Despite his fear, Drackonwulf glanced at his sword a few yards away. He wondered if he could retrieve it without being snatched up, devoured, and swallowed by the enormous beast.

The massive black dragon folded its mighty wings against its sleek body, its frilled neck arched in a menacing display. Slowly, it retracted its head before unleashing a stream of dark green acid mixed with blood from its gaping maw toward the unsuspecting barbarian.

Drackonwulf countered the dragon's deadly attack. He could feel the intense heat of the acid as it sizzled and burned on its way toward him. He sprinted to the other side of the mountain of treasure, where his sword lay partially buried beneath piles of glittering gold and jewels.

As he reached for his weapon, he heard the sound of the acid contacting the wall behind him, searing through solid stone. Then a thought crossed Drackonwulf's mind—could this be a chance for escape?

With his bastard sword in hand, Drackonwulf took a firm stance.

The black dragon drew back its head and spewed another stream of bloody, acidic liquid.

Drackonwulf rolled out of harm's way just in time. But he stumbled over a separate pile of treasure near the stone wall where the acid was eating it away.

The dragon wasn't finished with him yet; it swung its horned tail and sent the barbarian crashing to the ground again.

Jewels tumbled around Drackonwulf as he struggled to get up and make his way toward the hole in the wall where rays of sunlight shined through.

The monstrous creature shifted its weight and let out a wail that could make a man drop dead.

Drackonwulf wielded his sword, hacking away at the wall until he broke through. He stumbled out into the morning light, shielding his eyes from the sun peering over the horizon. Inhaling the crisp, clean air, it felt like he was taking his first breath in life.

He dropped his sword and sank to his knees. The cool breeze brushed against his skin. Behind him, the dragon thrashed about inside the tower.

Drackonwulf pulled himself back to his feet. His body was exhausted and weak from battle, but he needed to start his journey back home immediately.

As he glanced back at Castle Filmar, a faint light flickered from an upper window of the keep. Drackonwulf thrust his fist into the air and declared, "I'll have my revenge, Clive. And I'll be returning for your treasure." He knew once he arrived at Rosenbarrel, retaliation would be swift.

So Drackonwulf set foot on the winding road leading to Rosenbarrel—a three-day journey. He anticipated King Grinyard greeting him with open arms and listening to the accounts of his brother's corrupt ways and his pet dragon. But his luck was unfortunate this time. After only several minutes of walking, Drackonwulf was cut off by a group of soldiers mounted on horses. They blocked his path into the forest. Two horses parted ways, revealing Clive, who guided his horse front and center.

"So, you've found the entrance to the dragon's den," Clive growled. He unsheathed his sword. "Shall we have a little chat? Or would you prefer my blade pierce slowly through your gut?"

Drackonwulf tightened his grip on his sword and puffed out his chest, holding his head high. But as the tension between them grew, the distant sound of thunder echoed through the valleys. Drackonwulf's heart raced in anticipation. Something was about to happen.

Then, miraculously, a sight to behold appeared on the horizon. King Grinyard of Rosenbarrel rode atop his magnificent stallion, leading an army of skilled knights and archers that greatly outnumbered Clive's measly cavalry. The sunlight gleamed off their golden armor as they halted their horses, waiting for Grinyard's command.

Grinyard guided his horse down the mountain and caught up to Clive with malicious intent in his eyes. Without looking at Drackonwulf, he addressed the barbarian. "Your task is complete here now. Take a horse from the army and head to the kingdom. A ceremony awaits you."

Drackonwulf shook his head at the king. "I would rather join in the battle, Your Majesty."

"Your role is finished," Grinyard declared. "The rest is in our hands."

Clive gave a sly grin. "Do you honestly believe your army can defeat mine?" he scoffed.

"Surrender or face the consequences," Grinyard warned his brother. "Your treacherous crimes and murderous plots come to an end today. And how dare you turn against our father! No more. You hear me? No more!"

"He'll unleash the dragon," Drackonwulf spoke up. "I've seen it myself. It's massive!"

Grinyard showed no fear at the idea of a dragon. He drew his sword and roared, prompting his soldiers to charge down the mountainside.

Clive glanced at Drackonwulf with a smirk. "What do you say? Should I unleash the beast?"

With determination burning in his eyes, Drackonwulf drew his sword. "I have nothing to say to you," he cried and charged at Clive.

The clashing of steel filled the air as both armies collided, their weapons glinting in the sunlight. But despite their skill, Clive and his men were no match for the sheer numbers and training of Grinyard's forces.

Drackonwulf thrust his sword into Clive's side, knocking him off his horse. He fought evil with a newfound rage, his body fueled by adrenaline and the desire for revenge. Then he saw it—fear in Clive's eyes. And with one swift motion, Drackonwulf beheaded Clive, sending his head rolling on the ground.

Every soldier on the battlefield froze, seemingly unable to believe what they had witnessed. The air turned eerily quiet, broken only by the moans of injured men lying among the fallen.

A bellowing roar echoed in the distance, and the black dragon burst through the stone walls of the castle. It spread its mighty wings midair and hovered over the battlefield, looking down at the carnage below. But instead of attacking, the dragon gave a slight nod as if thanking the one setting it free. Then it turned and flew away, disappearing into the clouds and never to be seen again. Only stories of its existence remained.

"Treasure!" One of Clive's soldiers threw a fist in the air. In a frenzy, those still alive fled on horseback toward the castle.

Drackonwulf and Grinyard stood alone on the bloodstained ground, surrounded by the bodies of their fallen enemies.

Grinyard sheathed his sword, his golden armor now stained with blood. He placed a hand on Drackonwulf's shoulder and smiled. "Well done. Now, go claim your reward."

Drackonwulf acknowledged the king's words and mounted a nearby horse. And with determination in his heart, he rode toward Castle Filmar…a wealthy man.

January 10, 2017 / Revised November 20, 2024

While studying video production (2005–2008), I was required to enroll in a scriptwriting course as part of my curriculum. For our final assignment, we were to write at least ten pages. Knowing in my last year of film school that I would have to produce and fund my own short film, I took the initiative. I wrote a thirty-page script (and took it a step further and registered it with the U.S. Copyright Office).

The following year, in September 2008, I revised the script and gave it the green light as my final shooting project. From there, I took on all tasks: rewriting the script, holding casting auditions at a local recreation center, scouting locations, creating a shooting script and storyboard, directing and editing the film myself, and premiering it at an upscale apartment complex's elegant clubhouse on a large projector screen for the cast and crew. Afterward, I made DVD copies for each member involved in the movie's production.

We filmed at two different locations: an office building in Garland, Texas, that offered services for air conditioning, electrical work, and plumbing, and a ranch in Sulphur Springs, Texas, where the crew could set up camp.

My fellow film students were a big help during production. The assistant director brought a camper where my wife and daughter could stay instead of sleeping in a tent. I was fortunate to have my father play the role of Buck (he used to be a Boy Scout troop leader, so camping came naturally to him). He was perfect for the part, so there was no need for an audition.

Our grueling production on the rustic ranch in Sulphur Springs demanded a non-stop twenty-four-hour schedule. Exhausted from the previous day's filming at the office building in Garland, I overslept and woke up just before sunrise, realizing we needed to capture crucial shots before the lighting change. I had to cut a significant portion of the script and scramble to rewrite an ending on the spot.

Despite the challenges, the talented cast and crew were fantastic, making it all worth it. And if given the chance to recreate the film today as a feature, I would jump at the opportunity to do it all over again.

Watch my student film, *Deadline*, online:
https://wolfentertainment.net/deadline-therealwolfman

DEADLINE

EXT. WOODS—NIGHT

Frightened, TINA CHRISFIELD runs through
a wooded area holding a DSLR camera. She
leaps over a log and proceeds onto a dirt
trail.

GROWLING and SNARLING escalate behind
her.

EXT. FRONT OF LAKE HOUSE—DUSK

Tina enters a clearing and runs toward
her lake house. Seeing that her sedan is
closer, she detours to the vehicle instead.

Before opening the car door, she turns
and snaps a quick photo of a figure lurking at the tree line.

The figure dips back into the woods out
of sight.

Tina flings open her car door and tosses
her camera over the driver's seat and
onto the passenger seat.

                    TINA
                  (to self)
        Oh my God! David will go nuts
        over this story.

She glides into the car, slams the door
shut, shifts the vehicle into gear, and
drives away.

EXT. NEWS STATION—DAY

Tina drives her sedan through a small
parking lot and whips into a parking
space.

INT. VEHICLE—DAY

Tina grabs her camera from the passenger
seat. She pushes the car door open and
steps out of the vehicle.

EXT. NEWS STATION—DAY

Tina speed-walks toward the entrance of
her workplace, passing a small monument
sign that reads: LITTLE CREEK COURIER.

INT. NEWSROOM CUBICLE #1—DAY

Tina slaps her hand on the corner of the
desk.

DAVID KRENDAL works diligently at his
desk when he is suddenly startled.

                    DAVID
                  (looks up)
        What's wrong?

                    TINA
          I saw it with my own eyes!

                    DAVID
          Saw what? And why aren't you
          dressed for work?

Tina glances over her shoulder.

REPORTERS scurry back and forth between
cubicles, making copies, turning in re-
ports, and mingling with other reporters.

                    TINA
          It's true, David. Look at the
          photo.

Tina powers on her camera and hands it to
David.

                    DAVID
          What am I looking at? This bet-
          ter be good because your report
          was due on my desk a half hour
          ago.

                    TINA
          I hope you believe me when you
          see it.

                    DAVID
          See what? It's just trees.
          Listen, you've already got my
          attention. Lose it now, and I'm
          moving on. I've got work to do.

Tina takes a breath and then leans over
the desk, inches from David's face.

                    TINA
          Bigfoot is real!

                  DAVID
        What? Bullshit!

Tina swipes the camera from David.

                  TINA
        I guess this was a bad idea.

                  DAVID
        Wait a minute, Tina. Let me see
        that again.

Tina rolls her eyes and hands the camera
back to David.

David taps on the LCD. He presses a button feature to zoom in, then points to
something on the screen.

                  DAVID (CONT'D)
        Is this what you saw? This
        little speck here?

                  TINA
        That's it.

David reaches for his glasses on his desk
and slips them on. He inspects the image
thoroughly.

                  DAVID
        Is this a joke?

                  TINA
        No, sir. I saw this thing last
        night at my lake house. It's
        real! I never believed in Big
        foot. But it's true. This thing
        exists!

David shakes his head and chuckles. He
returns the camera to Tina.

> DAVID
> Find a better story. You have
> twenty-four hours.

Tina groans, spins on her heel, and
storms out of the office.

INT. NEWSROOM CUBICLE #2—DAY

Frustrated, Tina swipes papers off the
front of her desk and onto the floor. She
pounds her elbows on her desk and rests
her forehead in her hands.

ROBERT JENSON enters the room.

> ROBERT
> Are you okay?

Tina glances up at Robert.

> TINA
> Our boss just gave me one day to
> find a good story. I'm gonna
> lose my job, Robert! David
> doesn't believe me.

> ROBERT
> What's the story?

> TINA
> I told him the truth.

> ROBERT
> And that would be?

> TINA
> (sighs)
> Look for yourself.

Tina grabs the camera from her desk and powers it on. She hands it to Robert.

Robert looks at the LCD and squints. He turns the camera at different angles while trying to figure out the image on the screen.

                    ROBERT
              (jokingly)
         Who is this? Bigfoot?

Tina perks up from her desk.

                    TINA
         How'd you know?

                    ROBERT
         I was only kidding.

                    TINA
         I'm not! I saw it with my own
         eyes. This thing is real!

Robert nods and passes the camera back to Tina.

                    ROBERT
         Well, do you need help capturing
         it? I mean, for your story.

                    TINA
         Are you joking with me again?

                    ROBERT
         No. If you think you're about to
         get fired, I don't mind helping.
         But this better be Bigfoot.
         We're not working for the
         Enquirer.

Tina stands from her desk and pushes her
chair back. She throws her arms around
Robert.

                    TINA
               (excited)
          Thank you, Robert! You don't
          know how much this means to me.
          I owe you one!

                    ROBERT
          You don't owe me anything. We
          can't lose another reporter due
          to deadlines. What do you need
          me to do?

Tina thinks for a beat.

                    TINA
          Can you meet me at my lake house
          tonight? And bring a few camera
          operators?

                    ROBERT
          Isn't your lake house an hour
          away?

                    TINA
          Yeah. But it's an easy drive.
          Trust me. If we can capture this
          thing on video, we could be the
          next big thing in this industry.

Robert rubs his chin, thinking.

                    ROBERT
          Okay. I'll be there tonight. I
          sure hope you're right about
          this thing, or you're pretty
          much screwed out

                    ROBERT (CONT'D)
          of your job. I know David when
          it comes to deadlines.

Tina sits back down at her desk and
scratches her forearm.

                    TINA
          I know. I'm willing to take the
          chance. I've got to prove to him
          that there's such a thing as Big
          Foot. I've doubted it myself as
          well.

Robert snickers and walks out of the
room.

EXT. WOODS—NIGHT

A white van follows an SUV through a
winding road surrounded by dense trees.

INT. SUV—DUSK

SERIES OF SHOTS

- Finger presses a button on the radio.

- JADE JORDAN grooves to rock music.

- Robert sings along to the music.

- Jade plays air drums during the chorus.

- Robert turns down volume on the radio.

END SERIES OF SHOTS

                    ROBERT
          Thanks for coming out here with
          me.

                    JADE
          No problem. It's not like I had
          anything else better to do.

Robert grins and turns up the volume.

Jade continues grooving to the music.

EXT. FRONT OF LAKE HOUSE—NIGHT

Tina parks her sedan in front of the lake
house. She exits the car, shuts the door,
and walks swiftly to the front porch. She
fumbles with her keys, unlocks the door,
and pushes it open.

INT. LAKE HOUSE LIVING ROOM—NIGHT

Tina flips on the light switch.

INT. LAKE HOUSE KITCHEN—NIGHT

Tina opens the refrigerator door.

                    TINA
          I'm glad I left these here.

She swipes a beer bottle, closes the refrigerator door, cracks the beer open,
and chugs it.

EXT. FRONT OF LAKE HOUSE—NIGHT

The SUV and van pull up and park behind the sedan. Robert and Jade exit the SUV.

Robert steps to the driver's window of the van and taps on the window.

JASON HILL rolls down the window.

> ROBERT
>
> I need your crew to set up and be ready to roll in forty-five minutes.

> JASON
>
> Copy that.

Jason signals to his crew sitting in the back of the van.

The van's side door slides open, and MACK EVANS and DAN BOSTON exit. They begin unloading video equipment.

Robert returns to the SUV and opens the liftgate for Jade. He helps her remove various items, including a duffel bag.

Jade pulls a hunting rifle from the SUV and straps it over her shoulder.

Robert closes the liftgate and leads Jade to the lake house.

INT. LAKE HOUSE KITCHEN—NIGHT

Robert and Jade gather with Tina around a small table.

> ROBERT
> (to Tina)
> This is Jade.

Jade extends a hand to Tina.

Tina shakes hands with Jade and then glances at the rifle.

> TINA
> Is that thing real?
> (turns to Robert)
> You didn't mention anything about bringing weapons.

> ROBERT
> (sighs)
> It's just for protection. Besides, Jade is former military.

Tina nods slightly.

> TINA
> Okay. Well, thank you for coming. I hope this thing shows itself tonight. I guess having that weapon isn't a bad idea.

Robert's attention is diverted to the living room window.

> ROBERT
> I'm gonna see if the crew needs help.

Robert traverses the living room to the front door and exits the lake house.

Tina smiles at Jade.

> TINA
> Please make yourself comfortable.

INT. LAKE HOUSE LIVING ROOM—NIGHT

Jade drops her duffel bag on the floor beside an old, dusty sofa. She removes the hunting rifle slung around her shoulder and takes a seat.

Tina's curiosity leads her to the window. She slowly parts the discolored drape and peeks outside.

Mack suddenly rises outside the window and hoists a tripod over his shoulder.

Tina flinches from Mack, who startled her, and slaps a hand over her chest.

                    JADE
          What happened?

                    TINA
          One of the guys out there scared
          me. I'm fine.

EXT. FRONT OF LAKE HOUSE—NIGHT

Jason and Dan inspect the van to be sure everything is unloaded.

A TWIG SNAPS, THE SOUND FILTERING THROUGH THE WOODS.

Jason slides the van door closed and glances toward the woods.

                    JASON
          What was that?

                    DAN
          Probably a raccoon.

Jason turns, nearly colliding with Mack.

                    JASON
          Dude! Watch where you're going.
          And what took you so long to set
          up that tripod?

                    MACK
          My bad. I was talking to Robert.
          But I'm back now, so what else
          do you need help with?

                    JASON
          You can start by loading these
          memory cards into the cameras.

Jason hands Mack a memory card case.

                    MACK
          Sure.

EXT. LAKE HOUSE FRONT PORCH—NIGHT

Robert leans over the handrail, smoking a
cigarette.

Jason, Dan, and Mack step onto the porch
carrying the rest of their gear.

                    ROBERT
          You guys look like a bunch of
          amateurs.

He dabs his cigarette on the handrail and
blows smoke from his mouth.

                    ROBERT (CONT'D)
          Let's get inside for a
          debriefing.

INT. LAKE HOUSE LIVING ROOM—NIGHT

Robert, Tina, Jade, Jason, Dan, and Mack
gather around the sofa.

>   ROBERT
>   (to Jason)
> I need a camera set up at the
> window outside the kitchen and
> another outside this living room
> window. The third camera needs
> to be stationary inside the
> house and have a wide-angle
> lens.

>   JADE
> What do you need me to do?

>   ROBERT
> I need you to follow Tina into
> the woods.

>   TINA
> I'm not going out there!

>   ROBERT
> How else do you expect to
> attract this thing's attention
> if you say it exists?

>   TINA
> Oh, so now you're doubting me?

>   ROBERT
> I didn't say that. I said, 'If
> it exists.'

>   TINA
> You're still doubting me!

Jade steps between Robert and Tina arguing.

She reminds Tina of the rifle and shows
it to her.

                    JADE
          You don't have to worry, Tina. I
          got your back.

Tina takes a deep breath and exhales
slowly.

                    ROBERT
               (to Jason)
          Let's start setting up.

                    JADE
          Wait.

Jade pulls a pair of radios from her duffel bag on the floor. She hands one to
Robert.

                    JADE (CONT'D)
          The range on these is about a
          couple hundred yards. I left my
          good ones at home.

                    ROBERT
          Thanks!

Tina steps closer to Robert. Fear shades
her face.

                    TINA
               (softly)
          I don't think I'll be able to
          handle going out there right
          now, especially in the dark.

                    ROBERT
          Relax. You'll be fine. I didn't
          drive all this way to load in

                    ROBERT (CONT'D)
          gear just to load it out
          again. This could be the story
          of the century. If you want to
          impress our boss, I suggest you
          get this story before it's too
          late.

                    TINA
          I just don't want to get hurt.
          Nor you or anyone else that's
          here.

                    ROBERT
          You'll be fine. We all will be
          fine.

Tina slumps her shoulders.

                    TINA
          Can we bring a handheld into the
          woods, just in case?

Robert turns to Jason for a response.

                    JASON
          I don't see why not.
                    (to Dan and Mack)
          Is either one of you up for the
          challenge?

Dan and Mack glance at each other.

                    MACK
          I'll film. Let me get a light on
          my camera, and I'll be ready.

Jade pulls a flashlight and a roll of
gaff tape from her duffel bag and tapes
the flashlight under the rifle's
forestock.

                    TINA
          Got an extra one of those?

                    JADE
          Of course!

Jade pulls another flashlight from her
duffel bag and hands it to Tina.

EXT. WOODS—NIGHT

SERIES OF SHOTS

- Full moon.

- Treetops.

- Dirt trail leading into the woods.

- Tina, Jade, and Mack walking the trail.

END SERIES OF SHOTS

Tina points toward a deeper part of the
woods.

                    TINA
          I saw it near that tree line.

                    JADE
               (through radio)
          Robert, stand by. We're almost
          to the location of Tina's
          sighting.

INT. LAKE HOUSE LIVING ROOM—NIGHT

Robert sits on the sofa with his radio in
hand.

Jason and Dan set up the static camera
for recording.

                    ROBERT
          Copy that.

STATIC RIPS THROUGH THE RADIO, FOLLOWED
BY AN UNINTELLIGIBLE VOICE.

                    ROBERT (CONT'D)
          Come again?

                    JADE
               (through radio)
          I need you to . . . because we
          can't. . .

                    ROBERT
          You're breaking up. Repeat.
          Over.

Jason and Dan pause setting up the camera. They gather around Robert to listen
to the communication with Jade.

                    ROBERT (CONT'D)
          Jade. Can you hear me? Over.

STATIC CRACKLES THROUGH THE RADIO.

GUNSHOT ECHOES OUTSIDE.

                    JASON
          What the hell is she shooting
          at?

                    ROBERT
          I don't know.
               (into radio)
          Jade, what's going on out there?

Dan lunges for the camera he and Dan set up and unlatches it from the tripod.

                    DAN
          I'm going out there to see
          what's happening.

Robert leaps from the sofa and dashes to the front door. He blocks Dan from leaving.

                  ROBERT
          No, you're not!

He waves the radio in Dan's face.

               ROBERT (CONT'D)
          Not until I get a reply from
          someone out there.

                  JASON
          Should we call the police?

                  ROBERT
          Not yet. For all we know, it
          could be hunters.

Dan sticks out his chest.

                    DAN
          Not at night!

                  ROBERT
          Maybe they're boar hunters. It's
          cold enough out there for hogs
          to be moving around.

Dan clenches his hand into a fist.

                    DAN
          Move, Robert! I'm going out
          there.

                    DAN (CONT'D)
          This is Tina's story. I'm sure
          she wants us to get everything
          on video for her.

                    ROBERT
          I don't think you should do
          that. Mack is already out there
          getting what we need. Take a
          seat on the couch and cool down,
          man.

Dan steps back, rams into Robert's shoulder, swings open the front door, and
darts outside.

Robert drops the radio, and the batteries
eject onto the floor.

                    ROBERT (CONT'D)
               (yelling)
          For God's sake! I'll deal with
          you back at the office later!

Robert shuts and locks the front door. He
bangs his head against it once.

                    ROBERT (CONT'D)
               (shouting)
          Why can't he listen!

                    JASON
          That's Dan for you. He's always
          gotta have his way.

EXT. WOODS—NIGHT

Dan records footage while he jogs down a
dirt trail. Without a flashlight, he re-
lies on the built-in night vision through
the camera's LCD viewfinder.

He steps in something on the ground and
stops. Raising his foot, he inspects the
bottom of his shoe.

                    DAN
          What the-

He points the camera toward the ground,
revealing a pile of entrails and shredded
clothing through the viewfinder. He pans
the camera and sees Jade's radio on the
ground.

Dan picks up the radio.

                    DAN (CONT'D)
               (frantic)
          Robert, it's Dan. Do you copy?

WHITE NOISE CRACKLES THROUGH THE RADIO.

                    DAN (CONT'D)
          I ran into a pile of guts from
          An animal or something.

VICIOUS GROWLING PIERCES THE WOODS.

Dan pans the camera toward the sound.

                    DAN (CONT'D)
          Who's there?

He tilts the camera down at a nearby tree
and sees Mack sitting up against the tree
through the viewfinder. Mack's camera is
beside him on the ground, the lens separated from the camera's body.

Quickly zooming in on Mack's face, Dan
sees Mack's throat has been ripped out.
His shirt is soaked in blood.

INT. LAKE HOUSE LIVING ROOM—NIGHT

Robert picks up the batteries from his radio that spilled onto the floor. He re-inserts the batteries and secures the cover.

                    ROBERT
          Jade, do you copy? Over.

WHITE NOISE SCREAMS THROUGH THE RADIO.

                    DAN (V.O.)
          Oh my God! Help!

                    ROBERT
          Dan? Did you find Jade?

Jason moves in closer to Robert, his attention focused on the radio.

                    JASON
          What's going on?

                    ROBERT
              (into radio)
          Dan. Did you catch up to Jade
          and Tina? And where's Mack?

WHITE NOISE CONTINUES THROUGH THE RADIO.

                    ROBERT (CONT'D)
          Dan. Do you copy? Over.

Robert and Jason exchange glances.

EXT. WOODS—NIGHT

Dan strays from the dirt trail and runs deeper into the woods. He trips over a log but maintains his balance.

EXT. TRAIL—NIGHT

Dan finds his way back onto the dirt trail. He stops and pans his camera left and right, glancing at the night vision through the viewfinder. He is confused about his whereabouts.

He quickly decides which direction to take on the trail and proceeds, glancing behind him every few beats.

Headlights from an SUV round a curve in the trail and move toward Dan.

Dan waves his arms at the approaching vehicle.

The SUV stops, and BUCK steps out of the vehicle. He grabs his ranger hat from off the dash and secures it on his head. Then he shuts the door and walks toward Dan. One hand grips a holstered revolver on his hip, and the other reaches for a CB radio across his chest.

                    BUCK
          10-107 stand by.
               (to Dan)
          You okay? Are you lost?

                    DAN
               (frantic)
          It's out to get me!

                    BUCK
          What's out to get you?

                    DAN
          The creature!

                    BUCK
          What, a bear?

                    DAN
          No, it's vicious!

                    BUCK
          C'mon, guy. You gotta help me
          out here. What spooked you?
          Describe it to me. And what's
          with the camera and radio?

Dan takes a step back. The look of shock
floods his face.

Buck keeps on Dan, steps forward, and
leans into Dan's face. He sniffs.

                    BUCK (CONT'D)
          How much have you had to drink
          tonight?

                    DAN
          What? I haven't been drinking!

                    BUCK
          What cabin are you staying in?

                    DAN
          It's a lake house. I'm filming a
          news story, and this creature
          appears out of nowhere. I ran
          away from it, and I guess I took
          a wrong turn because I can't
          find my way back now.

                    BUCK
          If you want my help, you gotta
          tell me what you saw. Was it
          big? Furry?

                    DAN
          I don't know. It happened so
          fast. It growled at me, and I
          took off running. Can you help
          me get back to the lake house?

                    BUCK
          So, you never saw the animal,
          you're telling me? You only
          heard it?

Dan lowers his head and shrugs.

                    BUCK (CONT'D)
          I think I know where you're
          staying. Hop in the cruiser.

Dan follows Buck to the vehicle.

Buck opens the passenger door.

INT. CRUISER—NIGHT

Dan sets his camera and radio on the
floorboard and secures his seatbelt.

                    DAN
          Thanks for the ride.

                    BUCK
          No problem. Try and stay calm.

                    DAN
          You might want to call for
          backup.

                    BUCK
          Oh yeah? Why is that?

                    DAN
          Because whatever that thing is
          out here, it ripped apart my
          co-worker.

Buck brakes hard.

                    BUCK
          Someone's dead? Why didn't you
          mention this to me before?

                    DAN
          I didn't think about it. I'm
          scared, man!

Buck glares at Dan for a beat, then
drives along the dirt trail.

                    BUCK
          I'll get to the bottom of this.
          Show me where you saw your co-
          worker, then we'll drive to
          where you're staying.

                    DAN
          If this is the same trail I was
          on when I found Mack, then we
          should see him not too far
          ahead.

Buck rolls down his window and flips on a
spotlight. He drives slowly, shining the
light into the trees.

INT. LAKE HOUSE LIVING ROOM

Robert turns from looking out the window
and steps to the sofa.

                    ROBERT
                 (into radio)

> ROBERT (CONT'D)
> Dan, Jade, or Tina. Do you copy?

> JASON
> I'm calling the cops. Is there a
> phone in this place?

> ROBERT
> I don't know. I've never been
> here. But I think you're
> overreacting.

> DAN (V.O.)
> Robert, it's Dan. I found help.
> I'm on my way back. We gotta
> make a report.

> ROBERT
> Dan! What do you mean? What
> happened? Over.

Jason exits the room in search of a
landline.

SOUNDS OF GROWLING ESCALATE OUTSIDE.

Jason returns to the LIVING ROOM.

> JASON
> Tell me you heard that, too.

> ROBERT
> Yeah. Whatever it was, it's
> close.

Robert stands from the sofa and steps to
the window.

Before he reaches the window, a body
flies through it. Glass shatters into
pieces around the room.

Robert dodges the body soaring through
the air.

At the same time, Jason flinches as the
body hits the floor face down.

                    JASON
                 (softly)
          Who is that?

Robert steps toward the body. He stoops
and touches the shoulder.

                    ROBERT
          Jade?

                    JASON
          Is she . . . dead?

Robert presses two fingers on Jade's
neck. He glances up at Jason.

                    ROBERT
          No pulse.

                    JASON
          This is crazy! What do we do?

Robert flips Jade onto her back. Entrails
spill onto the floor.

                    ROBERT
          Ugh!

He steps away from the body.

                    JASON
          What did that to her!

A figure moves outside the window.

                    ROBERT
          Did you see that?

Jason shakes his head.

SOUNDS OF POUNDING ON THE FRONT DOOR FROM
OUTSIDE.

Robert approaches the door.

                    JASON
          Don't open it!

Robert places one hand on the door, and
the other grasps the doorknob. He looks
back at Jason.

POUNDING ON THE DOOR CONTINUES.

                    JASON (CONT'D)
          We need to get out of here! Is
          there a back door?

                    DAN (V.O.)
              (muffled)
          Open the door. It's me, Dan.

Robert unlocks the door and opens it as
Jason peers over his shoulder.

Dan and Buck stand shoulder to shoulder
on the porch.

                    JASON
          A park ranger?

                    BUCK
          I'm a game warden.
              (grips holstered gun)
          Park rangers don't carry fire
          arms.

Robert and Jason step away from the door.

Dan and Buck enter.

>   ROBERT
>   (points to body on floor)
>   What's going on out there? Jade
>   was just mauled and thrown
>   through the window!

>   DAN
>   (gasps)

Blood has pooled around Jade's body on
the floor.

>   BUCK
>   (into radio)
>   11-44. Coroner requested at the
>   lake house off County Road 1176.

VICIOUS GROWLING OUTSIDE.

>   JASON
>   It's out there again!

>   DAN
>   (to Buck)
>   That's it! That's the sound I
>   heard and told you about.

Robert steps toward the front door and
peers over Buck's shoulder, who's blocking the doorway.

>   ROBERT
>   What the hell is that?

>   BUCK
>   (throws up a hand)
>   Hold up a minute. Let me check
>   the scene.

                    ROBERT
          Wait! You're gonna get hurt out
          there.

                    BUCK
          Son, I'm on duty. This is my
          job.

Buck turns and walks out onto the porch.
He glances outside, then proceeds down
the steps and out of sight.

Robert closes and locks the front door.

                    ROBERT
          I don't know about that guy.
          Something's not right about him.

                    DAN
          It's fine. He's been helping me.

                    JASON
          We need to get out of here!

                    ROBERT
          Hey! Stop being a whiny little
          brat.

SNARLING SOUNDS OUTSIDE GRADUALLY BECOME
LOUDER.

Robert dashes toward the sofa.

                    ROBERT (CONT'D)
          Help me block the door! That
          thing's gonna slaughter that guy
          out there and come after us
          next!

                    JASON
          Oh, and who's whining now?

                    ROBERT
          Shut up and help me.

SHARP BANGING ON THE FRONT DOOR.

                         ROBERT
               Are y'all going to help me or
               just stand there with your
               thumbs up your asses?

The front door bursts open.

A WEREWOLF dressed in Tina's clothing
hurtles through the doorway and lunges
for Dan. It grabs Dan by his throat and
slams him against the back wall.

The werewolf stares into Dan's eyes,
snarling, then rears its head back before
sinking its teeth into his neck, ripping
out his throat.

Holding Dan's lifeless body against the
wall, his feet dangling off the ground,
the werewolf turns its head and locks
eyes on Robert. It rears its head back
again and bares its bloody teeth.

                    ROBERT (CONT'D)
                 (to Jason)
               Get out of here!

                    JASON
          Not gonna tell me twice!

Jason turns and runs toward the back of
the house.

The werewolf releases Dan.

Dan's body slides down the wall and bends

forward like a rag doll. Blood gushes
from the gaping hole in his throat.

The werewolf runs after Jason.

EXT. BACK OF LAKE HOUSE—NIGHT

Jason bursts through the screen door from
the back of the house. He soars over the
back porch steps and hits the ground,
tumbling head over heel.

A beat later, the werewolf leaps through
the back doorway, soars in midair, and
lands on top of Jason. It mauls him to
pieces.

EXT. FRONT OF LAKE HOUSE—NIGHT

Robert scrambles through the front doorway and leaps off the porch. He lands
next to Buck's mangled body on the
ground.

DISTANT GROWLING BECOMES CLOSER.

Robert grabs Buck's gun from the holster
and fires six rounds as the werewolf appears from the corner of the house and
runs toward him. The sixth shot sinks
into the creature's skull at point-blank
range.

A claw slices through Robert's forearm as
the werewolf falls.

Robert drops the gun and staggers to the
SUV, keeping pressure on his bleeding

arm. He opens the driver's door and
slides onto the seat.

The SUV reverses and then drives off the
property.

EXT. FRONT OF LAKE HOUSE—NIGHT

The werewolf lies on the ground,
motionless. It shape-shifts into Tina for
a beat, then shape-shifts back into the
werewolf.

The creature twitches, rolls onto all
fours, and pushes itself up. Then, it
runs into the woods.

EXT. NEWS STATION—DAWN

The SUV speeds into the parking lot and
whips into a space.

Robert exits the vehicle and limps toward
the entrance of the building, shirt
stained in blood.

INT. NEWSROOM CUBICLE #1—DAWN

Robert stands before David, who is
working diligently at his desk.

                    DAVID
                (surprised)
            You look like crap! Are you
            hurt?

                    ROBERT
            I have the story of the century!

                    DAVID
          Where is it?

                    ROBERT
          I don't have proof just yet.

                    DAVID
          Why not?

                    ROBERT
          You wouldn't believe me if I
          told you.

                    DAVID
          Try me.

Robert glances over his shoulder, then
back at David.

                    ROBERT
          Tina's a werewolf!

David shakes his head.

                    DAVID
          Do I need to request a random
          drug screening today?

                    ROBERT
          You wait and see. I'm going back
          to collect the evidence. It's
          all on video.

                    DAVID
          Why don't you have it with you
          now?

                    ROBERT
          Fear for my life!
               (lowers head)
          And I lost my crew.

                DAVID
          Where are they?

                ROBERT
          Dead. And Tina, too!

David's eyes widen. He slaps a hand over
his face.

                DAVID
          You gotta be kidding me!

                ROBERT
          No, sir.

                DAVID
          Tina called me yesterday to say
          she quit. I can't believe this.
                    (serious)
          Are you telling me the truth,
          Robert?

                ROBERT
          Yes, sir.

Robert scratches his forearm. He glances
down at a thick strand of hair protruding
from the laceration.

                DAVID
          Have you gone to the authorities
          about this?

                ROBERT
          Not yet.

                DAVID
          Don't.

Robert tilts his head.

                    DAVID (CONT'D)
          Go get your equipment and bring
          it to me. I want to review the
          footage. I'll have two of our
          security officers and a camera
          operator accompany you. And
          don't tell anyone about this.

                    ROBERT
                  (grinning)
          Are you serious?

David pauses for a beat and stares into
Robert's eyes.

                    DAVID
          You've got twenty-four hours.

Robert spins on his heel and exits the
office.

                              FADE TO BLACK.

On February 3, 1991, the Michelangelo computer virus was first discovered in Australia. In 1992, America faced the same computer virus scare. This malicious program was not only designed to destroy hard drives but also had the potential to plunge the computing world into chaos. Rumors circulated that it had a time-bomb feature, set to activate on March 6 of any year and wreak havoc. The virus was named after the birth date of Renaissance artist Michelangelo.

As a high school creative writing assignment, I wrote a story about the virus, which had caused quite a stir in America just five days prior. However, the virus's creator (who remains unidentified today) never followed through on their threat. It turned out to be a bust.

To pay homage to the failed execution of the Michelangelo computer virus, I brainstormed a story involving a time machine that successfully launched on March 6. I often wonder if time travel will ever become possible.

MICHELANGELO

March 6, 1992

Rumors of the destructive Michelangelo computer virus had reached Jacob months ago. Still, as a busy scientist devoting long hours to his work, he never gave it much thought today even though the virus was supposed to trigger at any time.

Jacob was putting the finishing touches on his time machine and finally getting ready to test it. He'd spent over thirty years researching, testing, retesting, and constructing his master craft.

The machine was a four-by-four box constructed of the same material used on the space shuttle as its outer shell—LI-900 tiles—high-purity silica (nearly pure quartz sand). Where he gained access to the material remained a mystery. Cables and wires of all sizes and lengths weaved in and out of the walls of the machine, each one serving different functions. Some powered specific mechanisms, while others transferred information to other sectors within the time machine. There were no windows on the machine, and the entrance was accessed through the top like a hatch on a tank.

Jacob climbed up the ladder outside the machine and crawled through the hatch on the roof. The interior was a spectacle to behold. He felt a surge of excitement as he descended. The walls were masterly crafted and well-insulated, lined with panels embedded with hundreds of buttons, switches, and screens flashing colorful digital readouts.

A soft hum resonated in the chamber, a soothing sound indicating the machine was alive and pulsing with energy.

In the center was a plastic chair where Jacob could manipulate all the buttons. He couldn't use a material like steel for the chair. With all the surrounding electronic gadgets and exposed cables, he'd risk getting electrocuted, and his invention would go down in history as a self-execution system. Jacob could imagine the headlines: *Don't call Dr. Kevorkian to end your life for you if you succumb to a terminal illness. Just call Jacob. His magic time machine would do the trick!*

The core of the machine was constructed behind the chair. It radiated a soft, pulsating glow that illuminated the small space in a heavenly light. The core was a marvel of engineering, a fusion of advanced technology. It thrummed with power, its energy source a closely guarded secret known only to Jacob.

The time machine sat in the center of Jacob's garage; its high-tech, computerized system was genius. Its programming was highly complex and unfathomable to anyone. Jacob had poured his heart and soul into perfecting every aspect of the machine.

For today's test, Jacob had invited a few witnesses to watch him execute the first launch. But his primary intention for having the witnesses was for his safety. If the thing caught fire, he'd need someone to assist with his escape. With one press of a button, every electrical connection and component and daisy-chained power and data cable would activate in unison. There was no telling what would happen during the first test run.

As Jacob sat in his futuristic time machine, anticipation and nerves swirling within him, he heard the familiar voices of his three best friends in the garage.

Austin, Brad, and Rhett had been by his side through thick and thin, supporting his wild scientific endeavors although they never understood the technical jargon and the gadgets he used to construct the machine. They were smart guys but not geniuses like Jacob.

"Jacob! Are you in there?" Austin called out when they entered the garage.

Jacob popped his head out from the top of the time machine. "Hey, guys! I'm about to perform the first test."

Each of Jacob's friends walked into the garage holding a can of beer. Rhett carried the party—a twelve-pack of Miller Light and his third opened beer. He'd already knocked back two cans on his way to Jacob's house.

Jacob climbed out of the machine and greeted his friends with fist bumps.

Brad said with his boisterous personality, "You've truly outdone yourself this time, Jacob! We've been waiting forever to see this thing in action."

Rhett cracked open another beer. His Iron Maiden T-shirt clung to his lean frame, the vibrant colors contrasting with his long dark hair. He raised an eyebrow at Jacob teasingly. "I hope this thing doesn't transport you back to the Stone Age. No time to find you. I've got a gig to play next week." He set down the twelve-pack next to a workbench and walked around the time machine, looking at every intricate detail. He had no clue what he was looking at, but the expression on his face could replicate a kid's excitement in a candy store.

Austin, the bashful friend, stood off to the side, watching Jacob with awe and apprehension. He adjusted his glasses nervously and muttered, "I believe in you, Jacob. Just . . . be careful, okay?"

Jacob appreciated Austin's support. "Thanks," he replied with a hand on Austin's shoulder. There was a mix of excitement and nervousness in his voice. He grinned at his friends, their diverse personalities a comforting presence amidst the high stakes ahead.

Rhett walked around the time machine and leaped to the twelve-pack he had placed on the floor next to the workbench. He pulled a beer can from the box and shoved it in Jacob's face. "Have a beer, man," he slurred. "You deserve it!"

"No thanks." Jacob politely pushed Rhett's hand away. "I'm still working."

Brad grabbed Rhett's beer and cracked it open. "Yeah, Rhett. He's working. That's something you know nothing about." He tipped a swig from the can.

Austin watched the interactions with a smile, milking his beer quietly.

"You're always so serious, man!" Rhett teased. "Lighten up a little! If this works, we'll be able to go back in time and redo all those embarrassing moments we've had."

Brad chuckled. "I don't know about redoing *your* embarrassing moments. They seem to fit your attitude just right."

"Suck a dick," Rhett barked.

Brad raised his beer to Rhett and winked.

Jacob looked at his watch. With a glint of determination in his eye, he gave a final walk around the time machine. He performed a thorough safety check, looking for loose wiring, damaged paneling, or anything unusual.

Rounding the corner of the machine back to his friends, he gave a thumbs-up. "Everything looks good to go," he said.

Austin approached Jacob and gestured at Brad and Rhett to join him. "C'mon, guys. Let's give this guy a proper send-off. He's worked night and day on this thing for the past three decades!"

"I guess," Rhett said sarcastically.

The guys huddled around Jacob like football players strategizing their next play.

"Okay, I think y'all are getting a little too comfortable," Jacob said, breaking from the circle. "I need to discuss my plan and safety measures."

"Lay it on us," Brad said.

"First and foremost," Jacob explained, "move the ladder away from the machine after I climb inside. Then most importantly, I need you guys to watch for any fires that may occur. Pull me out immediately if you see a fire or a hint of smoke. The time machine generates a lot of energy and can overheat instantly. Just place the ladder back where it is now, climb up, and open the hatch. I have a fire extinguisher inside and some extra ones by the toolbox.

"Also, stand back until the machine has powered down after the time travel process finishes. I don't want any of you hurt due to a malfunction."

Rhett downed the rest of his beer and belched. He crushed the can and threw it into the far corner of the garage, where it ricocheted off the corner of the roll-up door and landed behind a toolbox.

Austin glanced at Rhett and frowned. "Really? Why are you trashing his garage?"

"I'll pick it up after we witness this historical event," Rhett said. "Geez, relax."

"Hey, Jacob," Brad stepped forward, "at what point in time are you traveling? Back to 1985?"

The guys laughed.

Jacob shook his head. "Nah. I'm going to set it to yesterday at noon. I don't want to go too far back in time because the machine has been ready to launch for the past three days. I don't want to re-build the whole thing again if something happens too far in the past."

"Be careful in there," Austin said. "I'll be rooting for a successful launch!"

Jacob smiled. "Thanks. Now, it's time to move on. I'll see you guys again soon." He turned and climbed the ladder. Then, with a steady hand, he reached for the hatch and lowered himself into the time machine, closing the hatch behind him.

Austin dutifully moved the ladder away from the machine, careful not to disturb any wires or thick cables from the sides. He folded and carried it toward the front of the garage and propped it against the wall near the toolbox. His eye caught a glimpse of Rhett's beer can on the floor.

* * *

Jacob sat in the chair inside the time machine and pressed a series of buttons on a panel before him. Using the keyboard built into a small table, he typed some code, and the computer monitor displayed green letters that scrolled across the screen:

```
STARTING MS-DOS . . .
HIMEM IS TESTING EXTENDED MEMORY . . .
. . . DONE.

JACOB_TIMEMACHINE V1.8.1
INSTALLED AT PS/2 PORT

C:\>DIR
   VOLUME SERIAL NUMBER IS 0E5Z-19EC
COMMAND   COM          93,521
CONFIG    SYS             801
BOOTSECT BIN             512
            3 FILE(S)          94,834 BYTES
      1 DIR(S) 1,059,329,632 BYTES FREE
```

The computer made ticking noises as the files in the system loaded. Jacob watched the lines of codes zip across the screen until the software program displayed what he was waiting for:

```
CURRENT DATE IS FRI 03-06-1992
ENTER TRAVEL DATE:
A:_
```

Jacob typed in the date he wanted to travel back in time: 03-05-1992.

```
CURRENT TIME IS 13:02:45.29
ENTER NEW TIME:
A:_
```

He typed in the time he wanted to arrive: 12:00:00.00.

```
SYSTEM READY
PRESS ENTER TO LAUNCH
```

Staring at the screen momentarily, Jacob's heart thumped in anticipation with his finger resting on the button. He took a nervous breath and pressed the button.

```
LAUNCH SEQUENCE ACTIVATED
MODE CODE PAGE FUNCTION COMPLETED
STANDBY . . .
TIME REMAINING TO OVERRIDE/ABORT SYSTEM
00:01:00.00
```

Jacob watched as the one-minute countdown to abort the mission ticked closer to zero seconds. He had no intention of canceling the launch.

```
TIME REMAINING TO OVERRIDE/ABORT SYSTEM
00:00:45.00
```

***

Rhett cracked open another beer and surveyed the garage with bleary eyes.

"What?" Brad asked, confused by Rhett's behavior.

"You'd think he'd at least have some lawn chairs for us," Rhett grumbled.

Brad snorted. "This isn't a billion-dollar rocket launch, dummy. If you need a seat, just sit your drunk ass on the floor."

***

```
TIME REMAINING TO OVERRIDE/ABORT SYSTEM
00:00:22.00
```

Jacob's hands and face perspired. He hadn't been more nervous in his life. He felt the core behind him vibrating his chair as he watched the computer screen.

```
TIME REMAINING TO OVERRIDE/ABORT SYSTEM
00:00:00.00
DATA TRANSFER INITIATED.
'HELLO.',13, 12,' $'
```

***

A soft humming noise filled the garage. Before anyone could process it, the sound intensified into a roar, sounding like a jet engine starting up. Then, a high-pitched whistling joined in, growing louder by the second.

Brad and Rhett exchanged worried glances before hurrying to where Austin stood near the roll-up door in the corner of the garage.

"Should we open the garage door?" Brad shouted over the deafening noise.

"I don't know," Austin yelled back. "Jacob never mentioned it!"

"But what if there's carbon monoxide or something? We could get poisoned!" Brad exclaimed anxiously.

Rhett rolled his eyes. "Calm down. I'm sure we'll be fine."

As if on cue, the whistling noise transformed into rapid crackling sounds, almost like popcorn kernels popping in a microwave.

"Is it supposed to sound like that?" Brad said.

Shrugging helplessly, Austin replied, "Your guess is as good as mine!"

Suddenly, a spark flashed from one of the cables outside the time machine, followed by a loud crackle.

Austin, Brad, and Rhett flinched from the thunderous noise.

"What the fuck was that?" Brad said.

Austin shook his head, his eyes transfixed on the time machine.

"No fire, so all must be good," Rhett slurred.

Brad concentrated on where he saw the spark fly, hoping he wouldn't see any smoke or flames shooting from the wall. He did not want to witness a failed launch.

Another spark shot through the garage, followed by a crackling noise like an exploding firework.

The guys tensed.

Moments later, flashes like bolts of lightning sparked around the time machine. Puffs of smoke seeped from the electrical charges and quickly filled the garage.

"What do we do!" Brad said anxiously.

"I have no idea!" Austin said. He still didn't know if this was all part of the launch sequence. Jacob never explained in detail how any of this worked.

More lightning bolts engulfed the time machine. They flowed in the same direction in a continuous pattern. The garage was filled with so much smoke now that the guys could barely see each other through the thickness.

"I'm opening the garage door," Brad determined. "We're gonna suffocate in here!"

Austin coughed and waved his hand, thinking it would clear some of the smoke from his face. "Okay!" he agreed.

Rhett was silent.

Natural light crept into the garage as the roll-up door rose.

Austin stepped out of the garage for fresh air, and Brad darted outside soon after. But Rhett did not follow.

The lightning encircling the time machine finally eased, and the humming and high-pitched whining noises quieted. The machine was shutting down.

Smoke billowed outside from the garage, and Austin and Brad watched as it dissipated to where they could see inside. Rhett lay on the floor inside the garage, the can of beer still grasped in his hand.

"Rhett passed out!" Brad pointed. He rushed into the garage and knelt beside Rhett, checking for a pulse.

"Is he breathing?" Austin asked, stepping back into the garage.

"Yeah. Looks like he's just passed out from the alcohol."

* * *

Jacob thumped the computer screen and then typed on the keyboard. "Ugh!" he fretted. "Why now?"

The core behind him had powered down, throwing a code to the computer system.

```
A PROBLEM HAS BEEN DETECTED AND THE SYS-
TEM WILL SHUT DOWN TO PREVENT DAMAGE TO
YOUR COMPUTER.

IF THIS IS THE FIRST TIME YOU'VE SEEN
THIS STOP ERROR SCREEN, RESTART YOUR
COMPUTER.

IF PROBLEMS CONTINUE, DISABLE OR REMOVE
ANY NEWLY INSTALLED HARDWARE OR SOFT-
WARE. REBOOT IN SAFE MODE AND PRESS F8
TO SELECT ADVANCED STARTUP OPTIONS.

TECHNICAL INFORMATION:
```

```
*** STOP: 0X00000A.
(0X00000004A, 0X000000001, 0000000002,
0XDDDDD90003C8ABF)

COLLECTING DATA FOR CRASH DUMP . . .
```

"Nooo!" Jacob said, pounding his fingers on the keyboard. "Where's the damn error code that's pinpointing the problem? It's supposed to do this!"

***

Brad looked up at Austin. "Go check on Jacob, and I'll handle this."

Austin nodded, quickly grabbed the ladder, and carried it to the time machine. He placed the ladder where Jacob originally had it, extended the spreaders, and climbed up.

Brad continued shaking Rhett on the garage floor to get him to wake up. "C'mon, buddy, open your eyes," he said nervously. "This show is over, and we need to get you home."

***

Austin was on all fours on top of the time machine. He reached for the door handle, twisted it, and flipped open the hatch. Leaning and poking his head inside, he saw an empty chair surrounded by hundreds of flashing buttons. "Jacob?" Austin called into the small chamber from the ceiling.

Jacob did not answer.

"Hello?" Austin called again. "Jacob, are you okay?"

No response.

***

The smoke had mostly cleared inside the garage.

"Hey, hey!" Brad smiled when Rhett moved his legs. "Welcome back."

Rhett opened his eyes. "Where am I?" he said, his speech still slurred.

"You're in Jacob's garage, remember? We're leaving soon, so you need to get up."

"Okay," Rhett responded. He rubbed his forehead.

"Hangover already?" Brad laughed.

"Nah, just a little dizzy."

"Do you want to stand?"

Rhett nodded slowly. "Yeah. I should be good."

Brad grabbed the beer can from Rhett's hand, set it on the garage floor behind him, and then helped Rhett.

Rhett rested his chin on Brad's shoulder, his body weak. "Hey, Brad," he said, his voice slightly raised.

"Yeah?"

"Why are there tall buildings outside? I thought you said we were at Jacob's house."

Brad wrinkled his brow. "I dunno. Maybe you've had too much to drink."

"No," Rhett slurred. "A horse is standing out there with a man on it."

"Damn. Are you a lightweight today?" Brad said. He eased Rhett off him, spun around, and looked outside the garage.

A drunken smile etched across Rhett's face. "I told you," he said, stepping next to Brad.

Brad's jaw dropped open. "Hey, Austin," he said, speaking out of the side of his mouth. His focus was fixed on something outside the garage. "You and Rhett need to get over here and see this."

Austin poked his head out of the hatch on the roof of the time machine. "Jacob's not in here!"

"Where did he go?" Brad called out.

"No idea! He just…vanished," Austin replied with a confused tone.

"Well, get down here and check this out," Brad commanded.

Austin hesitated, looking back into the time machine before carefully descending the ladder.

He didn't need to join Brad and Rhett to see what was happening outside. But as he approached, his steps slowed as he took in the incredible sight before him.

A bustling city filled with tall buildings lined the road as far as the eye could see. Men in business attire and women in long cotton dresses bustled along the cobblestone street, running errands, conducting business, and chatting with neighbors. People rode past on horse-drawn carriages, creating a constant symphony of clip-clopping hooves and turning wheels. The smell of manure mingled with the scent of city smoke.

"You've got to be kidding me," Austin muttered as he stood alongside his friends, witnessing Jacob's time travel experiment gone wrong.

As people rode past, glimpsing at the guys from the future, they parted the center of the street where a police officer sat perfectly composed on horseback. He stared at them with a look of shock. He wore a neatly pressed navy blue uniform with a stovepipe hat and shiny black boots. He was very skilled at keeping his horse still.

"Why is Jacob's neighborhood replaced with all these old buildings?" Rhett wondered. His eyes, red and heavy, scanned each building.

Austin looked over at his friends. "Did we just teleport back in time and not Jacob?"

"It appears so," Brad said. "And that cop out there doesn't look so happy."

"But how?" Austin griped. "It looked like everything was working to me."

The officer tugged the horse's reins and steered it toward the three unusually dressed men. He eased the horse to a stop and stared down at them. "Might I ask where you gentlemen have come from?"

The guys looked at each other, unsure how to explain everything.

The officer waited patiently for a reply.

Brad decided he'd speak for the others. "We come in peace," he said.

"You idiot!" Austin gasped. "Why'd you say that?"

Rhett maintained a big grin on his face. "This is far out, man. It's like something right out of a Bill and Ted adventure! Jacob's time machine worked!"

Austin closed his eyes, knowing they were doomed.

"Excuse me?" the officer sneered. "A time machine?"

"I bet he probably thinks we're a bunch of aliens," Rhett laughed. But he fell silent as if he had an epiphany, then said, "Oh, shit! How am I supposed to play my gig next week?"

The police officer looked confused at Rhett, reached down inside the front of his uniform, and pulled out a whistle tied to a string hanging around his neck. He placed the whistle to his lips and blew it several times loudly.

Moments later, an army of police officers on horseback and a couple of horse-drawn carriages appeared and gathered around Austin, Brad, and Rhett.

"Arrest these fools!" said the officer who blew the whistle. "Take them to the station before they do something stupid to our city."

"Wait!" Brad said. "We didn't do anything! Rhett's right. It's just an experiment gone wrong."

A gang of police officers were swift in apprehending the unusually dressed men. "You'll get a fair trial in court," one of the officers said to Brad. "And a proper hanging if found guilty."

"Guilty of what?" Brad said, resisting his arrest.

Austin was already being escorted to one of the buggies when he glanced back at Brad. "Don't fight them. I'm sure we'll find a way out of this."

"Get in!" said the officer escorting Austin to the buggy. The officer pushed him inside and shut and locked the door.

Rhett was thrown in a separate buggy shortly after. But Brad continued to put up a fight. Until he was knocked unconscious by an officer with a stick.

The police officer who whistled the call for help stepped toward the structure in the middle of the street. "However this building got here, have it destroyed immediately." He mounted his horse and rode away.

* * *

Jacob stared at the blue screen of death on the computer monitor, depicting how his invention malfunctioned. The white cursor blinked as if the system was waiting for the input of a command. But the computer beat him to the punch. It exported a series of codes and text.

```
SYSTEM ANALYSIS COMPLETE . . .
CHECKINFECT: INFECTED.

'HELLO, MICHELANGELO.',17, 29,' $'
COPY VIRUS TO SECTOR 1

CURRENT DATE IS FRI 03-06-1992
ENTER TRAVEL DATE:
A:_
```

Jacob slapped his hand over his mouth. "Michelangelo!" he breathed. "I forgot about that virus! It will take me a long time to reprogram everything."

He quickly pressed buttons and flipped switches around him, then pushed himself up from the chair.

Climbing from the top hatch, Jacob descended the ladder and searched for his friends. Not seeing them, he looked at his watch in confusion: 13:17:22. He threw his hands in the air. "Where'd they go? The system malfunctioned, so nothing should've happened but the normal passing of time. Those idiots stood me up!"

Jacob walked the perimeter of the time machine in frustration. "Ugh! How did this happen?" He inspected the cables and wires weaving in and out of the machine.

After tracing the wires and their flowing patterns, he finally discovered a problem on the external side.

"Oh, how could I be so stupid!" Jacob said, disconnecting one of several hundred wires. "Of all the connections, it had to be the teleportation one. The damn thing is run backward."

March 11, 1992 / Revised November 18, 2024

A personal experience inspired a short film I created for a high school English IV class. Our assignment was to choose a scene from the book we were reading, *A Tale of Two Cities* by Charles Dickens, and either write about it, create a story based on it, or reenact a scene in a video. While most students opted to write an essay, I wanted to be unique and chose to produce a video instead. With the help of my family and a friend, we recreated the intense guillotine scene from the book in our garage. My father helped me construct a makeshift guillotine using my older brother's bench press machine and added fake blood using ketchup. For the decapitated head, we used a gorilla Halloween mask for a touch of humor.

Armed with a Panasonic VHS camcorder, I also took on the role of editor. I pieced together the footage within the camera itself.

Like in the original story, my middle brother Vince took on the role of Sydney Carton and sacrificed himself for Charles Darnay (also played by Vince). However, instead of reciting the line from the book, his final words at the guillotine were a comical, "I didn't do it!"

My father portrayed Dr. Alexandre Manette, a shoemaker who spent eighteen years imprisoned and kept himself sane by making shoes. Ironically, this scene left a lasting impression on me and inspired the following story. The theme of mental struggles in isolation was what fueled my character's journey as he found himself trapped within his own home.

This is one of my most memorable works. It combines actual events from my great-grandfather's manuscript, *Shall We Hang This Boy Twice?* (although significantly altered for this story). I have previously shared the tale of his manuscript and its journey in my book, *The Man I Never Met*, published in 2004. I am considering revisiting and updating that book.

THE UNFINISHED DIARY

1795
MONDAY
PM

My name is Randy E. Delray, I'm 32, and I'm a working-class citizen. I make shoes for a living and work part-time as a carpenter. My hands are always busy. I prefer to keep things simple. I have no wife or children. Growing up in Philadelphia, my older brother and I never had a close relationship. He left home at thirteen, and we haven't crossed paths or exchanged words since our parents passed away, having fallen victim to the yellow fever epidemic of 1793. I received word that my father had brought it home from work one day and unwittingly infected my mother.

I moved to New York when I was eighteen and lived there for many years, spending my days in solitude crafting shoes with careful precision and shaping wood with steady hands. The repetitive motions would later soothe my restless mind when I found out my parents had left this world—my years of crafting in New York landed me a better job, and I moved back to Philadelphia.

Do I have friends? Yes, there are a few I can count on. They were concerned by my withdrawal from the world outside since my parents died, trying to coax me back into the light of day before my relocation.

I live in my parents' home, where I grew up. I returned because I wanted to keep the house in the family, even if it's just me and my brother. He has a son. I'm glad the Delray family will continue.

This place may be small, but it provides me with much-needed tranquility. The house is secluded from neighbors and surrounded by towering trees.

I am writing this journal for two reasons:

1) To pass down the story of my grandfather to future generations.
2) To document the strange events unfolding in my home.

In 1700, my grandfather, Joe Delray, was a prominent attorney in Purvis, Mississippi, according to old documents I found stashed away in what used to be my parents' bedroom. He had successfully represented numerous clients ranging from misdemeanors to serious offenses. Sometime in the middle of his career, he took on a case of a man accused of a crime that he did not commit. In a turn of events, the true culprit was set free for the shameful acts pinned on this client.

What has become of justice in this world?

Although I have never met my grandfather or know anything about his client, I believe the accounts were accurate. My grandfather also spoke of the incident to my parents at the close of the trial. After all, what parent would fabricate such a tragic tale that would deceive their child?

As I write this first entry in the late hours of the night, the flame from the melting candle wax flickers before me, providing the only light source. I must hasten to finish this section before it extinguishes completely.

Everything is happening so quickly and unexpectedly. The past two days have been filled with inexplicable occurrences. It's as if a riddle or puzzle surrounding me eludes understanding. I am of sound mind, but I find myself constantly fatigued. This is very strange.

And so, I bring this first passage to a close as the candle flame dwindles into a mere pinprick of light.

TUESDAY
AM
I decided to take the day off from work and rest at home. Tomorrow, I may start waking up earlier to avoid the sweltering walk to work. It's been slower than usual at the shoe depot, and my work on the Ricketts Circus Amphitheater doesn't start for a few more weeks. Speaking of which, it's a remarkable place. Even President George Washington attended an event there once.

But I digress; this journal is meant for a specific purpose. I could write endlessly about my involvement in constructing props and background displays for the circus, but I'll focus on that later.

I discovered a document dated 1730, where my grandfather paid one dollar to purchase the rights to his client's story. The defendant's record was the first double jeopardy case of its kind. Despite being found guilty and sentenced to death by hanging, the rope broke during his execution, rendering him immune from being tried again under the law.

The details of this case are recorded here, in my house, in a worn but legible manuscript. My grandfather had serialized it in a newspaper, releasing one chapter per month.

PM

A sudden cramp in my hand caused me to pause writing. The tightness was foreign to me, a strange sensation I had never experienced before. So, I had to take a much-needed break. The muscles in my hand are sore and tense.

I ate lunch, grateful for the nourishment. The juicy chicken and crisp vegetables were very satisfying.

At the beginning of this journal, I mentioned my heightened senses and unexplainable occurrences. The sudden cramp in my hand adds to the list. Could it be connected to the bizarre sensations that have been plaguing me? Was it a result of my writing? It seems ironic that my hand, toughened from years of making shoes, would succumb to pain from simply dabbing a quill pen in ink and transferring words onto paper. The ache is a reminder of the physical toll of pouring one's thoughts onto paper.

I've been unable to sleep due to these unsettling events. It takes a lot to scare me, but the occurrences have left me anxious and uneasy.

On the first night, I felt a cold draft when I was getting ready for bed. Despite the warm weather and closed windows, the chill kept returning periodically through the night.

The second night was even more alarming. There were no drafts, but my chest felt tight, and my legs weighed down. I feared it could be an illness coming on.

While the physical sensations eventually subsided, I couldn't shake off the heavy feeling that seemed to follow me everywhere in my house, like someone always standing behind me and breathing down the back of my neck. I believe in the afterlife, but I never thought spirits could linger on earth among the living.

I'm anticipating more events that might unfold tonight, so I should try to get some more rest.

PM

It's late, and I rely on the candle flame to keep my room lit as I continue this entry. A sense of trepidation has crept over me. The events from the past few days have left me on edge, and the mysteries surrounding my grandfather's manuscript about the innocent client he represented seem to be seeping into my reality like ink bleeding through parchment.

I dipped my pen into the inkwell, and the scratching sound echoes in the room's stillness. Yet another breeze has swept through the room this evening, causing papers to flutter and items to fall from shelves with a clatter. My heart raced when I glanced around the room, trying to find a rational explanation for this unnatural occurrence.

I hear noises from the other bedrooms like whispers carried on the wind. My hand is shaking as I try to steady myself to continue writing. But an invisible force seems to be working against me. It's as if this unseen presence is trying to prevent me from uncovering the secrets hidden within the words of my grandfather's story. I've read his articles silently, end to end. However, it seems when I mention the story in this journal, it triggers a backlash. I think I've pissed someone, or something, off.

WEDNESDAY
AM

Once again, another sleepless night left me with more questions than answers. My home, once a place of comfort and security, now feels like a maze of unexplainable occurrences. I've resided here for almost two years, yet the sudden disturbances keep me on edge. Could it be my deceased parents, trapped between the real world and the afterlife? But the energy feels too intense to be their gentle spirits. It's as if an aggressive force is lurking in the shadows.

Last night was no exception.

I felt my linen sheets dancing in the darkness. At first, it was just a slight movement, barely noticeable. But then...something whispered at the end of my bed. The sound was faint yet unmistakable, sending shivers down my spine. I sat up abruptly, every hair on my body standing on end. Goosebumps prickled my skin. The presence grew more substantial, and I couldn't shake off the feeling of being watched. Something isn't right in this house, and I'm starting to fear for my safety.

I strained my ears, trying to make out the words from the whispering. It could be a language long forgotten. Ancient. Chilling.

A cold breeze crept through the room (again), swirling around me like ghostly fingers. Then, the unexpected happened. The silhouette of a figure appeared at the foot of my bed, its form blurry and indistinct. My heart hammered as I tried to understand what I had seen. The figure was clad in tattered robes that billowed around it in an unseen wind. Its face was obscured by darkness, but I could feel its gaze boring into me with an intensity that made me want to shrink back into the safety of my covers.

I opened my mouth to speak, but no sound or words came out. Fear had turned my tongue to lead, rendering me mute in the face of this unearthly visitor. I can't think of any rational explanation as to why I'm being haunted. If something is trying to push me out of my house, it will not win!

I must make haste, for I need to return to work today. More to come . . .

PM

Work today at the shoe depot was slower than usual. I spent most of my time polishing shoes on display. I have yet to discuss the unfolding events with my co-workers. There's no need to cause alarm unless there is an immediate threat. Plus, who would believe me anyway? I prefer keeping to myself in the workplace. I show up, do my job, and go home; why stir things up with my personal life when I'm already making a living without trouble?

The last few hours since I've been home from work have been uneventful. I haven't made as much progress writing about my grandfather for this journal as I was planning. However, I skimmed through his old manuscript again and reminded myself of his client—Henry Jones. He was convicted of murdering Jamar Smith, a Black farmhand living on a neighboring farm. Jamar was a peaceful man who ran afoul of a local gang and was brutally beaten. This incident was brought before the grand jury, which ruled in favor of Jamar.

After the trial, Jamar returned home later that afternoon on horseback with the farm owner. They traveled down a road cutting through a thick forest with few settlements. Unaware of any danger, they were chatting and enjoying their ride as they had likely done many times before. Little did they know, it would be Jamar's last ride. As they crossed a small stream surrounded by trees and vines, they were ambushed from a nearby blind.

A shot suddenly rang out from a Springfield 1795 musket held by an assassin hidden in the blind. With a groan of agony, Jamar fell from his horse, a dead man. A promising life was snuffed out in an instant.

Investigators traced the shot back to the house of Henry Jones, an eighteen-year-old man who lived with his poor parents. Without proper investigation, Henry was arrested and charged with the crime.

My grandfather, Joe Delray, heard about Henry's case and met with him. After learning his story, my grandfather believed in Henry's innocence and decided to represent him in court. Despite providing witnesses and an alibi, the jury still convicted Henry of murder after several days of trial. He was sentenced to death and returned to his cell to await execution.

This was the first case my grandfather had lost, but it would later become a double jeopardy that would work in his favor.

PM

Unusual events are happening again. I was interrupted from writing by a knock at the door. But no one stood before me when I opened it. I must have mistaken the knock for the outhouse door banging due to the wind. But the weather was calm this evening, and I stood outside for a few minutes to see if anyone would exit the outhouse. I don't get many visitors except for a few lost travelers inquiring about directions.

As I stood outside, the only things facing me were the setting sun dipping below the horizon and a hitching rail I had built recently. I'm excited to get a horse soon and can't wait! Joe Piedmont from the Piedmont Ranch will deliver the steed next week.

I've lit a new candle to burn tonight while I continue this journal. There's more that has happened since the ghostly knock at the door. Watching the candle burn while I think about how to begin this next entry has reminded me that I'm low on candles, and a trip to visit a tradesman will be required of me tomorrow after work.

After I heard the sound at the door and a brief investigation, I dipped back inside to slice some cheese and vegetables for dinner. It wasn't too long before another incident occurred. This one was more chilling than the last. Not only did my spine tingle from the startlement, but I nearly sliced my finger off with the knife! A faint voice whispered close to my ear, "Your life is my life." The voice was quite clear. It was masculine yet gentle.

I flinched as I sliced a thin piece of cheese from the block and spun around to face the intruder. Alas, no one was there. "Who said that?" I raised my voice, but all was still. Trusting my gut that there was no danger, I spun back to the cheese block and finished preparing my meal, which I consumed at a snail's pace.

I'm blowing out the candle now to turn in for some much needed rest . . .

THURSDAY
Early AM

It's still dark outside, but this must be a quick entry, for I'm jotting only highlights to remember and explain later.

- Grunting noise at the bedside.
- Swirling dark smoke above me.
- Shuffling footsteps.
- Clicking sounds close to my ear.

LATE AM

I'm off to work. I need out of this house for a few hours anyway. More to come . . .

PM

I've returned from work. Another easy day. It was slow again.

When I entered the house this afternoon, something was amiss. I had thought someone had broken in while I was gone. Items were missing, such as my boots, the quill pen I'm using to write in this journal, the ink, and my grandfather's manuscript. But after looking around, I found everything that was missing. They had been relocated elsewhere in the house. Funny, I don't remember moving these items.

So, back to the list I jotted down earlier this morning. The grunting noise I heard at my bedside last night was wicked. The sound was guttural, almost inhuman. It reverberated through the room, chilling me to the core. I sat up in bed, heart pounding in my chest, trying to understand what I was hearing. Then, a swirling dark cloud, or smoke, appeared above me and thickened and contorted, taking on eerie shapes that danced in the dim moonlight filtering through the window.

The shuffling footsteps began when I strained my eyes to focus on the smoke. The footsteps were slow and deliberate, like someone or something pacing back and forth around my bedroom.

Panic seized me. I could feel the hairs on my neck prick like a porcupine's quills in defense, and a cold sweat broke out across my forehead. The entity is becoming more sinister each night. It may be time I tell someone about my experiences before it's too late.

The clicking sounds followed next. The sounds were a sharp contrast to the guttural grunts and shuffling steps. They were rhythmic, almost like claws or fingernails tapping on a hard surface. They grew louder and more persistent, echoing in the room like a macabre symphony. I could feel my heart racing as I tried to pinpoint their origin, but they seemed to come from all directions. It was as if the very walls of my home were alive with some unseen presence, toying with me in the darkness.

Fear clenched at my chest, squeezing the breath from my lungs. I called out into the shadows, demanding to know who was there, but my voice seemed to get swallowed up by the oppressive silence that suddenly followed. Had I scared it off—whatever was making the clicking sounds?

With trembling hands, I reached for the matches on the bedside table and struck one, bathing the room in flickering light. What I saw made my blood run cold.

It was that figure again, hovering magically at the foot of my bed, cloaked in shadows despite the dancing flames casting eerie patterns on its form. It was hunched over, its back twisted and gnarly. The apparition was only visible for a few seconds before it vanished. Then the flame burning the matchstick stung my fingers, and I quickly shook it out.

PM

Before I turn in for bed, I need to conclude the summary of my grandfather's story. I'm dreading another night's rest, so I'll do my best to stay up late writing and make myself so tired that I may sleep through the night without incident.

But first, I need to light another candle . . .

Henry Jones stood upon the gallows in the presence of five thousand people. My grandfather was also present, according to his manuscript. Public hangings were customary in Mississippi in those days.

The sun crept above the eastern hilltops in all its glory and splendor that day. The birds caroled forth their mating songs, unconscious of the awful tragedy soon to be enacted. Men, women, and children journeyed on foot, on horseback, in carts, wagons, and buggies toward the scene of the great event.

Everyone in attendance expected Henry to make a full confession on the gallows. Instead, he protested his innocence once again, saying, "The man who killed Jamar Smith stands before me, and if he will come up and confess the crime, I will go free."

The sheriff and his deputies carefully adjusted the rope about Henry's neck. His feet and arms were pinioned. The black cap was placed and pulled down over his head. All was ready.

Five thousand people stood in breathless silence. Nothing was heard except for the persistent prayer of the minister wrestling with God to deliver Henry's soul.

Strong men trembled and averted their glances as the hatchet was drawn back to be followed by a swift descent, which would sever the rope that held the trap upon where Henry stood.

The blow descended. The trap fell. The body shot down in the twinkle of an eye.

But instead of hanging in the air, the body fell to the ground! No tongue, however versatile, and no pen, however facile, could describe the feeling of horror and terror that seized and held the vast crowd.

The crowd, dumbfounded, stood silent. Even the officials stood aghast. A moment previous, five thousand people were clamoring for the lifeblood of Henry Jones. Now, they were demanding his release.

The Fifth Amendment of the United States Constitution states: "No person shall be subject for the same offense to be twice put in jeopardy of life or limb."

The state of Mississippi awarded Henry $5,000, one dollar per person in attendance for his failed execution.

Henry Jones went on to live a whole life, and the man responsible for Jamar Smith's murder confessed on his deathbed years later, clearing Henry of wrongdoing.

FRIDAY

AM

WOW! I slept like a baby through the night. There were no disturbances (at least none that I can remember).

So, there you have it—the summary of my grandfather's story of Henry Jones. Crazy, isn't it? But what's more intriguing is the oxidized manuscript. I can't believe I have possession of the original document. Fascinating!

AM

While changing clothes for work, I noticed a few bruises on my wrists.

They weren't noticeable before I went to bed last night. There's even a slight redness around my neck area. Strange.

AM

I'm frantic! After eating breakfast, slipping on my boots, and attempting to head out for work, the door is jammed. No matter how much force I used, the door will not open. Now I'll be late for work because I can't escape my house! Even the windows are shut tight like they have been nailed from the outside.

What am I to do?

Something is keeping me from leaving my house. This is not good. And I'm low on ink. Unbelievable!

AM

I tried the door again—still refusing to budge. Panic is clawing up from the pit of my stomach.

My mind's racing with a thousand possibilities, each more terrifying than the last. Is someone playing a sick prank on me? Or is there something more sinister at play here, something beyond the realm of human understanding?

When I turned away from the stubborn door, my eyes fell upon the faint outline of a figure standing before me. My breath caught in my throat. The figure swayed as if suspended in midair, as it did at the foot of my bed once before. A chill swept over me like a cold wind. I took a hesitant step forward, my voice barely a whisper when I called out nervously, "What do you want?"

The entity did not respond. How could it? It's a spirit!

Then it vanished.

AM

I kid you not. Something is trying to hold me hostage in my home. I can't see straight, as my eyes are fogging. My throat is scratchy. I keep coughing.

Going to find another way out of the house . . .

PM

I can't get out! I'm afraid when night falls, I won't be safe. What becomes of me? My right eye is dark!

PM

The voice spoke again, saying, "Your life is my life." What does it mean?!

My hand shakes as I write.

I've vomited several times now.

I'm disoriented and can't keep writing.

I pray someone reads this journal. Please keep my grandfather's manuscript safe. That's all that's valuable to me.

Could the entity be Henry? Back from the dead? Did I do wrong by writing your story?

I'm weak and can't write anymore. My last breath may be soon. A heaviness surrounds me again.

My chest feels tight.

SUNDAY

Post Two Weeks

Brother, I'm adding my words at the end of your journal entries.

Word of your passing traveled far, reaching me in my distant home. Your journal was delivered to me by the local sheriff of my town. His face was grim as he handed it over, saying he found it clutched in your hand on the floor bedside. He also gave me Granddad's manuscript. Miraculously, it remained unscathed. It will now rest safely in my possession.

Your words are a jumbled mess, recounting a tale of a spirit or something that haunted you. And the swirling of a dark cloud, or smoke, hovering over your bed. Is this not why Mom and Dad sent you to New York when they could not care for you since you turned eighteen? I do remember you having an imaginary friend as a child.

Although you may have had some excellent crafting skills, you were not fit for release in New York so soon. And there was no need for the upkeep of Mom and Dad's home. I don't miss it. I'm not sure about your intentions.

How did the house catch fire? It seems to me you inhaled too much smoke, and you hallucinated. I heard good fortune was on your side, though, as some travelers happened to be passing through and were able to gather others to help put out the flames. I was told they used countless buckets of water to douse the raging inferno.

I do hope you did not suffer in the hellish blaze and were asleep. Anyway, say hello to Mom and Dad, wherever they may be spiritually gathered with you.

I hope to have some answers soon—how the house burned and all—

once the professionals complete their investigations.
  Until we meet again . . .

   —Andrew

October 2, 1995 / Revised September 29, 2024

During the 2024 holiday season, I had some downtime from my full-time work. It was during this time that I wrote "The Long Walk Home," inspired by memories of my father, who passed away in 2020.

In the last decade of his life, we grew closer through his teachings on deer hunting. One year, in Alto, Texas, we slept in a less-than-ideal camper available to us onsite instead of setting up a tent.

My father gave himself a black eye while testing a new rifle. We had just arrived at the campsite and were about to unload our gear when he decided to calibrate the scope before it got dark.

Unfortunately, the recoil was too powerful for him, and the scope hit him in the eye. I took him to the ER, and when my father was released, I drove him back home.

That trip would be our last one together.

THE LONG WALK HOME

I've kept my story to myself for years, convinced no one would believe me. With the recent bizarre events happening in the world lately, like drones flying over homes and people thinking they own the airspace above them, a pandemic supposedly manufactured in a lab, and the threats of nuclear warfare, I feel now is the perfect time to tell my story from that unforgettable night on November 11, 1989.

Just after the crack of dawn, I left the campground to head home after spending three days deer hunting. Old Blue overheated on the winding dirt road. I knew it was only a matter of time before the truck broke down; I had been experiencing issues with it for the past few weeks.

While my friend Drew was out of the country on a business trip, he permitted me to hunt on his extensive property. He had visions of constructing a mini resort, but it's been over a decade, and he has yet to progress. There's a camper on the property that I stay in during my hunting trips, but no house or cabin has been built on the property yet. Drew continues to rent out the land to hunters yearly—a smart way to earn extra money. If his camper were equipped with a landline, that would be nice. But you're living old-school when visiting Drew's property.

I usually go deer hunting at least a week after the hunting season begins. My wife and daughter don't like to camp, let alone shoot at deer for food, and especially not for sport. So, I take the trips alone.

After driving about a quarter mile on the trail from the campsite, I noticed smoke billowing out of my 1965 Chevy pickup's hood. I had about three miles to go before I reached the county road. Nobody traveled this dirt trail to Drew's property except Drew and whoever paid him to hunt. Not many people knew about this secluded location. It was tucked away well.

I was 139 miles from home. If Old Blue broke down now, there was no one to contact nearby for help. I didn't know where Drew's neighbors lived, but I knew they were four or five miles apart. Even if I reached the county road, the closest gas station or truck stop was at least ten miles in either direction.

I pressed my foot on the gas, and Old Blue sputtered and coughed as it moved along the trail. I knew this was the end of the line. And sure enough, the truck's struggling engine finally gave out. My surroundings were filled with tall weeds, blocking my view in every direction.

Fortunately, I had enough food and water for the next few days. Plus, I had plenty of ammunition for my rifle. Even though this trip hadn't yielded any results, I could still use my hunting skills to procure food if necessary.

If I hiked back to the camper and stayed there for one more night, it would buy me time to fix the truck. Drew usually ensured the camper on his property was stocked with extra canned food and several gallons of fresh water for his guests. He also had a four-wheeler parked outside the camper with some gas cans available. His rule was if the hunters used the ATV, they needed to fill the tank with gas and any cans they used before departing.

My family would wonder why I hadn't returned as scheduled, but I'd reach out to them as soon as I could use the ATV to get to a phone. I could also use the ATV to drive into town if I couldn't fix my truck. If I got stopped by the sheriff driving that thing on the road, I'm sure he would understand my situation.

I killed the truck's ignition, walked around the front, and popped the hood. A cloud of white smoke engulfed me. I checked the engine and found it was low on coolant, probably due to a leak leading to a blown head gasket.

I kept the hood up to cool the engine. Since I knew no one would come around here anytime soon, I didn't worry about my camping gear getting jacked from the truck's bed.

Zipping up my jacket, I grabbed my rifle and backpack filled with clothes, bottled water, and snacks from behind the seat. I walked back to the camper, which wasn't too bad of a trek and not as cold as I thought it would be that morning.

When I reached the campsite, I secured my rifle to the front of the ATV, placed my backpack on the rack in the rear, and secured it with some bungees. Then, I entered the camper and took a nap to allow more time for the radiator in the truck to cool.

Forgetting to set an alarm, I woke up nearly four hours later, my stomach growling for food. I opened a can of baked beans and Vienna sausages stocked in a cupboard. After my meal, I stepped outside the camper. And that's when I realized the weather had taken a turn for the worse. It was bitterly cold, so I returned inside the camper and turned on the battery-powered weather radio. I heard that the temperature had dropped forty degrees! It was in the teens, and the windchill factor was in the single digits. I wasn't expecting a blue norther to rip through the area while I slept!

Zipping up my jacket and pulling the hood over my head, I grabbed the keys to the ATV on a shelf and stepped outside. My hands were already cold, and I remembered I left my gloves in the truck.

I checked the gas level on the four-wheeler, started the engine, and rode to my truck. The bitter winds caused the ATV to swerve along the trail, making it difficult to steer.

The sky was darkening from a sudden overcast. It was looking much like snowy weather.

When I arrived at the truck, I kept the ATV engine idling as I retrieved my gloves. I didn't want to risk it not starting again because of the freezing temperature.

I remembered packing a beanie in my backpack, and I retrieved it from under a wad of clothing. Pulling the beanie over my head and ears, I walked to the front of the truck. But when I leaned over to check the engine, I found myself staring into a hole. The engine was gone! This was impossible. No one was out here but me. And no other hunters had reserved the location for another few more days. Drew never overlapped bookings.

I searched the field around my truck, thinking the engine must have been dumped in the weeds somewhere. But who would play such a game with me? It takes hours to remove an engine. How would anyone know I was even out here? The only ones who knew my whereabouts were Drew and my family. And Drew would have never told anyone to do this to me. We were best friends since childhood, and we've never had any beef with one another. This didn't make sense!

As I searched the area, the temperature felt like it was dropping every minute. And the sky was becoming darker. My only option was to return to the camper for warmth and drive the ATV to the gas station tomorrow to get some help.

A dark shadow moved over me, and I looked up. Something was falling from the sky, spiraling out of control.

A plane? A helicopter? A meteor?

I quickly hopped on the ATV and gunned the throttle, distancing myself from the inbound object. When I thought I was out of harm's way, I slowed the ATV and whipped it around. That's when I witnessed the object falling from the sky crash to the ground.

I sped up and followed the stream of black smoke rising from within the weeds several hundred yards from my truck.

Stopping off the side of the trail, I unzipped my backpack and pulled out a flashlight because it was strangely getting darker. I kept the ATV's engine idling and walked through the weeds toward the smoke, parting the weeds when I approached the crash site. I pointed my flashlight toward the object that had cratered the ground.

It looked like . . . my truck's engine?

"What the hell?" I said to no one in the middle of nowhere with puffs of frozen breath drifting from my lips. I stepped cautiously to the burning engine.

I wondered how an engine could fall from the sky. And how could the engine reach the sky in the first place? From an explosion? But the body of my truck was not damaged.

"This is impossible," I said, trembling from the cold.

The bulb in my flashlight started flickering, and I hit the side of the device a few times. I had inserted fresh batteries before I left home on this trip. There was no way they were already losing power. Maybe the extreme cold had something to do with it.

I looked up when something massive moved in the sky again. This time, I saw lights spinning above me. They moved slowly but gradually spun faster, so fast they became one solid light in the sky.

The last thing I remembered while standing in the weeds in the middle of nowhere was a flash of light that zapped from the sky and right down on me.

I woke to darkness. My body felt warm—not feverish warm, but cozy warm. It was a pleasant feeling. I didn't know if my eyes were open, looking in complete darkness, or shut, and only my subconscious was aware.

Something was pulling on my fingers and thumbs like they were hooked to a mechanical device. I felt the bones pop like when you crack your knuckles.

As my fingers stretched, they began to burn. I tried to call out for help but couldn't. My jaw was locked.

A few moments later, I sensed my arms rising over my head. I couldn't tell if I was lying or standing during this ordeal because my body felt weightless. My arms rotated backward in a full circle. I heard bones cracking and tendons snapping. My arms rotated without pain in three continuous revolutions like a contortionist.

From all that was happening to me, my eyes felt the strangest. Although painless, I could feel them sinking deep into their sockets. The pressure was constant for several moments before finally letting up.

I couldn't fight against this torment. Like a Stretch Armstrong action figure, my body went through a wringer of twists, turns, pulls, and squeezes.

A light suddenly flashed, and I saw in the blink of an eye my captor's bald head and colorless face inches before mine. The head was elongated, with three beady eyes lining the forehead, a shriveled nose and mouth, tiny ears, and a pointed chin.

Shortly after I saw the creature, it uttered words forever etched in my brain. I'm unsure if the speech was directed at me specifically. But, to this day, I still hear the low-pitched voice proclaiming, "No equivalence—send home."

A trap door flew open below me almost immediately after those words, and a bright light shone up from the hole. I could see Earth below me!

I fell from the sky.

I fell rapidly.

I fell for what seemed like an eternity.

I fell with my arms at my sides and my legs straight out.

I fell quietly.

I fell without feelings of emotion.

I fell smoothly.

I fell as my life flashed before me.

I fell straight down.

I fell into a body of water.

Sinking deep into the lake, I gained control of my arms and legs and swam upward until I burst through the water's surface. The feeling of oxygen filling my lungs was the most incredible ever.

I swam toward the shore until my feet could touch the ground. As I emerged from the water, I saw I was completely unclothed, with long, unkempt hair and a beard that reached new lengths for me.

I scanned my surroundings from the water's edge. The sun was beating on me relentlessly, and the weather was clear and hot. Before me was a wide-open field with a solitary windmill in the distance. This place looked familiar.

With no clothes to cover myself, I had to use my hands to shield my genitals.

I made my way across the field toward a freshly paved road. The pungent smell of tar overwhelmed me as I stepped onto the winding path and continued for approximately three miles. Although I hoped a car would pass by and offer me help, I also wanted to maintain some sense of dignity.

As I walked the final curve in the road, my eyes locked on a gated community. I continued toward the entrance, and a security guard manning a booth leaned out the side window. He raised a radio to his mouth.

Tired and dehydrated, I approached the gate guard and introduced myself.

The guard looked at me strangely.

I observed the arched entryway to this place. "What is this?" I asked.

"Forest Haven Resorts," the guard replied as if he didn't want to speak to me.

Behind me, several vehicles pulled up to the gate and rolled to a stop. The drivers and passengers held up devices like radios and were laughing. Some of the devices flashed like people were taking pictures of me. One passenger raised his device for a few seconds, placed it to his ear, and spoke into the device with a big smile. *Is that a telephone?* I thought.

I turned back to the guard, and someone driving a golf cart rolled up to the gate. The gate opened, and the golf cart drove through and stopped beside me. The driver was a man about my age. "Get on!" he demanded.

I gladly hopped on the golf cart, and the driver handed me a towel. "Cover yourself," he said, pulling a U-turn and driving back through the open gate. "Who are you, and why are you exposing yourself on my property?"

"Paul Fredricks," I replied, placing the towel in my lap.

The driver slammed on the brakes and turned to me. "Are you Paul Fredricks from Carrollton?"

"Yeah," I said, wondering how the guy knew where I lived.

The driver shook his head. "You went missing over thirty years ago!"

I stared at him. "Thirty years? How?"

The man glanced at me curiously as though attempting to recognize me. "Hunting trip. I leased my property to you and other hunters before building this place. Investigators said your truck broke down, and you must've wandered off to get help. You were never found."

My heart leaped into my throat. "Wait a minute. Are you Drew Bennings?"

"Yes," Drew replied. "Is it really you? You and I were childhood friends!"

"Yes, I remember!" I said gleefully.

Drew's eyes glassed over. Then, after some awkward silence, he said, "Welcome home!"

"Home?"

"Well, welcome back," Drew clarified. "But you're more than welcome to call this your home."

"I appreciate that, but I need to get back to my family so they know I'm safe."

Drew shook his head. "I'm not sure where your family is. They moved on since you've been gone, and I lost touch with them. Let's get you cleaned up and fed, then I'll take you to the authorities so you can report your return and close your case. You were all over the news for several years after your disappearance. There was a large search party involved in the beginning."

"No way," I said. I couldn't fathom how I lost over thirty years of my life! Did several minutes of darkness really turn into three decades?

Drew drove to a building that faced a water park surrounded by breathtaking views. He parked the golf cart under a carport and turned to me, looking deep into my eyes with a serious expression. "We've been friends since before we could count on our fingers, right?"

"Yeah," I replied, wondering where this was going.

"We've always been honest with each other after all these years."

"As far as I can remember," I agreed.

"Whatever you say to the authorities and the media about what happened to you, please tell me the truth," Drew said. He crossed an "X" over his chest. "I swear I'll take it to the grave."

I was at a loss for words.

"I mean it," Drew pleaded.

But I couldn't be utterly truthful with Drew yet. I couldn't even come up with a believable story about my disappearance. It felt like I was heading home from my hunting trip only hours ago.

Drew raised an eyebrow, waiting for my response.

"Okay," I finally said. "I'll tell you everything."

"Thank you," Drew said sincerely. "Consider this your home until you're ready to get back on your feet. Take all the time you need, my friend."

I smiled gratefully, relieved to have a place to stay. It felt like I was starting my life over again.

December 23, 2024

I have a record of submitting my story "They're Under Our Beds" to multiple magazines for publication, but I can't find it. I don't even remember what the story was about.

When I wrote the story in 1997, a coworker asked me what lurks under our beds when I told her the title. But before I could respond, she answered her own question.

Even to this day, I struggle to remember what inspired the story.

While searching for another poem to add to this collection, this story's title stuck out. So, in this new version, I used my coworker's suggested answer to reveal what was hiding under the bed.

Thank you, coworker!

THEY'RE UNDER OUR BEDS

Beware the ankle biters under your bed,
Their jaws snap when they're not fed.

Even without souls, they are tough,
For they always love to play rough.

They chomp and gnaw on fresh or filthy skin,
Their lust for hunger never seems to end.

With every step, a little nip,
From heel to toe, they love to grip.

Whether you're running or jogging,
The ankle biters keep chewing and stalking.

Their tongues lash out to taste your feet,
Even blisters are a savory treat.

People plea that nothing goes wrong,
But the ankle biters continue with their haunting songs.

With a serenade of clicks and snaps,
Their teeth for eyes set their traps.

Mind your step and guard your ankles,
Hunger awaits from every angle.

Under your bed, they lie dark and deep,
And shuffle closer while you sleep.

If you work late-night shifts, they especially love to feast,
Including if their victims are deceased.

And as soon as your feet touch the floor,
The ankle biters snap hungrily for more.

They'll chew through leather, laces, and soles,
Every bite makes feet less than whole.

Hunger grows with every stride,
No sock or shoe can block the tide.

Ankle biters love to smile,
For making humans run is worth their while.

But when they catch up, they love to mock,
At work or even while you walk.

Everywhere you go, ankle biters skitter and crawl,
There's no escaping their flapping jaws.

Whether working hard or taking a break,
Another human they will take.

When chaos erupts, they create a symphony of screams,
And the ankle biters look forward to fulfilling their dreams.

Whenever you're too busy to be aware,
The tiny terrors are most likely lurking there.

And when they plague a group of feet,
A crowd unites, determined to defeat.

Organized by a cobbler with steel-toed boots,
He forges weapons from iron and roots.

The man in the hat offers to bring his traps,
Designed to crush those wicked little chaps.

And the scientist, with potions green and blue,

THE REAL WOLF MAN

Concocts a serum to melt them through and through.

A nimble-fingered thief may join the ranks,
Where he'll prepare his lockpicks to spring their planks.

Even the witch, with spells so old,
Prepares to banish the creatures so bold.

Her chants and incantations she did learn,
To make the ankle biters writhe and burn.

A hunter can track their patterned trails,
While a priest's holy water will never fail.

And then the survivors, with their ankles bandaged,
Gather in secret, their spirits undamaged.

When people rumor to end their plight,
They vanquish the ankle biters in the dead of night.

An exterminator can also join the team,
His potions and powders will vanquish them clean.

He can promise to fumigate every nook,
Where ankle biters might lurk and look.

So, when you fall asleep at night,
Be wary of those concealed things, ready to take flight.

And in the morning, when you're about to scoot,
Remember them under your bed, those filthy boots.

December 9, 1997 / Rewritten December 24, 2024

The idea for "Seventh Floor" came to me as I stood in the shower, surrounded by steam. It's strange how my stories come together during cleansing, as if the hot water massaging my neck unlocks my creative mind.

I wanted this final tale to be entirely new and unexpected. And so, the haunting and suspenseful journey of being trapped in an elevator, riding the cable toward an unknown destination, begins on the next page. This small metal box is suffocating and disorienting. The only sounds we hear are the creaking cables and the distant screams of other passengers trapped in this nightmare in the other elevators beside us.

With each passing floor, a sense of dread and anticipation grows stronger. When the doors open, I know this tale will stay with me long after the shower has turned off and reality sets back in. But what horrors await when the elevator doors open? I don't know yet as I type this short synopsis before diving into the story.

Let's check this out together.

SEVENTH FLOOR

Eight elevators were available in the hotel lobby area. Four lining one wall and another four elevators on the opposite wall. George Little waited impatiently for one of the elevator landing doors to open. He checked the time on his watch and tapped his foot. He could've taken the stairs and reached his destination by now. There were eight elevators for crying out loud, and no one else waiting for one to open. What was the deal?

Finally, the elevator landing doors in front of George slid open with a soft chime, and George stepped inside and pressed the button to the twenty-second floor. He stood alone as the doors slid closed, adjusting his coat and tie.

The Ironclad Ventures International's annual conference always excited him, yet he dreaded the drawn-out general sessions. And like many corporate conferences, the break-out sessions were boring, too. Thankfully, he'd made it through the panel discussions of talking heads. The events George enjoyed most at the three-day conference were the second evening after-party and the independent entrepreneurs' demonstrations of their weapons systems on the third day. Today was the last day, and the final event was beginning soon on the twenty-second floor.

Ironclad Ventures International was a global tech corporation specializing in investments in independent entrepreneurs creating weapons of mass destruction. This was George's fifth annual conference with the company. He consulted new entrepreneurs onboarding with the company and loved every aspect of his position. He got dibs on learning new developments with various weapons created by people young and old. However, the more advanced weaponry he saw was usually made by young entrepreneurs in their early twenties. He believed those who played video games as kids grew up with ideas for advancing or altering a specific weapon they selected in their games. With some brainstorming and tweaking, the weapons could be introduced to and used in the military in return for an insane amount of money. One sale could instantly send an entrepreneur into retirement and provide for their family for a lifetime.

George had seen it before and could see it happen again today. One lucky chap would surprise everyone attending this event with a weapon that would blow their minds.

He looked up at the digital display showing which floor the elevator was climbing to next. The number flashed "2," and the elevator slowed to a stop. The doors swished open, and a woman wearing a crisp black suit and holding a leather portfolio entered, her heels clicking against the polished floor. She nodded curtly at George before turning to face the doors. She looked like an executive in the company. Probably filthy rich and stuck up. Most of the executives were in this company.

"Going to twenty-two?" George asked the lady.

"I am," she replied softly.

The elevator doors slid closed, and the metal box ascended again.

The subtle, intoxicating scent of the woman's perfume filled George's nostrils, instantly awakening his senses. A delicate blend of orange and lime wafted through the air. The fragrance of essential oils drew him closer to the attractive woman. The scent was like a potion, casting a spell over him and making him want to stay near her for as long as possible.

Then he sneezed.

"Bless you," the woman said, turning her head slightly but avoiding eye contact.

"Thanks." George sniffled. He dug into his pants pocket, pulled out a handkerchief, and wiped his nose. Not many people used handkerchiefs anymore. But George was old-school. He always followed in his father's footsteps. Whatever his father did in life, George repeated almost to a T.

He missed his dad. But after accepting his loss nearly three years ago, George's life was getting back on track. His father had left him with a plethora of advice, life hacks, jokes, and more that only his father could have taught him to carry forward. The only thing he didn't receive from his father was money. Oh no, George's father made sure he always had to work for his income—no matter the situation or how hard life got at times. If his father could make it through struggles, so could he.

The digital display flashed "3," and the elevator slowed to a stop.

"Are we going to stop at every floor?" George murmured. He noticed the woman shrug slightly at his comment like the inconvenience of stopping at every floor didn't bother her.

The doors slid open. Another lady stood outside holding a briefcase. Her smile grew when she noticed the woman on the elevator. "Stacey!" she exclaimed and stepped onto the elevator. Her silky smooth, straight blond hair bounced with each movement. Even her breasts jiggled slightly underneath her tight outfit.

"Hey, girl!" Stacey smiled in return, her teeth white as snow. She either took good care of her teeth with whitening toothpaste or she'd recently visited the dentist. They were spotless, which made her smile even more attractive.

George found himself in heaven. With the sweet aroma of Stacey's perfume lingering and now two beautiful women on the elevator accompanying him, he couldn't resist feasting his eyes on the two pairs of perfectly peach-shaped buttocks staring up at him as the ladies stood shoulder to shoulder.

The elevator doors closed, and the metal box proceeded to climb.

George cleared his throat. "Going to twenty-two?" he blurted, directing the question to the lady who just got on.

"Yes," the lady chirped. She flicked her hair over her shoulder. Like Stacey, she refused to make eye contact.

George rolled his eyes. Another executive, he thought as he glanced at the woman with her briefcase. She probably had more power than Stacey, who was now just a lower-level manager. Two office drones sharing the elevator with him. Great. He knew he wasn't the most handsome man, but they could have looked in his direction and acknowledged him being there. Was it his bushy beard that made them uncomfortable? Too intimidating? Or was it his bald head? Many women liked bald guys these days.

The digital display flashed "4," and once again, the elevator slowed to a stop.

"You gotta be fucking kidding me." George threw his head back. "There are eight freakin' elevators, and this one has to stop at every single floor?"

Stacey and the blond looked at each other in judgment of George's comments. Still, they would not make eye contact with him.

The doors opened. A tall amazon woman stood outside, holding a backpack by its strap. She glanced at Stacey and the blond and stepped onto the elevator.

George felt the elevator shake when the tall woman turned and faced the doors as they closed. He got a foul body odor from the amazon woman like she hadn't used deodorant for days. He turned toward Stacey in hopes her perfume would dilute the stench. But his senses were used to Stacey's scent, and the new smell in the elevator lingered.

This time, George kept his mouth shut as the elevator ascended. If the amazon woman wasn't going to the twenty-second floor, it was her fault for not checking the floor selection buttons. No one was talking to him anyway, so why should he care?

The amazon woman turned to Stacey and the blond. "Going to the twenty-second floor?" she asked, her voice on the verge of sounding masculine.

George threw his hands in the air.

Stacey and the blond nodded.

"I'm Brooke," the amazon woman said.

"I'm Tammy," the blond replied. She glanced at Stacey and back at Brooke. "And this is Stacey."

"Nice to meet you." Brooke smiled.

George felt ignored. Did none of them realize he was on the elevator, too?

The digital display flashed "5," and the elevator slowed to a stop.

George clenched his hands into fists and gritted his teeth. He couldn't take this elevator stopping on every floor. Someone must've played a joke before he stepped onto the elevator. Perhaps some snot-nosed bratty kid pressed all the buttons to every floor and dashed out of the elevator. But no, only the button for floor 22 was lit.

The doors slid open with a soft swish, and an elegant, very short older black woman entered with a rollaboard suitcase. She didn't appear to be attending the event on the twenty-second floor. Probably a hotel guest. A warm smile graced her face as she greeted the other women in the elevator. Her teeth were just as white as Stacey's. But she wasn't dressed as stylishly as the others. Instead, she wore a church crown hat and a cozy knitted sweater over her blouse.

George migrated to the far corner of the elevator as the other women made room for the elderly lady.

The doors closed, and the elevator climbed.

George glanced at his watch. The event was to start in ten minutes, and he couldn't be late. If he wasn't one of the first consultants from his department to visit the entrepreneur and vendor booths, his chances of selecting the best candidate to onboard were slim.

The elevator was getting hot from all the body heat. George could feel the sweat running down his back. He couldn't take much more of this elevator stopping. He decided to get off and take another car if it stopped again.

The digital display flashed "6," and the elevator slowed to a stop.

George adjusted his coat and tie, ready to get off. But before he spoke up to excuse himself off the elevator, the doors slid open, and an obese woman sitting in a heavy-duty, wide-seat electric wheelchair blocked almost the entire doorway. A large backpack stuffed full was strapped to the back of the chair.

The ladies standing in the center of the elevator parted to allow the next passenger on.

The middle-aged woman pushed forward on the chair's joystick, and the wheelchair rolled onto the elevator. The elevator sunk about a quarter of an inch from the hoistway. "Thank you," the woman said. "I'm going to twenty-two if someone can push the button for me."

"It's the only button that's been pressed," George replied with annoyance.

The woman in the wheelchair peered around Stacey at George. "Oh, hehe. I didn't see you there."

George pursed his lips.

The doors closed, and the elevator ascended.

Everyone was quiet as the hydraulic drive system raised the car through the shaft. George could hear the pistons working below. The hotel elevators weren't very insulated.

George needed to get off on the next floor because he felt his life depended on it now. He was sure the elevator was moving slower than usual due to the excessive weight. It was going to get stuck, he thought.

The digital display flashed "7," and the elevator slowed to a stop.

George hugged the side wall of the car, excusing himself past Stacey, who barely moved to allow him to position himself to the front.

The woman in the wheelchair watched George's movement as he made his way to the front of the car. "This is your stop?"

George paused in front of the car operating panel. He huffed loudly, waiting for the doors to open. "Yup," he said, avoiding eye contact with the woman in the chair.

But the elevator doors and the landing doors remained shut. The car was not moving.

George pressed the door open button on the panel. He repeatedly pushed the button when the system did not respond to the command.

The elevator doors remained shut.

"What did you do?" the woman in the wheelchair whined.

"Nothing," George said, pushing and holding the door open button. He saw button 22 was still the only button illuminated on the panel.

"You pushed a button," the wheelchair woman said.

"I need to get off here," George lied. "This is my stop." His heart raced as he realized the elevator wasn't responding to any other button commands, including the emergency call button, which made no sound from the speaker. The silence in the car was deafening.

Suddenly, a muffled scream echoed through the shaft from one of the adjacent elevators. George pressed his ear against the cold metal wall, straining to hear more. The other passengers trapped with him exchanged worried glances of a shared crisis.

"Did you hear that?" Stacey whispered.

Before anyone could respond, a series of dull thuds reverberated through the shaft, followed by what sounded like metal scraping against metal. The noise grew louder, seeming to come from multiple elevators surrounding them.

Then, faintly at first but growing louder, came more sounds of commotion from the neighboring elevator shafts. Muffled voices echoed through the shafts, a rattle of confusion and alarm.

"Hello? Can anyone hear us?" a man's voice called from the shaft to the left.

"We're stuck! The elevator's not moving!" a woman shrieked from the right.

"Is this happening in all the elevators?" the woman in the wheelchair asked.

The elderly woman wiped a bead of sweat from her face. "It's getting stuffy in here."

"How are all the other elevators stuck, too?" Brooke wondered. "We still have electricity in here, so the power's not out."

Tammy adjusted her dress over her bosom. "I can't stay cooped up in here. If this wheelchair hadn't rolled on, everything would've been fine."

"Excuse me?" the woman in the wheelchair scolded.

The elderly black lady feathered the woman's hand in the wheelchair with her fingertips. "Oh, sweetie. I'm sure she didn't mean it that way. What's your name, hon? I'm Phyllis."

The woman in the chair smiled at Phyllis and replied, "I'm Audrey. Thank you for being so kind."

Funny, no one asked George his name. Feeling singled out, he decided not to interact with anyone and just kept pressing buttons until, hopefully, the elevator responded.

As the minutes ticked by, the atmosphere in the elevator grew increasingly tense. The women exchanged worried glances.

Stacey, ever the executive, took charge. "Alright, ladies, we need to think this through logically. There must be a way out of here."

Tammy nodded, her blonde hair bouncing. "Maybe we could pry the doors open? I've seen it done in movies."

Brooke stepped forward. "I'm strong. I could try."

George, still frantically pressing buttons, scoffed. "That's ridiculous. These doors are designed to withstand tremendous force. And that's way too dangerous. You shouldn't—"

But Brooke was already wedging her fingers into the thin gap between the doors. Her muscles strained as she pulled, veins popping on her forehead.

"They aren't budging," Phyllis said, worried that Brooke should save her strength in case they needed her help later.

Audrey had no room to turn her electric wheelchair around. She shifted in the chair so she could glance behind her. But after seeing Brooke struggling, she readjusted back into position in the chair, realizing there was nothing she could do to help.

Brooke released her grip on the doors and shook out her hands. "Why aren't they opening? I've pried them open once before."

"Yeah, let's not try that again," Stacey intervened.

George rolled his eyes. An executive realizing the dangers of opening elevator doors while the car was stuck after an attempt to open them was brilliant. He loved how she heeded his warning. He stopped pressing buttons, realizing it was useless, and retrieved his smartphone from his back pocket. He held it over his head and waved it around, trying to get a signal. "Does anyone have a signal on their phones?"

Tammy glanced up. "Isn't there a door or something on top of this thing?" she asked, ignoring George. "Maybe someone can climb up and check if something is stuck on the cables."

"That's not a good idea, either," George said, just like his father would've probably warned. Again, no one paid any attention to him.

The heat blasting through the car intensified the body odor. Brooke's armpits and the sweat accumulating under Audrey's skin folds were emitting a stench that was becoming unbearable.

"There's no signal on my phone," Audrey said, repeating what George did by waving her smartphone above her head. She struggled to breathe; the air was dense. Storing her phone down into her shirt between her oversized breasts, she asked, "What do you suggest we should do?"

George took shallow breaths. The more he inhaled, the more intense the smell, making him gag. If he breathed through his mouth, he could taste it. He wondered why the others weren't cringing from the stench. Had they lost their sense of smell?

"Well, like our executive here suggested initially," George said, referring to Stacey, "we should collect our thoughts and talk this out. Find a reasonable and safe solution. On the upside, if other elevators are also stuck, I'm sure it won't be long before someone on the outside figures it out and security is notified so they can start working on a solution."

Audrey nodded silently in agreement.

"What's your name, young man?" Phyllis stepped forward.

George was shocked. The old lady noticed him! Had his suggestions enticed others to recognize him in the elevator? "My name's George, ma'am."

"George Ma'am?" Phyllis teased.

George chuckled. "Just George."

"Oh. Well, that's nice. Thank you for your suggestions."

George gave Phyllis a thumbs-up. But what was with Stacey, Tammy, and Brooke? Why hadn't they acknowledged him and thanked him for anything?

The car fell silent momentarily. More voices could be heard from the cars stuck in the shafts on either side. But what were once nonstop frantic voices now came in delayed, random bursts.

"Have the others found a way off their elevators?" Audrey wondered. "I don't hear anyone talking much anymore."

Phyllis slapped her hands to her face. "Oh Lord, I hope they haven't suffocated!"

"Yeah, the oxygen doesn't seem to be circulating much in here," Audrey acknowledged, taking deeper breaths.

George shook his head. "I'm not sure what's going on with the others."

A loud bang suddenly erupted in another elevator next to them.

"Oh my God!" Stacey jumped. "Was that a gunshot?"

More popping sounds came in random bursts, followed by screams. Then, the hydraulic system malfunctioning echoed within the elevator shaft, and the screams faded quickly.

"That sounded like a free fall!" George said.

They listened with bated breath until they heard the elevator crash to the concrete ground seven stories below them. Immediately, they felt the impact reverberating through the shaft.

Everyone but George screamed in terror, clutching at each other and the walls for support as the floor beneath them trembled.

Before anyone could recover from the shock, another snap echoed through the shaft—the sound of steel cables giving way under immense strain. George's stomach lurched as he realized what was happening. The elevator on the other side of them had just broken free.

The plummeting car displaced the muffled screams, followed by an agonizing silence. Then came the deafening crash as tons of metal and machinery collided with the concrete pit at the bottom of the shaft.

"Good Lord!" Phyllis cried out. Her eyes grew as big as silver dollars. "Are we hanging by a thread, and we drop next?"

Another round of gunfire blasted through the elevator shafts.

"Who the hell is shooting?" Audrey blurted.

Like a free fall ride at an amusement park, screams echoed through the shafts as another car was released from its cables and plummeted.

George lowered his head, feeling defeated. But Audrey spoke up with an idea just as he was about to accept that there was no way out.

"Stupid me!" Audrey said. "Can someone get the backpack off my chair for me?"

George looked up, wondering what Audrey wanted with her bulky backpack.

"I got it, dear," Phyllis said, her tiny body gliding between Brooke and Tammy behind Audrey's wheelchair. She grasped the shoulder straps and pulled with all her strength. The bag didn't budge. "Whew!

What do you have in this bag, girl? A ton of lead?"

Brooke moved over and grabbed the bag as if it were filled with air. She set it in Audrey's lap, then turned and winked at Phyllis before folding her thick-boned arms across her chest. She was interested in what Audrey had in the bag.

Stacey and Tammy locked eyes on the oversized backpack, too.

Interested but not hopeful, George watched as Audrey unzipped the bag.

Audrey rummaged through her backpack, her face lighting up as her hand closed around something. "Ah, here it is!" she exclaimed, carefully extracting a sleek, metallic device about the size of a large smartphone.

George's eyes widened in recognition. "Is that… a plasma cutter?" he asked, his voice a mix of awe and disbelief.

Audrey grinned, her earlier distress replaced by a spark of excitement. "Not just any plasma cutter, Mr. George. This is the PlasmaBlade 3000, my own creation."

The other women in the elevator leaned in, curiosity momentarily overriding their fear.

"You're an entrepreneur?" Stacey asked.

Audrey nodded, her fingers dancing over the device's smooth surface. "I am. I'm here for the Ironclad Ventures International conference. And this beauty is my ticket in." She held up the device, which gleamed under the elevator's flickering lights.

Audrey's eyes met George's, a glimmer of recognition flashing across her face. "You're a consultant for Ironclad, aren't you? I remember seeing you at last year's conference. I didn't want to mention that I knew you until later, during the event when we got off this elevator."

George nodded, surprised. "That's right."

"Your insights on the future of compact energy weapons were fascinating," Audrey said, her earlier frustration melting away. She held out the PlasmaBlade 3000 to George. "Here, why don't you give it a try? I'd love to get your professional opinion."

George hesitated, his eyes darting between Audrey's eager face and the sleek device. "Are you sure? This is your invention, your chance to showcase it."

Audrey smiled warmly. "Consider this a pre-conference demonstration. Besides, I trust your steady hands more than mine."

George took the PlasmaBlade 3000 from Audrey, marveling at its lightweight design and ergonomic grip. As he examined the device, Stacey and Tammy exchanged envious glances.

Phyllis moved closer to the front of Audrey's wheelchair to examine the device. Brooke joined her, standing tall behind the tiny elderly woman, creating a dynamic of the tallest and shortest women in the world in one location.

"How does it work?" George asked, his fingers tracing the smooth contours of the weapon.

Audrey's eyes lit up as she explained. "It uses a concentrated plasma beam to cut through virtually any material. The energy output is adjustable, allowing for precision cuts and more aggressive slicing. It's powered by a miniaturized fusion core I developed, giving it unprecedented longevity and power."

George whistled, impressed. "Incredible. You think it can cut through the elevator doors?"

"Like a hot knife through butter." Audrey nodded confidently.

As if on cue, another sickening snap echoed through the shaft, followed by the now-familiar whoosh of a plummeting elevator car. The muffled screams of its occupants pierced the air, growing fainter as the car accelerated downward.

"We're running out of time!" Stacey said, her voice tight with fear.

George wiped his sweaty palms on his pants before adjusting the PlasmaBlade 3000. He pulled a strap from a hidden compartment underneath and secured it around his hand, ensuring a tight grip on the device. "Alright, everyone step back," he ordered, positioning himself before the elevator doors.

The women pressed themselves against the walls, Brooke helping Audrey maneuver her wheelchair as close to the opposite wall as she could, considering the size of the chair. With everyone hugging the walls, she was able to spin the wheelchair around so Audrey could watch her invention at work.

Phyllis, the tiniest one onboard, stood protectively in front of everyone.

George steadied his nerves as he positioned the PlasmaBlade 3000 against the elevator door. With a gentle press of the activation button, a brilliant blue-white beam erupted from the device, illuminating the cramped elevator car with a soft glow.

As he carefully traced the outline of a large square, the door's metal seemed to vanish. There was no sparking, molten metal dripping to the floor, or even the slightest wisp of smoke. Instead, the powerful beam left behind a perfectly clean edge, as if the door section had never existed.

George's movements were precise and controlled. The PlasmaBlade 3000 hummed softly, its energy output adjusting automatically to maintain the optimal cutting power as it encountered different densities within the door's structure.

As George completed the final cut, the square section of the door fell away with a thud, revealing a dark landing. Yet even more impressed, George realized the device had sliced through not only the elevator doors but also the landing doors!

Before him, another woman stood in the shadows on the landing, waiting for the elevator doors to open. Ignoring her, George marveled at the clean, precise edges of the opening he had cut. It didn't look hand-cut but rather like a machine had laser-etched it.

"Incredible," George murmured, turning the PlasmaBlade 3000 over. He ran his fingers along its sleek surface, feeling the faint warmth from the device. Despite the intense heat it had generated, the handle remained cool to the touch, a testament to its advanced thermal management system.

He accidentally pressed a small button on the side, and a holographic display sprang to life above the device. It showed a detailed readout of the PlasmaBlade's power levels, cutting efficiency, and molecular analysis. "This is far out!" George said, pressing the button again to shut off the holographic image.

"Is there a problem?" a voice called outside the elevator.

George looked up. The woman waiting to ride the elevator stepped onto the door panels that had crashed to the floor. She acted as if them lying there in her way was no big deal. George moved aside as she stepped onto the elevator, her hips swaying hypnotically, drawing every eye in the cramped space. She was striking, her presence immediately commanding attention. Her deep purple dress clung to every curve of her hourglass figure. The neckline plunged daringly low, revealing a tantalizing glimpse of cleavage. Her legs seemed to go on forever, ending in four-inch heels.

Her face was a masterpiece of delicate features—high cheekbones, full lips painted a matching shade of her dress, and intelligent eyes that sparkled with a hint of mischief. Her raven hair cascaded down her back in loose waves.

George felt his face flush as Lisa Ironclad, the CEO of Ironclad

Ventures International, stood next to him. He was motionless and speechless.

Phyllis grabbed the extended handle of her rollaboard suitcase. "I ain't standing on this elevator forever," she griped and skillfully maneuvered around everyone, the first to escape onto the landing.

"Ma'am, please move before I run you over with my chair," Audrey warned Lisa.

Lisa slowly turned to Audrey. "Excuse me? You have no right to talk to me that way. Do you know who I am?"

Audrey chuckled, knowing Lisa had no authority over her. "I don't care who the fuck you are! You don't own me. Now move!" She pushed the joystick on the chair forward, and the wheelchair advanced.

Lisa stepped aside just before the wheelchair ran over her foot. Then she turned and watched Audrey try to fit the chair through the cut-out door panel. "Look who's moving now," Lisa said.

Audrey thrust herself back in the chair, pissed that the hole George had cut was not big enough for her to fit through. The elevator car shifted and rattled with her temper.

"You'll cause this thing to fall like the others, thrashing around in your chair like that," Brooke said. Surprisingly, she, Stacey, and Tammy were not in any hurry to escape the elevator.

Audrey paused for a breather. Her blouse had dampened with sweat. After she collected herself, she spoke in a calm voice to George. "Mr. George, can you cut out the other door so I can fit through?"

Lisa suddenly grabbed George's arm, noting the PlasmaBlade 3000 gripped in his hand. "I wouldn't do that if I were you."

George instinctively jerked his arm away and took a step back. "Ms. Ironclad, I assume you've read the employee handbook, which I'm sure you helped write? Remove your hand from me."

Stacey and Tammy made it clear they didn't want to get involved in the argument.

Meanwhile, Brooke stood in the corner, ready to intervene if necessary.

Phyllis remained outside the landing, keeping watch probably in case things escalated, and she needed to be a witness for any potential lawsuits.

Lisa's eyes bored into George, unflinching and determined.

As he stared back, mesmerized by her gaze, George noticed something unsettling. Lisa's eyes, initially a deep brown, began to shift.

The irises swirled like liquid mercury, transforming to a vivid electric blue.

George caught his breath. This wasn't Lisa Ironclad, the CEO he'd met at previous conferences. This was something else entirely—a highly advanced android that had somehow infiltrated the company, posing as its leader. George had heard rumors of the company's secret robotics division, but this was beyond anything he could have imagined.

His mind raced as he processed the revelation. Without hesitation, he activated the PlasmaBlade 3000. The device hummed to life, its blue-white beam illuminating the cramped elevator.

"What are you doing?" Lisa's voice remained eerily calm.

George raised the weapon, and in one fluid motion, he brought the plasma beam down on Lisa's forehead. The beam sliced through her synthetic skin and skull with frightening ease, cutting a precise line from her hairline to her chin. There was no blood, only a faint sizzling sound as the beam made its cut.

Lisa didn't flinch or scream. Her face split open, revealing a complex network of circuitry and metallic components where brain tissue should have been. Tiny sparks danced across the exposed electronics as her systems began to fail.

George stumbled backward in shock. But strong hands gripped his shoulders from behind before he could fully process what he'd just done.

Brooke's voice, devoid of human warmth, spoke directly into his ear. "That was unwise. You shouldn't have done that."

George spun around, bringing the PlasmaBlade 3000 up defensively. Brooke's eyes had transformed, matching the eerie electric blue of Lisa's.

"What the hell?" George gasped, his gaze darting toward Stacey and Tammy as their eyes changed, too. All three women underwent the same transformation with electric blue eyes.

"What's happening?" Audrey yelled.

George's heart raced as he faced the three android women, their eyes fixed on him with predatory intensity. In a split second, he made his decision. With precision, he swung the PlasmaBlade 3000 in a wide arc, the plasma beam slicing through Brooke's midsection.

Brooke's synthetic body separated cleanly, the top half sliding off with a thud. Sparks erupted from her severed circuitry, the smell of melted plastic filling the air.

Stacey lunged forward, her movements unnaturally fast.

George ducked under her outstretched arms and brought the blade up, cutting diagonally across her chest. The beam carved through the synthetic flesh and internal components with ease.

Stacey's face froze in a rictus of simulated shock as her systems failed.

Tammy, moving with robotic precision, reached for George's throat. He ducked under her grasp and thrust the PlasmaBlade 3000 upward, piercing through her chin and into her skull.

Still outside the elevator on the landing, Phyllis stood with her jaw gaping.

To make matters more terrifying, two elevator shafts over, a fifth car released from its cable into a free fall. The sound of metal scraping against metal echoed through the building as the box crashed to the floor seven stories below.

George stood amidst the sparking remains of the four android women, his chest heaving. The acrid smell of melted circuitry filled the car.

"We need to get out of here, now!" Audrey panicked.

George positioned himself before the intact elevator door, raising the PlasmaBlade 3000, and flicked a switch to activate the weapon. The device hummed to life. He noticed Phyllis still standing on the landing. "Phyllis, step back so you don't get hurt," he cautioned, positioning the weapon's blue-white beam on the door and quickly slicing through the metal.

Phyllis took a few steps to the side and rolled the suitcase with her, watching for the door panels to fall to the floor.

George traced a larger opening this time, ensuring it would accommodate Audrey's wheelchair. The clean edges of the cut glowed faintly as he worked.

Halfway through the process, the PlasmaBlade 3000 suddenly sputtered. The beam flickered, its intensity wavering.

George frantically adjusted the settings, even though he didn't know what he was doing, but the device continued to falter.

The elevator car jolted.

"It's jammed or something," George said, tapping the device. But the blue-white beam didn't activate.

Audrey opened the backpack on her lap and dug inside. "I have more," she said, pulling another PlasmaBlade 3000 prototype from the bag.

George unstrapped the broken device from his hand and exchanged the plasma cutter with Audrey's backup. "You're a lifesaver!" he said, strapping the device to his hand, powering it on, and continuing cutting where the previous weapon jammed.

As he completed the final cut, the elevator and landing doors fell away, overlapping the other doors on the landing.

Ecstatic, Phyllis clapped and cheered.

Audrey moved her wheelchair through the doorway and out onto the landing.

Phyllis threw her arms around Audrey's neck. "Yes! You made it, girl. I'm so happy!"

A cold metal hand clamped around his ankle as George stepped off the elevator. He stumbled, nearly falling face-first onto the landing. Twisting around, he saw android Lisa's mangled form, sparks flying from her exposed circuitry. Her eyes blazed red as she pulled him back toward the damaged car.

"You can't leave," Lisa's voice crackled, distorted by her failing systems. "The demonstration must continue."

The elevator car shuddered violently, the metal groaning under the strain. A deafening snap echoed through the shaft as one of the main cables gave way. The car lurched downward several feet before catching on the remaining cables, the sudden movement nearly throwing George off his feet.

George raised the PlasmaBlade 3000 and sliced it through Lisa's hand. He kicked his leg violently, sending the hand off his ankle and flying into the elevator. Then he stumbled over the door panels on the floor as he moved away from the elevator.

The elevator broke from the remaining cables that kept it in position, and the metal box plummeted through the shaft. Screeching metal filled the air as the elevator car scraped against the shaft walls during its rapid descent. Sparks flew in brilliant cascades, illuminating the darkness as the box hurtled downward until it crashed to the ground.

Echoes of electronic circuitry reverberated through the dark elevator shaft as Ironclad Ventures International's highly advanced robotic systems failed, their once efficient movements now ceasing to function. Then, an eerie silence filled the shaft, broken only by the occasional creaks and groans of metal structures.

George took a moment to survey the surroundings. Like the ground-level hotel lobby, the hallway had eight landing doors.

In a flurry of movement, two landing doors slid open with soft chimes—the doors to the only two elevators that had not dropped. Without hesitation, small groups of passengers scrambled out of the elevators, their hurried footsteps following one another toward the glowing red emergency exit sign, where they cascaded down the stairs in a chaotic frenzy.

George leaned in and handed the PlasmaBlade 3000 back to Audrey.

Audrey shook her head and threw her hands up. "No, keep it as a thank-you for saving me," she insisted. "But on one condition."

"What's that?" George asked curiously.

"We become business partners. I have other ideas in mind," Audrey proposed.

"You do have a fantastic product," George admitted, admiring the weapon. "But with a little more attention to its power and configuring it to withstand more aggressive cutting without faltering so quickly, it should be ready for market."

Phyllis suddenly interjected. "What about me?"

George chuckled. "What about you? Do you want to be our lawyer or something?"

Audrey giggled along with Phyllis.

"No, silly," Phyllis replied, collapsing the handle of her suitcase. She set the bag on the floor and unzipped it, pulling out an object. She held a spherical device the size of a softball. Its metallic surface gleamed with an iridescent sheen, shifting colors as it caught the light. Intricate patterns etched into its surface pulsed with a soft, white glow.

"This here's my baby," Phyllis said, her eyes twinkling with pride. "I call it the Shadowstep."

"Damn, you're an entrepreneur, too?" George said. "It doesn't look like much of a weapon, though." His eyes traced the delicate patterns on the orb's surface.

"That's because it's not just a weapon, honey. It's a teleportation device."

Audrey's eyes widened. "Teleportation? But that's…"

"Impossible?" Phyllis finished for her. "This will get us downstairs without having to take another elevator."

"Oh, trust me, I'm never getting on an elevator again," Audrey said. "It may take me a while to walk stairs, but I'll take them any day from now on."

"The good thing is your wheelchair can teleport with you." Phyllis smiled.

Audrey's eyes lit up. "Oh?"

"Why didn't you whip this out while we were trapped on the elevator?" George asked.

"I haven't figured out yet how to get the orb to teleport with the one who possesses it," Phyllis said. "I could've teleported *you*, yes. But how would I have retrieved the orb if I had teleported from the elevator? It would've plunged with the rest of them robots."

"She's got a point," Audrey said.

"Sounds like you need to reconfigure some settings with your product." George smiled.

Phyllis held the Shadowstep orb out to them. "If you want to get out of here, touch the orb and think of where you want to go. It'll do the rest."

George hesitated, his hand hovering over the device. "How are you sure this is safe? Based on what you mentioned about the orb being unable to teleport with the person using it, your invention may have more problems."

Phyllis chuckled. "Honey, I've been using this on my friends to get them to bingo nights for years. It's safer than those death trap elevators."

Audrey reached out first, her fingers brushing the cool metal surface. "I'm game if you are, Mr. George."

George gave a hopeful sigh, flexed his fingers, and placed his hand on the orb beside Audrey's. The pulsing patterns intensified when their flesh contacted the device, casting a soft glow over their faces.

"Now, picture the hotel lobby," Phyllis instructed. "I'll take the stairs back down and meet you there. Ready?"

George and Audrey closed their eyes. A brilliant white light emanated from the sphere, enveloping their bodies in a pulsating aura before they vanished into thin air.

As the light dimmed and faded into the orb, Phyllis carefully placed the silver sphere back into her suitcase and securely closed it. She then extended the handle of her rollaboard and pulled it behind her as she made her way toward the exit.

* * *

George and Audrey materialized in the hotel lobby with a soft whoosh of displaced air. The world around them came into focus as the tingling sensation of the teleportation faded.

They found themselves amid chaos.

"Oh my God," Audrey breathed, her eyes wide as she entered the scene. Her wheelchair wobbled slightly as it settled onto the polished marble floor. She gripped the armrests tightly, her knuckles white, as she took in the pandemonium around them.

The once-pristine lobby was now a scene of frantic activity and panic. People rushed in all directions, their faces etched with fear and confusion.

Firefighters in full gear pushed past them, dragging heavy equipment toward the elevators. The sound of grinding metal echoed through the lobby as they worked to pry open the elevator landing doors that had bent outward due to the impact of the elevator cars crashing to the ground.

George stood beside her, his hand still clutching the PlasmaBlade 3000, his eyes wide as he surveyed the devastation.

Teams of paramedics rushed by with stretchers.

A figure caught George's eye as he and Audrey took in the chaotic scene. Phyllis emerged from the emergency exit, her rollaboard suitcase trailing behind her. She weaved through the crowd with ease.

George waved, catching Phyllis's attention.

Phyllis made her way over to them, her face a mixture of relief and excitement. "Well, I'll be," she said, walking toward Audrey. She placed a hand on her new friend's shoulder. "Looks like my little Shadowstep worked like a charm."

"It's incredible," George marveled, still processing the instantaneous journey he and Audrey had just experienced. "The potential applications are mind-boggling."

Audrey nodded in agreement, her eyes sparkling with newfound enthusiasm despite the chaos around them. "Between your Shadowstep, my PlasmaBlade 3000, and George's expertise, we can grow a new company together." She looked up at George from her electric wheelchair. "What do you say?"

George flashed a warm, genuine smile down at Audrey. He then turned to Phyllis, who stood at Audrey's height in her chair. "I believe we would make an unstoppable team," he declared confidently.

Two ambitious entrepreneurs and a savvy business consultant fled the luxurious hotel, united in conquering their next venture. Armed with determination, drive, and innovative weapons, they were ready for success.

January 9, 2025

In today's competitive market, books from indie authors often find it challenging to catch readers' eyes. Whether or not you liked *The Real Wolf Man*, please leave a review on Amazon or Goodreads.

Thank you!

- Phillip Wolf

EXTRAS

MEET THE AUTHOR

PHILLIP WOLF is an award-winning writer, producer, and director. In addition to writing and producing independent films, he creates real estate videos for multifamily communities. Wolf also works as a supervisor, camera operator, and audio/video tech within the live event industry for entertainment, corporate, and industrial events.

To learn more, visit WolfEntertainment.NET.

SPOILER ALERT!

The following chapters are excerpts from the sequel to *Jack Stinger and the Haunting of Whitlock Manor*. It's advisable to read the first book before continuing, as these chapters continue where the previous story leaves off.

JACK STINGER
AND THE DÉJÀ VU EXPERIENCE

Available Soon.

CHAPTER ONE

The Gang Is All Here

1

Jack lay in a fetal position on a metallic floor, cold and wet.

Drawing his knees firmly against his bare chest, he breathed deeply, then stretched his legs. His head ached. He pushed his naked body from the floor and twisted at the waist, sitting in a puddle of thick, transparent liquid. But he wasn't *totally* naked; he was still wearing the nifty antigravity boots he had on when he had first entered the pod.

His mouth was a cotton ball. He licked his lips—bitter and salty.

The liquid surrounding him peeled from the floor and transformed into small spherical shapes that floated around him before quickly dissolving. Fascinating.

For a moment, he thought he had awakened from a nightmare—the events at Whitlock Manor still playing in his mind. Gazing upon the six otherworldly pods lined before him with piles of clothing beside each one, Jack realized he was no longer in Rusty, Texas.

The pod in front of him—second from the left—jiggled, diverting his attention from his state of wonder. He scooted further from the pod, his rear end gliding along the cold floor. He watched as the pod's encasement vibrated violently, the growth inside it on a desperate mission to break free.

Jack cringed. The thought of a face hugger from the movie *Alien* sent a chill down his spine. Was something preparing to leap from the crust of the pod and latch onto his face? The movie had scared him as a kid, and he remembered sleeping in his brother's room for two nights, thinking this would save him from having nightmares. "What the hell!" he moaned, readying himself to parry whatever was hatching from the pod.

With several aggressive vibrations, the pod finally regurgitated a black ball of slime from its belly, the remaining liquid inside the textured shell sliding out and spreading rapidly across the floor like an overturned bucket of chum. But without gravity, the substance peeled from the floor and floated in the air, combusting into thousands of tiny spheres that popped like soap bubbles and evaporated.

The thick and wet dark mass glided to Jack's feet and paused within reach.

Jack kept his eye on the glistening thing as he inched away. He cocked his head, his eyes gleaming down at the mass. *Is that thing . . . breathing?* he wondered.

Thin legs slowly uncurled from a tight tuck out the side of the black glob. Next came the head, the neck stretching out and gentle eyes locking with Jack's.

Jack face-palmed himself. "Of course . . . Bosco! Duh!"

Bosco looked like a large wet rat struggling to his feet. His hind legs splayed apart when he attempted to stand. He tried again. Success! After shaking his head, body, and tail, he whimpered with excitement and pounced into Jack's lap, greeting him with mad licks to his face.

"Ha-ha, I missed you too, boy!" Jack laughed.

Bosco pulled away and sat on his haunches.

Looking over his best friend, Jack admired the Chow-Chow with his purple tongue hanging out the side of his mouth—tiny bubbles accumulating at the tip. He felt safe reuniting with his dog. Jack couldn't fathom how the puppy had grown to full size within a matter of days! Or had Jack been sleeping in that pod for a year or two? He certainly didn't feel any older.

Surely this is a dream? Jack thought, assuring himself he was back home in his bed, having a crazy nightmare. Any moment now, he'd wake up to the aroma of bacon his mother cooked in the kitchen.

But everything around him was surreal—and very real. He remembered being with his friends just a short while ago, each one being consumed into their respective pods. Everyone was supposed to be resting before the ship landed, according to Delanore Bagleweed.

But had it already landed, and therefore, Jack had awakened on the cold floor? Wherever he and his friends were going, he had many questions, yet he had no idea when he'd find the answers. Jack felt imprisoned on this spaceship without a clue of what time or even what day it was.

Bosco's ears perked. He woofed and turned his fluffy head toward the row of pods behind him.

"What is it?" Jack leaned to one side, peering around Bosco. His eyes widened when the furthest pod on the left moved. "Oh, this again."

Bosco gave a high-pitched whine and took a few backward steps, his body close to the ground with his head even lower. His lips rolled back on his gums, exposing his ferocious teeth. He growled, tongue lashing.

Quickly getting to his feet, Jack felt the pressure from his antigravity boots against the floor. They were noticeably heavy, but his feet felt very comfortable. The boots reminded him of the limited-edition Reebok Alien Stompers released in '86. Those had been too expensive for him to own a pair.

With all eyes on the pod, Jack and Bosco anticipated something bursting from the encasement any second. Ooze seeped from the belly of the pod. Then pop! Like the bursting shell of a cherry cordial, the pod regurgitated a river of slime. Within the flowing liquid, Daisy glided from the burst egg in a fetal position.

Once again, the liquid peeled from the floor and transposed into popping bubbles.

Daisy's smooth flesh glistened in the fluorescent lighting. It didn't take long before she became aware of her surroundings and sat up, rubbing her eyes. "What happened?" she said, glancing about the room as her eyes adjusted. "I dreamt of a parade." Her eyes finally locked on Jack's. She glanced down and then quickly back up at him and giggled.

Jack cupped his hands over his crotch. The beauty of Daisy's flawless body sent a warm feeling down there.

Realizing Jack was not the only one in a birthday suit, Daisy gasped quickly, shielded herself, and turned her back to Jack and the dog.

Jack cleared his throat. "Our clothes are next to those pods," he said. "Grab the pile that looks like yours and put 'em on."

Daisy targeted the three pods where she, Jack, and Bosco were flushed. Each was still dripping remnants of odorless slime at their bases and transforming into popping bubbles like boiling water in a cauldron. Not a single drop of liquid had soaked into the clothes piled on the floor next to the pods.

Inspecting herself, Daisy noticed the slime she had been covered in had dried, much like hand sanitizer does shortly after it has been rubbed on the skin. "I'll grab my clothes, but please don't look at me," she said, embarrassed.

Recalling he had already seen her naked just before they entered the pods to drift into cryosleep, Jack nevertheless respected Daisy's request. He cleared his throat again as if something was lodged in it. Perhaps he was recovering from being intubated. But the feeling of time while inside the pod was like he blinked and woke up; he had no clue what went on with his body while he was sleeping. For all he knew, his body could've been violated and probed while all kinds of tests were being performed on him.

Daisy glanced over her shoulder to be sure Jack wasn't watching her, and then she stepped toward her neatly folded pile of clothes.

Keeping his eyes away from her as promised, Jack killed the time by petting his dog. Bosco's fur was soaked like a sponge. It was weird feeling the slimy substance squishing between his fingers as if he were giving the dog a bath with a shampoo that produced never-ending suds. "You're a good boy, aren't you!" he said, his face in Bosco's.

Bosco panted happily, enjoying the lengthy massage.

"Jack, help!" Daisy suddenly yelped.

Immediately ending the bonding session with his dog, Jack quickly spun around just as Daisy pulled up her panties. She had already managed to throw on her blouse, which hung to her thighs, but her pants were still on the floor, as were her antigravity boots. She was drifting weightlessly several feet in midair, flailing her arms and legs and trying to swim her way back down to the rest of her clothes on the floor.

Jack burst out laughing while watching her total loss of control. Her body was naturally rotating into a somersault. "If you were a gymnast, I'd say you'd take the gold!" he teased.

"Get me down!" Daisy pleaded. She tugged on the hem of her blouse to keep herself covered as she exited the rotation. "This isn't funny!"

Bosco gave a single bark, probably letting Jack know it wasn't funny anymore, either. His fur was drying now that Jack wasn't kneading it like biscuits. His coat shone beautifully as if the slimy substance was made of protein or vitamins.

"Why did you take both of your boots off?" Jack calmly said. *She's not going anywhere; she just needs something to grab onto.* Knowing he still needed to get dressed himself and was in no rush, he took the opportunity to put his pants on.

"What are you doing?" Daisy griped, still treading the air.

"You're fine," Jack assured her. "Gonna change right quick." He removed his right boot, eyeballed his underwear, and then looked at his jeans. *Screw it, I'm going commando.* While his left boot kept him weighted to the floor, he slipped his right leg into the pant leg, then put the right boot back on. He rinsed and repeated with his left boot and leg.

Daisy let out a frustrated sigh. She was approaching another rotation.

"And that's how it's done." Jack zipped up and buttoned his jeans. He bent down and grabbed Daisy's boots, then stepped underneath her. He raised his hand for her to grab.

Daisy latched onto Jack's hand and forearm and was eased back to the ground. "Thanks," she said, nearly out of breath. "But you could've shown me all that *afterward*."

"Just thought it was funny."

Daisy slipped into her boots, and they automatically (and silently) sized and secured to her feet with built-in sensors. "Well, it wasn't funny to me."

2

Within the isolated, alien-like chamber, the remaining three pods, looking like collapsed lungs, stood erect, unscathed, and uneventful. Jack's brother, Victor, and Jack's other two friends, Tommy and Billy, were inside those things. But why hadn't they been discharged like Jack, Daisy, and Bosco?

Bosco approached the pods, his nose twitching. Something must've been out of place for him to have wandered over to them. He sniffed a bit longer at the third pod from the right—Victor's pod. He stretched his neck around one side of the egg-shaped organism, then retracted it to smell the crusted tip.

With his keen sense of smell, Bosco seemed to know who was inside the pod. Finally, he sat and stared, waiting for something to happen. His fluffy black tail stretched in a cautious position horizontally on the floor.

Now fully clothed, Jack and Daisy joined Bosco in observing the other pods. Seeing no activity, they were as confused as the dog. Or did Bosco know something they didn't?

"Sooo, do we wait, or can we pull them out of there somehow?" Jack said.

Daisy shook her head. "No clue. Maybe the thingies malfunctioned and haven't woken them up yet?"

"But I remember they entered those things before us," Jack said.

Daisy returned a shrug.

Since there was still no movement from the pods, Jack took the opportunity to glance around his surroundings. There hadn't been much time for him to scope the place out before entering cryosleep. The room was vast, with pillars spaced throughout, probably holding up the roof of this colossal ship. The walls looked thick, textured, and . . . wet? Tilting his head, he scanned the domed ceiling. He figured the crown of the arch was maybe twenty feet up. There was no lookout. Only a very long single, dimmed fluorescent light wrapped entirely around the dome's base just above the walls.

Unlike the space shuttle he'd seen on TV and in textbooks, there were no cables connecting to electronic devices, computer monitors, gauges, or other flight instruments used for powering and navigating the spacecraft. How was this thing flying? Perhaps everything was behind the walls. Then again, the holographic crew members in the control room he saw when he and his friends had teleported into the ship were probably the brains of the operation.

How are we breathing in this thing? Jack wondered, not seeing any air ducts either.

There wasn't much room behind him, where he had glided across the floor after bursting from his pod. Most of the abundance of space flowed on the other side of the pods before him. Observing the floor, Jack assumed it had to be made of steel or some other type of metal to have magnetized their boots. Then he realized something strange: Why was Bosco not floating around if no antigravity boots covered *his* paws?

Peering over the pods before him, he saw a pathway curved to the left. *The way out*, he thought. He reached down and stroked Bosco's head, relieved to know this room was not a holding cell where he and his friends couldn't escape. But where would they go if they tried to flee? Their demise would happen in minutes outside the ship with boiling bodily fluids and frozen limbs within the vacuum of space.

Jack eyed the pods for a moment again, then turned to Daisy. "Nothing's happening."

"I know," Daisy replied, her eyes still transfixed on the pods.

Bosco woofed.

Jack's eyes shot back to the pods. Seeing no movement, he stared down at his dog. But Bosco wasn't looking at the pods. His head was turned away from them, peering at something approaching to the left of Jack and Daisy.

3

A split-second burst of light brightened the room.

Jack and Daisy synchronized their attention toward the flash, which had already transposed to a solid vertical beam when their eyes locked on the image.

The illumination continued its approach toward the teens from afar. As it advanced closer, it flickered in rapid succession before the holographic image of Delanore Bagleweed appeared.

"Ms. Bagleweed!" Jack blurted.

Daisy looked on with a grin stretching across her face.

"Your pods prematurely discharged you," Delanore said, the digital projection glitching as the microscopic electronic chips were still booting to display her image. Three-fourths of her body was visible, but it was enough for Jack and Daisy to recognize the old cafeteria lady from high school. The effects of the fascinating technology gradually roaring to life appeared like a movie actor stepping from the shadows and into the light—subtle, yet translucent.

"We weren't supposed to have woken from cryosleep yet?" Daisy asked.

Delanore clasped her hands together. "I sent a signal to the pods to wake you early. I have some important information that only pertains to you two."

"This is all a dream, and we're gonna wake up soon," Jack hoped, the words rolling off his tongue.

"Sorry, Jack." Delanore sustained a straight face. "This is no dream. We are orbiting Obuathea and about to reenter the atmosphere."

"Mirror Earth!" Daisy said.

Jack turned to Daisy. "Huh?"

"Obuathea. Remember she said it means 'Mirror Earth' when she briefed us before cryosleep."

"Oh."

Delanore's imagery was solid now. She looked, moved, and sounded like she was human. "Yes, Mirror Earth," she said. "I must brief you before landing. It will take you some time to get accustomed to your surroundings where we are going."

Jack looked confused. "Why can't you tell all of us at once?"

"Because this pertains to your new abilities," Delanore said. "Including your dog's."

Bosco tilted his head and perked his ears.

"The Adrotomytes infesting Earth have begun communicating with a potential host on our planet," Delanore continued. "There's a very high threat and probability that the transformation process has already begun on our planet as it has on yours since our briefing a few months ago. We cannot allow this species to spread amongst our people. We cannot let them win!"

"Wait!" Jack intervened. "A few months ago? We've been in those pods for *months*?"

Delanore nodded. "We had to remain in orbit around Obuathea because of the threat shortly after you settled into the pods. But now we haven't much time. I need you to pay close attention." She focused on Daisy. "As you are aware, you possess the power of the orb. It remains guarded by Gerald until needed. I'll be handing it off to you shortly after our arrival. Keep it safe and never let it out of your sight—I'm sure you already know based on your previous experience."

The fluorescent light ring around the room flickered.

Bosco whimpered.

"What was that?" Jack glanced around.

"We are nearing atmospheric entry," Delanore said, turning to Jack. "On that note, let me explain quickly that your services will be needed once we settle on land. We have a few days to detect if a suspect we captured and are holding at the base is being used as a host for an Adrotomyte. You'll use your power of sight to look into the eyes of the prisoner and determine if he is infected."

"How am I going to know that?" Jack said.

"You can foresee the future just as you did with your friend Stewart. During sleep, your pod taps signals into your brain to enhance your ability. You'll understand when you meet the suspect. The foresight will happen naturally."

The ship suddenly dipped, and Jack's and Daisy's bodies were thrown forward. They would have shot across the room if their antigravity boots hadn't been secured to the floor.

Bosco, surprisingly, didn't budge.

"We're getting closer," Delanore said. "I need to shut down and signal your friends' pods to wake them. I should've woken you sooner to explain more. There's no time to brief you about your dog, but he will play a key role in helping wipe out the Adrotomytes. We will reconvene upon arrival."

"Wait!" Jack reached out. "Don't we need to be seat-belted or something? I mean, we're gonna bounce around like pinballs!"

"Your boots will keep you secure during reentry. There shouldn't be any more turbulence than what you just felt. Everything should be smooth, and you won't realize we have landed. I'll return once we've touched down."

Delanore's holographic image glitched and fizzled out.

Jack scratched behind Bosco's ear, wondering what power his dog possessed.

"Okay, this is getting way too weird," Daisy said. "And I think I might be getting homesick."

"You're telling me!" Jack agreed.

Without warning, Bosco snapped his head from Jack's hand and leaped toward the pods. He repositioned himself like before, sitting and staring with his tail stretched horizontally on the floor.

Jack and Daisy whipped around. The pods were vibrating.

4

Floods of thick, clear slime burst from the bellies of the pods one after the other, their liquids collecting along the floor as one large puddle, then transposing into bubbles bursting in the air.

The bodies of Victor, Tommy, and Billy in fetal positions glided across the floor to Jack's and Daisy's feet. They all woke up in unison.

Bosco took a few backward steps from the teens, their bodies glistening with slime, and belted a couple of barks.

Victor was the first to stand and stretch. "Ugh, what's that nasty taste?" he said, smacking his lips. He looked at his hand and spread his his fingers apart. Strings of slime stretched between them like thick egg albumen and then dissolved. "Gross! What is this crap?"

Jack burst out laughing at Victor, standing naked with his back turned to him and wearing only a pair of antigravity boots—his brother's bare butt cheeks in full view. "You look like a nude cowboy!"

Daisy giggled.

"What?" Victor turned around.

Daisy squeaked and quickly shielded her eyes.

"You sick bastard!" Jack flinched. "Put your clothes on. Now I'm scarred for life!"

"What the—" Victor covered his privates with his hand and the stump of his other arm, then turned back around to scan for his clothes.

Tommy and Billy stood from the floor like two rising zombies. Disoriented, they mirrored Victor's reactions and scrambled for their clothes.

"Make sure you take one boot off when putting your pants on," Jack warned.

Bosco approached Jack and sat, observing the teens while they re-clothed.

"What the hell is going on?" Victor said from afar. "And whose underwear is this on the floor?"

Jack looked at Daisy and grinned.

Daisy rolled her eyes.

"We've been cryosleeping for several months," Jack replied to Victor.

"What?!" Tommy cried out.

"Yep. According to Delanore, an infestation on the planet caused the delay."

Victor slipped his shirt over his head. "Who's Dela—oh yeah, the old broad." He stepped to Jack and Daisy and raised the stump of his arm. "I see I still don't have a hand. And it feels like I've lost a few years of my life!"

"Nope, just a few months," Daisy clarified.

"Well, look on the bright side," Jack said, "at least you have a permanent fire 'arm' at your side."

"Very funny, douchebag."

Tommy and Billy finished dressing and joined the group.

"How long have you been awake, Jack?" Tommy asked.

Jack gestured to Daisy and Bosco. "Just a short while. Delanore woke us earlier than expected to give us a quick rundown. But she didn't have time to explain everything; she just told us it would take some time to get used to our surroundings once we're off this ship."

"I haven't even gotten used to *this* surrounding," Victor said.

"Why did she wake just y'all and not us, too?" Tommy said.

"I asked her that as well. We are more important, I guess."

"Or our abilities are in higher demand right now," Daisy added.

"When do we land?" Billy chimed in.

"Dunno," Jack said. "Soon. Delanore mentioned she'd return after we touched down. As you can see, this room has no windows, so we won't know for sure. This ship must be well insulated because, according to Delanore, we won't be able to feel the reentry nor the landing."

Victor glanced at Tommy. "You think we're still in a simulator surrounded by fake backgrounds and images?"

"Who knows anymore." Tommy exhaled. Appearing somewhat distraught, he stepped away from the others and looked around the room.

Billy spun around on his heel. "What are you doing?"

"Just looking," Tommy said, scanning the walls and then looking down to check out his boots. "And thinking."

"About what?" Billy asked.

Tommy fell silent for a moment. "Mom."

"Oh . . . yeah," Billy said, bowing his head. Now that his brother mentioned it, he suddenly missed his mother. With all the events that transpired, his mind had been diverted from the grief of their mother, who was no longer with them.

"I just had a random image pop into my head of her in the bathroom covered in all that blood," Tommy said.

"Sorry, guys," Daisy sympathized with the brothers. Although she didn't know all the details, it was the thought of losing another parent that swept across her mind. And knowing Tommy and Billy weren't home to plan their mother's funeral must have been devastating.

Jack didn't know what to say. He knew their mother had problems after their father passed, but he didn't think it would come to her taking her own life over it. *So tragic*, he thought.

Tommy peered up at the ceiling and gave a long, heavy sigh. He felt embarrassed grieving in front of his friends. It was something he rarely did. However, experiencing the imagery of death firsthand was different. He felt empty on the inside. His body may have been weightless on the ship, but the weightlessness he was currently feeling was very different.

The fluorescent light ring around the walls flickered.

Tommy snapped back into the now, and he rejoined the group. "What just happened?" he asked.

There was a brilliant flash, followed by a solid vertical beam that stretched from the floor to the ceiling and moved toward the teens. It transposed into the holographic image of Delanore.

"Looks like we may have landed," Jack said.

CHAPTER TWO

SSO Alliance

1

The teens heard the spaceship's engines powering down from within the chamber. But the insulated room muffled most of the high-decibel noise, gradually leveling to a barely noticeable rumble.

The signals from Delanore's holographic projection never glitched upon power-up since the ship was closer to the command center on Obuathea. It was a strong signal.

Jack and his crew gathered around the lifelike image, anticipating the reveal of the age-old question, "Is there life on other planets?" The tension in the room was rising.

Bosco obeyed and heeled next to Jack. He didn't seem to care where he was. Eat, sleep, poop, and repeat were all he probably cared about.

Delanore stood silent, concentrating on the teens one at a time as if making sure they could tolerate a new atmosphere. She made eye contact with them first, as if reading their minds, then scanned them head to toe before turning to the next person.

"What's she doing?" Victor said without moving his lips. He didn't realize it, but he was standing at attention. Either Delanore was using a mental force on him or his body was naturally adjusting. "She's freaking me out."

Jack also stood at attention, as did everyone else. His body was stiff and straight, with his feet together and both arms at his sides. He spoke out the side of his mouth in response to Victor. "Shut up."

When Delanore finally finished her inspection, she announced, smiling, "Welcome to Obuathea!" Her eyes gleamed with excitement, making her look like a travel guide greeting vacationing guests on a secluded island. But this was not even close to a weekend getaway.

The young crew turned to each other, unsure if they should be excited or scared about this new place. Could it get any worse than the craziness on Earth that led them to this point?

An unusual sucking sound coming from the pods caught the crew's attention. Glancing over, they witnessed the pods rejuvenating to their original states. The holes in the bellies were closing and resealing themselves like flatworms regrowing their decapitated heads and retaining their trained behaviors.

"What in the world?" Victor said, wrinkling his nose.

The others moaned in disgust.

"Resealed and ready to use again," Delanore explained with a tickle of exhilaration. Then, snapping the teens from their states of wonder, she added, "Please follow me." She proceeded past the group, stepped around the pods, and shuffled to the curved pathway at the opposite side of the chamber.

Leading his friends, with Bosco at his side, Jack followed Delanore at close range. He still couldn't fathom how lifelike her illusion appeared when they rounded the corner and walked down a lengthy corridor. From Delanore's bouncing hair to her aged flesh and the fine wrinkles in her clothing, it was hard to identify her as a digital image. The only odd thing about her that he could distinguish between reality and the digital deception before him, save for the thin, blurred line that outlined her body, was how she walked. For an old cafeteria lady at school whom he knew moved slowly, Delanore sure had quick steps!

2

They walked in a staggered line down the passageway. LEDs lining the ceiling sensed their movement and sparked to life a step ahead of them. The lights illuminated separate chambers branching off the hallway. Each room was identical to the cryosleep chamber the teens had awakened in.

Daisy remembered passing these rooms shortly after arriving on the vessel, when Delanore led them through to their pods. The only difference this time was the garments lying next to each pod were missing.

Rounding another corner, Jack took note of a small plaque inscribed with *SSO Alliance—2B* secured to the wall. He'd seen another bronze plate like it before when they turned the first corner, right outside the cryosleep chamber. "What is SSO *Alliance?*" he asked.

"Spaceship Obuathea *Alliance.*" Delanore's voice carried through the corridor. "It's one of seven."

"There's seven of these big-ass things?" Victor was quick to comment.

Amused at Victor's response, Delanore replied, "Yes. And when they are berthed together, they form a single starship called *The Battalion.* It's designed for war."

"Oh, like a Transformer," Jack said.

"Not exactly, assuming you're speaking of the toy robots from several hundred years ago," Delanore said.

Jack and Victor looked sharply at each other.

"Hundreds of years ago?" Jack murmured.

Delanore picked up on Jack's comment. "Obuathea is hundreds of years ahead of Earth's time," she reminded him. "And those toys here faded quickly."

"Interesting," Tommy said. "I used to collect those toys, but Billy here got a hold of them one day and decided to toss them up in the trees."

"You told me I could play with them!" Billy said in his defense.

"Yeah, but not throw them like they were rag dolls!"

Daisy broke up the bickering between the two brothers before it got out of hand. "What happened to the clothes in those chambers?" she asked.

Delanore escorted the crew down another long corridor to the mess hall at the other end. This time, everyone noticed the next nameplate on the wall when they turned the corner: *SSO Alliance— 2A.* "The cadets have exited the ship and are awaiting their assigned living quarters," she said.

"So, there *were* other people on this ship," Daisy said.

"Several," Delanore replied. She approached the bay doors to the mess hall, and they swooshed open.

The teens followed her into the room single file. Behind them, Bosco left a trail of bright green paw prints that faded one after the other.

3

"Well, this place sure looks familiar," Victor said.

"Food!" Jack smiled. And there was plenty of it.

Rows of a wide variety of hearty meals—arranged buffet style—covered two transparent glass tables in the center of the room. The menu listed fried chicken, fettuccini alfredo, perfectly cooked hamburgers, thick juicy steaks, baked potatoes, garden salads, cherry cobbler, and cheesecake. There were even meaty bones for Bosco. What a treat!

"Wow," Tommy said, grabbing from the corner of the table a crystal plate and silverware wrapped in an elegant satin cloth napkin. "We're being fed like kings!"

"You'd think it was the end of the world or something," Victor teased. "Er, no pun intended." He snatched a plate and paused before a dish stacked with rib eyes, the juices still sizzling. With the plate grasped in his good hand, he looked at the stump of his other arm. The struggle was real, and there was no room to set his plate down to dish his food.

"Looks like *you're* not eating today," Jack chuckled.

"That's what you think," Victor said. "No way in hell I'm going to miss out on something like this."

Tommy grabbed the tongs opposite Victor across the table, picked up a rib eye, and placed it on Victor's plate.

"Man, I'm sure glad someone here is kind enough to help me," Victor said. "Thanks, Toms."

Delanore whisked to the corner of the room, then turned and faced the crew. "Enjoy the meal prepared for you," she said. "I'll return shortly to guide you off the ship, where we'll process the paperwork that will grant you access to our planet."

"Paperwork?" Victor mumbled, moving down the table and pointing to the food he craved for Tommy to slap onto his plate. "I feel like my rights are about to be stripped away."

Delanore's holographic image faded and fizzled out like an old, boxed television powering off. A tiny dot remained stationary in mid-air for a moment before it slowly dimmed and then disappeared.

4

324

The teens sat around the table stuffed with delicious food. Even Bosco looked satisfied, lying on the floor fast asleep next to Jack's feet.

"Ugh! I can't eat any more," Tommy breathed.

"That was the best food I've ever had!" Billy leaned back in his chair and rubbed his stomach.

Victor was still picking at the gristle on his plate.

"You know there's more where that came from," Jack told his brother.

"Nah, I've had enough."

Daisy did not comment on the food. Instead, she observed everyone around the table and saw how each one reacted differently. But when she glanced over at Billy holding his stomach, the thought of him losing all that weight triggered a memory of when he went missing back home. It was when Daisy and Jack found him locked in the cage beneath Whitlock Manor.

Then fear struck her as she sat at the table, watching everyone mingle after the delicious meal. The thought of the Adrotomyte snatching her from within the darkness at the old house and dragging her to its lair suddenly popped into her head. She could smell that awful stench like she was there again. All she could see was pitch-black while she pounded her fists against the creature's rubber-like flesh. She heard it grunting as it carried her deeper beneath the house. At one point, her arm smacked against the wall, but she was so frightened—adrenaline pumping—she did not feel the pain. No matter how much she kicked and screamed, she could not wiggle free from the clutches of the creature's massive hands. When the thing finally flopped her onto the moistened soil, her head hit so hard she blacked out.

Daisy jolted in her chair at the table, snapping from the hallucination.

Jack placed his hand over hers. "Hey, you okay?"

"Yeah," Daisy said. She felt all eyes on her. "Just had a flashback is all."

"The food isn't that bad now, c'mon," Victor joked.

"It's not that," Daisy said.

Jack squeezed her hand. "Wait, was it when you were lost at Whitlock Manor?" he guessed.

Daisy lowered her head and nodded.

"PTSD!" Victor proclaimed.

Daisy looked up from the table at Victor.

"I have it now and then," Victor said.

"So do I," Jack said back at his brother. Then he patted Daisy's hand to assure her everything would be okay.

"I get it, too." Billy sat up straight. "It happens to me quite often actually."

"Me, too, but not too often," Tommy admitted. He looked at Daisy inquisitively. "What triggered it? Nothing's happening here but a *fantastic* meal."

Daisy shook her head in embarrassment. "Never mind. I'm fine. Really. Don't worry about it."

"Sorry," Tommy said. "I was just curious how and when it affects you. Just wondered if the same events I experience sometimes also trigger it to happen in someone else."

Billy sank back in his chair. "So, we all suffer from this? I thought it was just me."

Daisy positioned her elbow on the table and rested her head in her hand. Then she cut her eyes up at Billy. "It was when you were rubbing your stomach and saying you were full," she confessed.

Billy shot back up. "*What!* Why?"

Tommy returned a confused look toward Daisy.

"At school, you were always heavyset—excuse my rudeness—"

"No worries," Billy broke in.

"That's how I've always known you," Daisy explained. "But after you went missing for all those days, and we found you in that cage, I noticed you lost a lot of weight. I mean, I'm glad to see you've kept it off, but when you rubbed your stomach just then, I suddenly remembered being dragged away by that hideous monster! Oh my God, it seemed so real!"

"Yeah, it can be pretty lifelike sometimes," Billy said.

The young crew fell silent. No one touched on the subject any further. Just thinking of an Adrotomyte could spark a frightening memory. They each fidgeted in their chairs uncomfortably until, finally, the projected image of Delanore returned to the corner of the room—the precise location where it initially vanished.

"Good," Delanore said. "It looks like everyone has had dinner. Did you enjoy your meals?"

"Delicious!" Tommy was the first to respond, and the others echoed him. Jack ended with, "Thank you."

Delanore dipped a curtsy at the teens, then turned and waved her hand at the wall behind her.

A small hidden compartment slid open, the tiled piece rising vertically. The motors of the contraption buzzed softly behind the wall.

Delanore reached inside the small hole and retrieved the orb. The spider (Gerald) was still frozen on top.

The orb magically floated in midair and moved with Delanore, creating the illusion that she was holding it.

When Delanore stepped toward Daisy, Bosco perked up from the floor next to Jack and settled on his haunches, his head and ears shaking nervously. He must've been sensitive to whatever pheromone the spider was producing.

Delanore reached out her hand, and the orb glided to Daisy. "Take it."

Daisy could only focus on the spider with its long, hairy legs clutched tightly around the sphere.

"He'll come to life once you take the orb," Delanore said. "You've interacted with Gerald before. You know he will not harm you."

"But it's gross!" Daisy snapped.

Jack and his other friends looked on curiously, anticipating what would happen when Daisy took the orb.

The holographic image paused. Delanore appeared as though she wouldn't move until Daisy fulfilled her wish.

With trembling fingers, Daisy slowly reached for the floating sphere. *It's going to move, and it's going to be gross!* she thought. The tip of her middle finger first touched the orb between two spider legs. Then, her ring finger, and finally, the rest of her fingers contacted the sphere with a gentle touch.

One of the spider's legs twitched, then rose gently.

Daisy held her position, afraid if she moved, it would only make matters worse.

The remaining spider's legs followed the pattern like Daisy's fingers when touching the object—one leg at a time. Each fuzzy leg peeled from the orb like the reincarnation of old bones.

"That's nasty!" Billy shrieked, scrunching against the back of his chair. "Get rid of that thing!" Even though he'd witnessed the evilest, gnarliest creature on earth, he'd probably never overcome the fear of spiders.

Delanore moved her head, and her eyes targeted Billy. "Trust me, you'll want Gerald around," she said. "It'll take some getting used to, but you'll see."

There's that word, trust, again, Tommy thought. Although Delanore had said it once before, he still didn't have much faith in that digital projection of an old woman. Something about a programmed talking, walking ghost of an image would never sit well with him. He could say he was old-school but just a teen. He hadn't lived long enough to determine what was old-school yet.

Daisy's face stretched with fear as she watched the tarantula come to life. It moved from the orb to her wrist, then scurried up her arm and to her shoulder, where it perched. "Get it off me!" she said through clenched teeth. She could feel the spider's hairy legs brushing against the side of her neck. Even with all the anxiety shocking the core of her soul, she managed to keep ahold of the orb—tightening her grip and keeping it from dropping to the floor.

Bosco maintained a sharp eye on Gerald. Not for his own sake but to be ready to lurch and protect Daisy if the arachnid tried to harm her. Smart dog.

Delanore waved her arm at Gerald, and he leaped from Daisy's shoulder and zipped across the floor.

The spider crawled up the wall and back into the hole, and the tile lowered back into place.

"I've misplaced the velvet pouch for the orb," Delanore said. "But follow me to the cargo bay where you can grab your packs."

"Packs?" Jack called out.

Delanore faced the group. "Yes. All of you. Follow me."

"Welp, here we go!" Victor said, pushing himself up from the chair with his good arm.

"I know, right?" Tommy responded. "We're getting closer to discovering what's outside this ship."

"I'm getting butterflies in my stomach," Billy said, gathering with his friends.

Delanore stood with her hands in front of her, her fingers interlocked. "Now, now. There's no need to get all worked up. Trust me, you'll love it here."

Tommy raised an eyebrow at her.

5

The crew followed Delanore through the *Alliance*. Walking past the ship's bridge, they glanced at the advanced electronics surrounding the command deck. A roll-up barrel steel door covered the large window that overlooked the area—the only window the teens had seen where they could look out into space when teleported onto the spacecraft. Unlike what they had seen before their sleep, no holographic crew members were moving about the room manipulating the computers. Since the ship had docked, all was quiet.

Moving on, Delanore ushered the teens down a narrow, winding corridor to the freight elevator. Thousands of blinking LED panels lined the walls. The aroma of the interior of a factory-new car lingered in the air.

As they finally approached the elevator, the upper and lower door panels swooshed open automatically when Delanore stepped within the boundaries of the motion sensors. The inner cage door was also raised automatically, and the rattling chain on the pulley system was the only sound carrying through the area.

The young cadets stepped onto the car, spacious enough to occupy at least fifteen people or several large wooden cargo crates. A single row of caged fluorescent lights lined the ceiling.

"Please stand away from the doors," Delanore warned.

Everyone behaved as if they were unknowingly partaking in a social experiment and stepped back with empty emotions and no hesitation.

A loud buzz signaled that the elevator cage door was lowering, followed by the upper and lower exterior panels closing together smoothly. Delanore waved her hand in front of the elevator's control panel buttons, and the car descended slowly.

"Sit," Jack commanded Bosco, and his dog immediately lowered his haunches. He stroked the dog's head while noting the labels on the buttons on the control panel from top to bottom: FOUR, THREE, TWO, ONE, and CB.

"How old is the spacecraft, if you don't mind me asking?" Tommy said.

"Pretty old." Delanore faced him. "Older than the sum of all the ages in this elevator."

"But it all looks and smells new," Victor said. "So, what's on the upper levels?"

The button labeled ONE lit up, but the car continued to descend.

"We just passed the support module on the first level, where you'll find the engineering systems, the med bay area, and the shuttlecraft," Delanore said. "Above us, on level two—which you have already seen—is the main bridge where the command center, the mess hall, and the sleep chambers are located. Level three consists of the main computer core and science station, and level four is recreational."

"This is far out!" Billy pronounced. "We're on a real spaceship, guys!"

The others seemed uninterested rather than impressed. "Homesick" was written all over their faces.

"So, what happens after wherever you're leading us to?" Tommy asked. "Do we go home? Do we even *get* to go home?"

"We'll exit the vessel, where a medical team will check in and examine you."

"We're gonna get probed!" Victor blurted.

Billy's eyes enlarged, and his jaw slacked.

"No, no." Delanore cracked a smile.

The button labeled CB lit up, the elevator eased to a stop, and a PING projected from a small speaker below the panel. The inner cage rose, and the upper and lower panels opened to the cargo bay area.

6

The cargo bay was dark and cold. The only light giving way was the fluorescents inside the elevator until the side panels closed, and then it became dark again.

"I can't see a damn thing!" Victor cried out.

Not a second later, a brilliant light shot across the room from several LED diodes that separated from part of the projections of Delanore's holographic image. They transformed into tiny spinning semiconductor discs that illuminated the cargo bay.

"Ah, there we go," Victor said, relieved.

"Whoa, what is all of this?" Jack said, scanning the place as he and the crew continued slowly. Pieces of equipment were scattered in this vast area of the *Alliance*, some of which were important to the spacecraft's operations. Additionally, between solid pillars throughout, large wooden crates entombed additional items, such as machinery, supplies (weapons?), and other miscellaneous things.

But the only interest Delanore had down here was with a rectangular opened crate nestled at the far end of the cargo bay. Its lid was propped against the side. The crate was placed separate from all the others, near the stairway that led to the airlock.

Delanore moved to the crate, and the teens gathered around it. "There's a pack labeled for each of you inside," she said. "Please find yours and strap it on."

"What's in them?" Tommy asked, reaching into the crate. He found his bag and secured it to his back. Its bulkiness was like a military recon pack, but it was dark blue instead of camouflage.

"Your packs are filled with items for survival," Delanore said. "Do not open them until you have been checked in at the base."

"These are heavy!" Daisy said. She turned her back to Jack. "Can you help me with mine?"

Jack secured his pack first, then assisted Daisy with hers.

"How'd these get here specifically for us, with our names already printed?" Billy wondered, smoothing his hand over his name stitched to the bag.

"Exactly." Daisy wondered the same thing. She shifted her hips and bounced on the balls of her heels to adjust her backpack. "It's creepy that someone—or something—we don't know, knows us."

"What the hell are we doing, preparing to go to war with this shit or what?" Tommy fussed. "I don't recall getting voluntold for this!"

Delanore did not respond. Instead, she moved toward the stairs leading to the airlock. "When you have secured your packs, follow me this way."

Bosco nudged his snout at the back of Jack's hand.

"Hey, what about Bosco?" Jack said. "Does he not get anything?" His friends chuckled, although he was being serious. How would his dog survive outside this spacecraft if he wasn't given any supplies? Were animals immune to the atmosphere?

"His supplies are packed with yours," Delanore said.

Jack felt better knowing Bosco would not be left out. He stroked the dog's fur, then patted his leg for Bosco to heel as he proceeded toward the stairway.

Victor stepped away from the crate to catch up with Jack. Looking around the area, he murmured nervously, "The moment of truth is near. I hope our bags are packed with weapons; we don't know what the hell we're up against outside this ship."

"I don't know, man," Jack said, taking to the stairs. "This is gonna be crazy!"

Daisy, Tommy, and Billy quickly caught up and proceeded up the stairway behind Jack and Victor.

Daisy, still struggling to get used to the heavy pack, leaned backward on the stairs, almost losing her balance. Thankfully, Tommy was there to catch her. "Thanks," she gasped. "Whew! That was close!

Tommy acknowledged with a big smile.

The teens scrunched together at the top of the stairs with their backpacks in each other's faces like military paratroopers lining up to parachute from a plane. They peered around one another to see Delanore standing at the airlock door.

"This is as far as I go," Delanore said. "You'll exit through this door and proceed down the corridor to a second door. Pull the handle out first, down, then push the door open. A member of our team will greet you outside." She glanced down at Bosco, then to Jack. "Your dog will need to stay aboard the ship for now. I'll lead him back to the main bridge."

"What? No! Why?" Jack felt his heart sink to his stomach. He didn't want Bosco to be alone. Perhaps the atmosphere *wasn't* fit for animals after all.

"Don't worry; our team will take excellent care of him, and you'll reunite with him soon," Delanore promised. "You will need to adapt to your new home here first. Things will be a little . . . overwhelming right now if your dog isn't gradually introduced to these new surroundings. Trust me, I've seen other animals not adapt well when they were let loose, thinking they could just roam around as they please."

Tommy eyeballed Delanore. *Trust me*, he thought. The more he heard her say it, the more agitated he got.

Jack patted Bosco on the head and bent down to let him lick his face. It was the most kisses Bosco had ever given him in seconds! Bosco must've sensed they were about to be separated.

Jack's friends felt sorry for the duo having to break up. Daisy slapped a hand over her chest and frowned, disheartened at the temporary goodbye. Even Victor almost shed a tear watching his little brother saying his goodbyes.

Jack gave a final scratch behind Bosco's ear. "Stay," he said, choking on his words.

Bosco sat, then pawed at Jack's leg. He seemed to understand that he couldn't tag along. He whimpered.

"It's okay, boy." Jack looked down at Bosco with glassy eyes. "I'll catch up with you again soon. I promise!"

Delanore nodded at Jack, acknowledging that Jack understood why his dog could not be with him and accepted the situation. She then turned to an electronic keypad next to the door. Another group of spinning computer chips formed from part of her image projection and floated to the keypad. A red laser beam shot through a sensor above the keypad and overrode the system.

The door cracked open.

"I'll see you all again soon!" Delanore said. "Welcome to Obuathea."

7

Natural light soaked through a frosted ceiling, stretching the length of the corridor, lighting the way for the teens.

Jack fought his nerves as he led his team to the second door. He stopped at the door and stared at the handle protruding from it.

"Well, it's not going to open itself," Victor said after a long pause. "If you don't want to open it, I will."

"I got it!" Jack said. He exhaled, still nervous, and grasped the handle.

Everyone looked on, just as nervous as Jack.

Jack gave the handle a firm pull, then pushed it down with more force and heard and felt the latch pop loose. He glanced back at his friends. "Here goes nothing."

"Do it!" Victor said, adrenaline pumping through his veins.

Jack slowly pushed on the door, and the hinges squeaked. Bright light slapped him in the face.

A portable staircase led to the ground below. The soil appeared to be the same as Earth's.

At the base of the stairs, a lone child waved up at him.

Jack froze.

"What's out there?" Billy projected his voice from behind.

"Well?" Tommy said impatiently.

Victor squeezed his way through to the doorway and saw the child below. "*What the hell?* That's our guide? He looks like he's eight years old!"

"Hey, guys." The child grinned, still waving at the teens. His voice was high-pitched, like he hadn't reached puberty yet. "Welcome! Step down."

"Who is that?" Daisy finally spoke. "What do you see?"

Victor took a long, deep breath, daring to test the atmosphere against his lungs. The air was odorless and thick yet pleasantly refreshing. He scanned the area like a climber atop a mountain he'd just conquered. The view was spectacular. The colors were rich. The sky was deep blue and clear. From as far as he could see, the land was flat. But it was the child's clothes that offset the scenic view. They appeared oversaturated, like in a poorly retouched photo.

The child was still waving. Was he real?

"Welp, we got nowhere else to go," Victor said, stepping onto the portable stairs.

Jack held back, waiting to see if it would be safe for Victor to step foot on the ground. Then, when Victor was halfway down the stairs, Jack noticed something odd about his brother. His figure appeared to change, like in a distorting mirror at a carnival. Jack rubbed his eyes to be sure he wasn't hallucinating, then saw Victor remove his backpack and toss it to the ground.

The child was still waving.

Victor stopped and grabbed the railing with his good hand. He glanced back up at Jack.

"Victor!" Jack shouted, his voice soaking into the atmosphere. It was like it hit a brick wall, unable to project.

"What's going on?" Daisy said nervously. "Is he okay?"

Tommy and Billy gathered closer to the hatch to try and see what was happening.

"I don't know," Jack said, keeping an eye on his brother, who turned to wave his good arm at him and smiled.

But something was out of place. Victor's face was changing. His hair seemed longer, too. And before Jack could wave back at his brother like a lunatic, Victor's pants and shirt ripped.

"Victor!" Jack yelled into the thick air. "Your clothes!"

Daisy, Tommy, and Billy crammed through the hatch, looking at Victor halfway down the stairs.

"*Oh my God!*" Daisy gasped. "Is he . . . aging?"